Tales from The Lake

Volume 3

edited by:
Monique Snyman

Crystal Lake Publishing
www.CrystalLakePub.com

Copyright 2016 Crystal Lake Publishing

All Rights Reserved

ISBN: 978-1-945176-25-8

Cover Design:
Ben Baldwin—http://www.benbaldwin.co.uk/

Interior Formatting:
Lori Michelle—http://www.theauthorsalley.com

Interior artwork:
Luke Spooner—http://www.carrionhouse.com

Proofread by:
Paula Limbaugh
Jan Strydom
Sue Jackson

This is a work of fiction. Names, characters, businesses, places, events and incidents are either the products of the authors' imagination or used in a fictitious manner. Any resemblance to actual persons, living or dead, or actual events is purely coincidental.

No part of this publication may be reproduced, stored in a retrieval system, or transmitted in any form or by any means, without the prior permission in writing of the publisher, nor be otherwise circulated in any form of binding or cover than that in which it is published and without a similar condition including this condition being imposed on the subsequent purchaser.

WELCOME
TO ANOTHER

CRYSTAL LAKE PUBLISHING
CREATION

Welcome to another Crystal Lake Publishing creation.

Thank you for supporting independent publishing and small presses. You rock, and hopefully you'll quickly realize why we've become one of the world's leading publishers of Dark and Speculative Fiction. We have some of the world's best fans for a reason, and hopefully we'll be able to add you to that list really soon. Be sure to sign up for our newsletter to receive some free eBooks, as well as info on new releases, special offers, and so much more.

**Welcome to Crystal Lake Publishing—
Tales from the Darkest Depths.**

Other Anthologies by Crystal Lake Publishing

Gutted: Beautiful Horror Stories edited by Doug Murano and D. Alexander Ward

Tales from The Lake Vol.1 edited by Joe Mynhardt

Tales from The Lake Vol.2 edited by Joe Mynhardt, Emma Audsley, and R.J. Cavender

Fear the Reaper edited by Joe Mynhardt

For the Night is Dark edited by Ross Warren

Or check out other Crystal Lake Publishing books for your Dark Fiction, Horror, Suspense, and Thriller needs, and join our newsletter while you're there.

Table of Contents

Foreword from the Editor

The art of storytelling has evolved over millennia, but folkloric elements are as rife in our stories as ever. Urban legends of fantastic creatures lurking within our midst, mad men with bloodthirsty appetites, ghosts of our pasts, and the cautionary tales of our youth, all play an important role in society as a whole. These stories may have changed over the years, but they're still told around campfires or whispered at slumber parties . . .

When I was asked to oversee the compiling of *Tales from the Lake: Volume 3*, I instantly knew that I wanted to create an anthology filled with new, modern urban legends. I wanted memorable stories from diverse authors, stories that could potentially be retold when the opportunity arises. I also knew that I wanted to do an open call, in order to discover new authors and unique voices. With the staggering amount of stories that were submitted, however, my biggest problem was not finding what I required to create this diverse urban legend vision—there were so many fantastic stories from so many spectacular authors— but instead I struggled to choose the best ones out of the hundreds sent to me. The process was tiring, but eventually I was able to put together this book you see before you.

Tales from the Lake: Volume 3 is compiled with a specific criterion in mind—in some instances it aims to scare, in others the purpose is to be thought-provoking, and sometimes it goes out of its way to showcase the problems we deal with on a daily basis. Furthermore, I tried to balance the book out as much as possible—not only based on the stories' "creep factor" but also to give equal opportunity based on gender, race, or sexual preference.

I hope that you, the reader, will find as much entertainment from the adventures, horrors, and explorations of the art of storytelling in *Tales from the Lake: Volume 3*, as I had compiling them together.

Monique Snyman

Editor of *Tales from the Lake: Volume 3*

The Owl Builder

D. MORGAN BALLMER

I cried the first time I learned about owls eating," Ashlynn says.

"Why?"

Travis studies the narrow form of his cousin. She rests uneasily against the open screen door of the ragged single-wide. The setting sun paints red highlights in her chestnut hair. He has trouble reconciling this young woman with the same cherub-faced child he climbed sugar maples with many years ago.

"The pellets," Ashlynn says, "Made of all the bits the owl can't swallow. Mostly bones, claws, and fur. Tiny graveyards, you know. All the stuff they hold inside until they just can't do it anymore."

Chill evening air spills down the mountainside and through the trailer, causing Ashlynn to rub one bare foot on top of the other. Travis glances around the room for something warm she might wear. The home is a maze of old newspaper, dusty cosmetics, take-out bags, and teetering ashtrays. The labyrinth of refuse stands like a monument to the life and vices of the missing Maebeth Henshaw, Ashlynn's mother.

D. Morgan Ballmer

"That what the sheriff wanted to talk to you about? Owl pellets?" Travis says.

"No."

He waits for her to continue, though it's no mystery why Sheriff Coleman came to see her. Nothing secret happens among the rusty trailers and leaning outbuildings known as Alpine View. Gossip is a widely traded commodity among the indigent mountain dwellers. When the news first reached him, Travis thought Ashlynn might be taken into custody. Her mother was three weeks gone by then.

"Your Pa ever mention the Owl Builder?" she says.

"Aww Jesus, Ashlynn. Don't tell me you gave the sheriff some cockamamie hoodoo story while Aunt Maebeth is missing. Are you trying to go to jail?" Travis says.

The twilight emphasizes the narrowness of his nose, the sharpness of his jaw. Long shadows impart a Faustian aspect to his dark and intense stare.

"I know you two have your differences, but Uncle Maynard has always been kind to me. He knows things about these mountains that most have forgotten," Ashlynn says.

Travis removes his ball cap and sweeps his hair back. The pomade leaves a residue indistinguishable from the motor oil already staining his palm.

"My dad is crazy as a four way stop on a one-way road. That's no secret. Sure, he served his country and all that. Then came home nuttier than a squirrel turd. You start repeating the things he says and folks will say you've gone soft in the head."

He watches her stare listlessly at the mountains and wonders if perhaps she hasn't gone a bit strange.

From this angle her profile reveals striking similarities to Maebeth's. Her supple form and high cheekbones lend her a haughty air of elegance. She has the same frosty blue eyes as her mother, a color unique to the Henshaw clan. Locals call the tint 'Husky Blue', after the Alaskan dog.

Yet for all their physical similarities the two women have little else in common. Maebeth is a wildfire recklessly burning her way through the small town. Her ferocious passion for life drew men like moths. Ashlynn dislikes attention, choosing solitude over company whenever the choice is offered. She is a ghost, forever skirting the edges of conversation.

"So your Pa never told you about him?" she says.

Travis fishes in his shirt pocket for a cigarette. He listens to the chirrup of crickets pulsing through the twilight air and wishes he were a part of that conversation instead. Mindless chirping would be more satisfying than rehashing the myths of his crackpot father.

"He told me about that old feathered witch doctor. Back when he and Aunt Maebeth were kids they had a feud with the Whitley twins over a fishing spot. Said the twins threatened to kidnap them, take them to the Owl Builder. A little after that their dog went missing."

Ashlynn nods, her gaze never leaving the treetops.

"That was mom's dog, Bandit. He was all white with black feet," she says.

"Might I finish? That okay with you Ms. Ashlynn?"

Travis stares at her through a curtain of cigarette smoke.

"Dang. Can't get two words in edgewise around here. It's almost like Maebeth never left. Yes, Bandit.

The dog with the black feet. Hell, we both know this stupid story, what's the point?"

Travis waits to see if her hide is any thicker. When she was a child and he barely a teen the two would play hide-and-go-seek together. She'd skulk after him, eyes downcast, obediently waiting for him to tell her whether to count or hide. He found her mannerisms strange, her little waddle-walk, the way she'd stand perfectly still and look straight ahead when waiting. One day he told her to stop acting like a dumb animal. She burst into tears and ran home. His father forced him to apologize, something Travis still resents. A man shouldn't have to apologize for telling the truth.

"So you know the Whitley twins came and took Bandit. Stole him in the dead of night and delivered him to the Owl Builder. They wanted to teach our folks a lesson," she says.

Travis takes another drag on his cigarette. He glances at the spider-webs crisscrossing his knuckles, mementos carved by the teeth of other boys. Reckless boys who teased him about his father and said he never had a mental breakdown overseas. Ones who said insanity ran through their bloodline like red hair through the Irish. A right hook silenced most of them, but it never eased his fears that they may be right. Listening to Ashlynn prattle on about the Owl Builder makes his knuckles ache.

"They walked the trails calling for him, begging Bandit to come home, but he never did. One day they hiked out to Old Soldier Peak. That's where they found something terrible. Do you remember?" Ashlynn says.

Travis drops his head back and exhales a plume of smoke. It billows across the mildewed ceiling creating a reverse night sky, black dots peering through a field of white.

"They found some fur," he says.

Ashlynn nods.

"White fur. No blood. And when they looked in the tree what did they spy but the largest owl this side of the Kanawha River peering back down at them. An owl the size of a toddler. White plumage covering the whole body except the wingtips and feet. Those were black."

"Yep. That fat owl probably ate their damn dog," Travis says. "If there even was an owl. Hell, if there even was a dog. Don't be naïve about the old folks. My dad is an unreliable witness to life in general, and Aunt Maebeth . . . well . . . she'll tell any story that livens up the party. Don't look at me like that, you know it's true."

He shifts uncomfortably under her pale blue stare. Like her mother, Ashlynn has mastered the art of pinning a man down with her gaze.

"You sure don't seem to miss her all that much," Ashlynn says.

"What's that supposed to mean? She's family. I'm worried about her. Worried enough. Still, it's no secret that she never had two good words to say about this place or anyone in it. Maybe she finally split town. Could be one of her ex-boyfriends finally acted out an old grudge. Either way you ain't got much family left in these parts. I've been talking with Pa and we don't like you being out here alone, especially with that cross-eyed sheriff trying to sniff up a headline for himself."

Ashlynn shrugs. She moves into the trailer. Her

weaving path carries her by a table of junk mail and past a pyramid of soiled clothes. When she reaches the far wall she kneels in front of a weathered trunk and touches the latch.

"So the local hens are already clucking about me and you and uncle Maynard want to help? That's what brought you out here?"

Travis stubs his cigarette out in the nearest ashtray. An avalanche of lipstick-stained filters cascade to the floor.

"Yeah, something like that. We want you to stay with us till everything blows over. Till Maebeth comes back or . . . whatever."

Ashlynn opens the lid of the trunk and begins digging through it. Travis hopes whatever she's grabbing will fit in the back of his Firebird. Blood may be thicker than water, but it doesn't fill a gas tank. Not to mention the winding country roads which turn treacherous in the dark.

"Mom isn't coming back, but that doesn't mean you can't help me," Ashlynn says.

Travis pauses, waiting for her to finish. She quietly sifts through the contents of the trunk. Somewhere beyond the forty-watt glow of the porch light the hoot of an owl pierces the night. Travis shivers, blaming the cold mountain air for setting his body atremble.

"What do you mean, Ashlynn? Are you saying you know what happened to Maebeth?"

"Like you said, she hated this town. She wanted to fly this dump 'cept I needed looking after. Every man she ever met here was a liar or a deadbeat. Always losing their jobs or changing their minds about moving. Some lied to get close to her. Swore they would take her to the city, or a whole other state. It was the only way she'd give them the time of day," Ashlynn says.

Travis snorts.

"Kinda looking through rose colored glasses, Ash. Your ma is a man-eater, pure and simple. She never liked any of them guys, and when they fell on hard times she showed them the door. Remember Clive Radford working those double shifts at the lumber mill for her? Two years he slaved away. The day he was fired she changed the locks and chucked his suitcase on the porch. Truth is I half suspected him when she went missing. Or maybe Martin Bales finally did something after she stood him up at the altar. Or Tyler Adkinson. Need I go on?" Travis says.

Silence fills the room, broken only by Ashlynn resuming her excavation of the chest.

"You hear anything I just said? What are you looking for? We got the essentials back home, just grab some clothes. We can pick up the rest of your stuff tomorrow," Travis says.

Ashlynn lifts a bulging sack from within the trunk. She uses both hands to heave the awkward bundle high enough to set upon the kitchen counter. The air is poisoned by a musty odor, one that leaves an unpleasant and salty tang at the back of Travis' throat. He coughs and lifts his shirt collar over his nose.

"Whew lordy! I don't know what you got in that bag but it stays here."

Ashlynn turns toward him. Her jaw is defiantly set in an unfamiliar way. The sudden change in her demeanor is alarming.

"Thought you came to help, Cousin Travis. This

bag has to come. Sheriff will be back with his hounds tomorrow and I don't have a car," she says.

"Whoa now, hold on just a minute. Why is the sheriff coming back with dogs and why do you need to ditch that bag? This all sounds mighty suspicious."

Ashlynn leans her elbows on the kitchen counter. Her lips pull into a tight line. No trace remains of the hyper-sensitive girl from summers gone by. Seeing her like this dredges up old memories. Disdainful recollections of Maebeth affecting the same posture before taking a man down a peg or three with her rattlesnake tongue.

"You seem awful particular about the help you want to give," Ashlynn says.

"Don't use that tone with me, Ash. You're not your momma. You're a little girl who won't last a month in these mountains alone. Now get yourself some clothes and get into the car. I got other things to do than worry about you vanishing, too. You can fill me in on what happened to Maebeth while we drive."

"She'd be touched to know you care," Ashlynn says.

"I don't care. She never liked me. I never really liked her neither. She thought she was too big for Alpine View and everyone in it. Just some tumbleweed runaway blown in from a bus station acting like she's the Queen of England. Still, I'm not aiming to become your accomplice. If you did something to Maebeth I expect you to say so."

"I did," Ashlynn says.

Travis blinks. He makes a sound like one of the old diesel engines back at his shop, sputtering and kicking but not going anywhere.

"Buh . . . uh . . . huh? Wait a second, you just said she ran off!"

"She did," Ashlynn says.

Travis slaps his palm against his forehead. His feet splay out across the threadbare carpet.

"Lord if I don't have the craziest relatives in all the Blue Ridge. Tell me straight, Ash, what happened to your mom? Do you know? Did you do something to her?"

Ashlynn lifts the bulging sack with both hands. The weight causes her to fall back a half-step before she steadies herself.

"Tried to tell you before. Mom always swore she'd fly this dump. She said it for years. I did my best to ease her burden. Got good grades, hoping to transfer schools. Sold secondhand clothes to make money. Learned to make soap and sell that, too, but the money I made was never enough. It wasn't until Uncle Maynard told me about the Owl Builder that I knew there was another way."

Travis moves to the edge of his chair as Ashlynn approaches. She is cradling the sack in her arms like a bundle of laundry. He pulls the keys to his Firebird from his pants pocket and clutches them until their teeth bite into his palm.

"I went up to his old cabin. The one past the abandoned church, just on the other side of the hemlock grove. I met him there. He was everything Uncle Maynard says, but worse. Moonlike eyes peering through a feathered mask. They aren't human, those eyes. Not animal neither. I thought he would be old, but he wasn't. More like, ageless. Hands curled up like they had arthritis, the skin all leathery."

Travis stands up before she gets close enough to hand him the bag. He clamps his ball cap over his nose with one hand and waves a fist jingling of keys with the other.

"Stop your crazy talk and get that damn thing away from me. I'm not playing anymore. Go to the car. If we weren't kin I'd say to hell with ya and leave right now."

Ashlyn takes a step back, just enough to hold Travis fully in view as she continues.

"I wore a rodent necklace. Like the legends say. Bound their tails and paws together. It was hard. They squirm so much, like they know what's coming. Biting, shrieking, clawing my neck with their back legs. I thought I might faint. When he leaned in close I wish I had. I didn't move a muscle, though. Not until he chewed the last screaming field mouse from my neck. Then I told him what I wanted. What Mom had always wanted. I didn't know what he would do. Not until I saw it happen."

Travis steps forward shoving the lumpy bag against Ashlynn with enough force to send her stumbling. His hand recoils from the strike as if snake-bit, but not before the sack smooshes inward like a pillow case holding a rotted turkey.

Ashlynn peers at him through her ragged bangs as he races for the door.

"All those things in life we can't swallow, they have to be spit out before the change can happen. The Owl Builder made her vomit up the bones that weighed her down. This town had left an awful lot stuck in her craw. We have to bury mom's pellet, Travis. You said you wanted to help."

Travis is not listening. He's running full bore into the moonlit night. He doesn't believe her. He doesn't believe Maebeth was anything more than a gold digger who finally got her comeuppance. Whether her daughter did it or some ghost from the past is something he can puzzle out on the ride home.

A swift thump sounds loudly from the front yard, a noise like a dirty rug being beat against a tree. Ashlynn hears the telltale shriek that follows and knows the owl has snatched her prey. Her wings are so quiet. They never hear her coming. Ashlynn reaches the door in time to see the massive owl swoop upward towards the moon. The body of a young man hangs limply from her great talons. For a fleeting second she sees the creature swivel its downy head and regards her kindly with ghostly blue eyes. Husky Blue.

The moment is broken by a metallic glint flickering like a lightning bug from the darkness of the yard. Keys. Ashlynn lifts them up to eye level, staring through the keyring at the Firebird parked a short distance away. She smiles, knowing the time has come for her to fly this place as well. A heavy price, perhaps, but she'll swallow the costs.

She'll miss Travis, of course. He may have been wrong about a number of things but he got two absolutely right; Maebeth doesn't like him much, and she is a man-eater.

BIOGRAPHY: *D. Morgan Ballmer lives in a small town just outside of Seattle. His previous work has appeared in* Three-Lobed Burning Eye Magazine *and the* Not Your Average Monster Anthology. *Upcoming releases include stories in the* Silent Screams anthology *and on the* Pseudopod.

Tragedy Park

CHRIS PEARCE

Everybody who's heard of Crimson Sea Water Park has heard the stories about it; it's part of the fun of going there. Everyone knows, for example, about the time they tested a new ride by having a teenage employee go down it and he came out the other end with a broken neck—just nobody knows which ride it was, exactly. That is supposed to be part of the fun, I guess.

There's nothing actually dangerous at a waterpark—it's all just for fun.

There had been deaths at the park—you can't run a place for thirty years and have a completely clean record, I guess, but when the papers had tried to nickname it "Tragedy Park" it hadn't really stuck and people had kept on lining up to ride the rides anyways.

I knew all the stories, obviously, because I find that sort of thing fascinating—hence explaining why I was down to so few friends. Pretty much just one to be exact, Jason. And with the last day of summer fast approaching we had decided to spend the day at the park.

Chris Pearce

Well, Jason had decided and asked me and Lisa to come, and the next thing I knew my mom was dropping me off at the park. I made her leave me at the other end of the parking lot because Jason already had a learner's permit and I didn't want him to see me getting driven around by my mother.

I was only thirteen, the youngest in our group of friends, so I still had to wear a wristband. It was only a few weeks away from my birthday so my plan had been that I would lie and say I was fourteen so I wouldn't have to, but when we got to the ticket booth I instinctively held out my hand and before I could pull it back I already had the loop of paper firmly wrapped around my wrist. I immediately tucked my right hand into my pocket—a pretty meaningless gesture since you could still see it and I wasn't going to be able to keep my hand buried in my pocket for the whole time we were at the park.

"I'm almost fourteen. I shouldn't have to wear one," I said to Jason as we headed to the changing room.

"I hear the reason they make you wear one is because of all the kidnappings," he said. "Back a few years ago, there were like five kids who got abducted, but nobody could prove that it happened at the park, so they started making everybody who was underage wear wristbands so you couldn't leave with anybody you didn't come in with."

"That doesn't make any sense," I said.

"You never believe anything," he said, giving me a shove before disappearing into one of the shower stalls to change. I walked along the row of stalls, looking for one that was open but the curtains were closed on every single one. I thought about trying to peek in one to see if anybody was in it but that seemed like a bad idea. I could hear the showers running in most of them, so I just stood there waiting for Jason to finish so I could use his stall.

It seemed like pretty much everybody, including Jason, had decided to take their sweet time that day, and I wasn't the only one waiting for a stall to open up. Somebody walked in soon after Jason disappeared into the shower; I glanced over at them, trying to not make it obvious I was looking because waiting here was already making me so nervous. He glanced over at the shower stalls and when he realized they were all occupied he started to change right there, without missing a beat. I must've made a noise or something because he finally looked over at me—he hadn't seemed to have noticed me when he first came in.

"What are you doing?" he said as he put on his bathing suit. It was one of the lifeguards—I could tell by the red bathing suit he wore, the same as every lifeguard everywhere. He was older than me—he was just a teenager, but seventeen still seemed like it was an eternity away.

He had a tattoo on his arm, which seemed kind of weird. I thought you had to be an adult before they let you get tattoos. I couldn't exactly make out what it was—at first I thought it was an octopus because I had spotted what looked like a tentacle on the side of his arm but I couldn't see what it connected to. I tried to follow it with my eyes but it traced down his arm and the side of his chest and I couldn't tell where it went from there.

"Hey, you there?" he said, smiling at me. There was

something about his eyes—something about the way he was looking at me—I couldn't explain it, it made me shiver. "What are you doing?"

"I'm waiting for a shower," I said, glancing over at him, squirming in the chair.

"They're all pretty much open," he said, nodding towards them. That didn't make any sense—I knew they were all full—at least I had thought I did but now that I looked over there I realized they were all empty, except for the one that Jason had gone into. I looked over to say something to the lifeguard, but he was already gone, and Jason was stepping out of his stall.

"Slowpoke," he said, grinning. Everything was always a competition with him, which I was pretty much okay with; it meant that he would actually listen to me when I started talking about something morbid like death rates at theme parks, even if it was only because he was trying to think of a way to top me— most people would just tune me out.

So then we headed out to look for Lisa. Jason chattered away about how he was going to try out for the basketball team and he was sure that he'd make it this time, and he asked me if I was going to try out even though he knew the answer was no.

Jason asked me to let him and Lisa go down the Vertical Leap together; I pretended to be a little miffed at them but honestly I was relieved; I hated that slide, I hated how it felt like you were going to go flying off the inner tube, I hated how fast it went, I hated the feeling in my stomach that I got going down it. I headed off to the Lazy River to wait for them to be done, ignoring the twinge of anger perking inside me as I figured out why he had asked to go on the ride with just Lisa, and why he had probably asked me here in the first place. If he had needed cover for a date he could've just told me and I would've gone along with it but I would've liked to have known what I was being involved in.

After about fifteen minutes or so I figured that Jason and Lisa had enough alone time together and since I had been invited I didn't want to just spend the whole day floating on a raft, looking up at the sun and thinking vaguely resentful thoughts about my last friend. I got off of the river and started to look for them. The Vertical Leap was grouped with a bunch of other slides—so there were always a bunch of people there, which made finding Jason and Lisa harder than it should've been.

I headed towards the line, trying to pick them out of the crowd, but I couldn't see them. They were either on the stairs or at the pool at the end of the slide. I backed up, looking up the stairs to see if I could spot them; at the top of the slide I saw a middle aged woman in a black bathing suit, a lanky teenager, and a little girl who looked like she probably should've had a parent with her but didn't. I looked to the end of the slide, waiting for each of them to come out: first the woman, and then the girl, and then someone I hadn't seen at the top of the slide, and then another, and another. I looked back up, wondering where the teenager had gone; I couldn't see him anywhere in the line or even near the ride. I was just about to go to the stairs to try and look for him when I felt Lisa tugging at my arm.

"C'mon Finn," she said.

"What," I said as she dragged me along the

sidewalk. I wished that Jason hadn't invited her, when he called me he hadn't said anything about her, just that it was going to be with some friends. "Where's Jason?"

"You'll see," she said, dragging me along to the far end of the park—to one ride that towered above all of the others, a long twisting mix of black plastic and wooden scaffolding, the sort of ride that everybody always just had to go down because you're chicken if you don't, the sort of ride that had taken me almost fourteen years to finally get to where I was willing to consider even going down:

The Black Vortex.

It was the biggest slide in the whole park, and I had heard that it was the biggest water slide in the whole state, and not a single person had ever gone down it. They had been advertising it all year long, or at least it seemed like it, on TV and in the newspapers. Come down to Crimson Sea Water Park and disappear into the Black Vortex! And everybody had lined up to ride it the first day the park had opened—and they hadn't let anybody go down it yet.

"They tested it and it's too dangerous," said Lisa. "They'll tear it down once the park closes for the year and next year they'll act like it never existed at all."

"Why do they keep the water running then?" I said.

"Because it's not really dangerous," said Jason. "It's all a stunt. They'll open the ride at the end of the season."

"It is the end of the season," I said.

"There are still a couple of weeks left," he said, and then he pointed to the top of the ride. "See, they have the water going and everything. I'll bet the lifeguards take turns going down it when the park closes."

You could hear the sound of water coming from the slide, and if you looked at the places where the tube opened up you could kind of see water flowing through it. It was kind of hard to tell because the whole slide was black, other than a few whirling purple designs painted on its side in a couple of places.

"I'm going to ride it," said Jason, walking up to the gate before looking back at me and Lisa. "And you two are coming with me."

I swallowed, trying to think of some excuse to get me out of this, suddenly wishing that I had just let Jason and Lisa hang out on their own—I could've called my mom and told her I was feeling sick or something. I wouldn't really have wanted to go down the Black Vortex normally, but since it wasn't even open I really didn't want to.

I looked over at Jason and then at Lisa and realized I wasn't quite ready to give up—maybe I could talk some sense into him, and maybe I wouldn't even need to—probably we wouldn't be able to get anywhere near the slide in the first place.

There was a big old padlock on the gate, which I thought would be the end of this little adventure, but Jason kept looking until he found a part of the fence that he could pull up just enough that somebody could probably slide under it, probably. Jason certainly was able to, and Lisa too, which left just me standing on the side of the park we were actually supposed to be in.

"Come on, Finn, somebody's going to see you," said Jason, his face peeking out from under the hole in the fence. "Throw the inner tube over, okay?"

I considered just throwing the tube over and then hightailing out of there, but just for a second; then I threw the inner tube over, just like he had asked me, and crawled under the fence. Jason and Lisa were already at the bottom of the stairs, which was farther away from the gate than I would've expected—I started to run over to them but then I noticed something out of the corner of my eye.

I stopped; there was something curled up in the grass behind the gate, right where the edge of the park gave way to the wilderness. At first I thought that—well, that it was somebody's arm or something because that's what it looked like, and I about shouted but I stopped myself. Then it moved a little and instead of screaming I jumped about a foot backward, stumbling into Jason, which was maybe worse than screaming.

"Did somebody throw up?" he said, leaning over my shoulder to look at whatever it was curled up in the grass. It could've been; there had been an outbreak of some bad bug a couple years back, rumor was that the park had been skimping on the cleaning chemicals, which led to half the attendants getting sick. Jason had been the one to tell me the story; he liked the way I gagged when he told me stuff like that. He looked down at the pink thing and scrunched up his face, before grabbing a stick off of the ground and poking it. It moved when the stick touched it, circling in on itself—it was a snake, a sickly pink snake—it must've been shedding its skin.

"Oh, gross," said Lisa, jumping back from the snake. "Leave it alone, guys."

"I wonder if it's poisonous," said Jason as he dropped the stick and continued towards the Black

Vortex. I kneeled down, still far enough from it that I was pretty sure it wouldn't be able to bite me.

"You can play with your worm later, let's get going," said Jason, as he headed towards the stairs. There was a gate over those two but they were easy enough to jump. The universe was making it pretty clear to me that I didn't need to be here.

"Why can't you just go with Lisa?" I said as we started to climb the stairs.

"C'mon, Finn, don't be a spoilsport," said Lisa, looking back at me and sticking out her tongue. I rolled my eyes at her, stopping immediately when Jason glared at me, and returned to walking up the stairs behind them. They seemed to go on up forever. I vaguely remembered reading that the Black Vortex had included the largest wood structure in the state, but that couldn't be right, surely there was something bigger than some stupid waterpark ride? Regardless, you could see pretty much the entire park, and the parking lot too, and a little bit more—and looking out at all of that I realized something.

"Where is everybody?" I said, looking down at the park below. It had been kind of late so people should've been filtering out of the park but it seemed almost completely empty. I could just see a handful of people, and it looked like most of them were employees. I looked out at the parking lot. It was still mostly full, which didn't seem to make any sense.

"Stop stalling," said Jason, pushing me forward and up the stairs. We were almost to the top of the slide now. Had this been a regular ride it would've been too late to chicken out, to force myself to march past all the other people waiting in line, half of who would be younger than me, but there was nobody else here other than me and Jason and Lisa.

"This is a bad idea," I said just as I stepped onto the landing at the top of the slide. "I'm going back down."

"No, you aren't," said Jason, stretching out his arms and legs and wrapping his hands around the railings on both sides of the stairs. I tried to push my way past him, but he didn't budge an inch. "We've gone this far and I'm not going to let you chicken out now."

"Let me go!" I said, trying to tense up so he'd have a harder time dragging me onto the slide, but I shuddered when he grabbed a hold of me and I felt myself go relatively limp—limp enough that Jason didn't have any trouble sitting me down on the tube. He sat in front of me and Lisa in front of him. I definitely didn't want to sit at the back of the tube so I tried to get up again but when Jason glared at me I sat back down again. Jason started to count—one, two— and then he pushed us forward, shouting three as we sped down into the Vortex.

The Vortex was one of those slides that were mostly covered, except for a few spots where it was open to the air. Maybe so the people waiting in line could hear the people on the ride screaming. And it wasn't very steep. It was mainly long and winding. At least, that's what I thought. But we were going so fast, it made me think of the time I had gone down the Vertical Leap. My stomach was churning—I kept waiting for the parts where we would be under open air, even for just a second, so I could tell how close we were to the bottom, but everything just stayed dark, and we were going so fast. Every turn we took my head would whip back and forth because I couldn't brace myself. I realized I was holding on to Jason—I hadn't even noticed it, and he hadn't pushed me off of him. He would surely make fun of me when we got to the bottom, but I kept my grip as tight as I could.

And then we stopped, but there was still only darkness.

"What the hell?" said Jason. I could feel him stumbling off the inner tube. I grabbed his hand and pulled him back down.

"Don't," I said as he landed beside me on the inner tube.

"Just stay here with Lisa, I'm going to go look around," he said, pulling his hand away from mine and getting back up again. "Okay, Lisa?"

Nobody answered.

"She's not here," I said, drawing my knees to my chest and wrapping my arms around them; I was glad it was so dark and that Jason couldn't see me.

"Crap, she must've fallen off of the tube," said Jason, and I heard him start running in the direction that the slide had been. "We are going to be in so much trouble," he started to say but his words trailed off just as the sound of his feet hitting something—that definitely wasn't pavement—stopped.

"Where's the slide?" he said.

I heard the sound of him fumbling with something, and then saw a light, a tiny flickering flame that lit up his face and the top half of his chest. Finally I could look around and see something—but I didn't see anything at all, not the slide, not the park, not anything in any direction. It was just me and Jason and the inner tube and the ground. At least, that's what it was at first. Then I heard the sound of somebody walking towards us, making a squishing sound in the ground as they got closer, and for a second I wished so much that Jason hadn't wandered off from me. There wasn't really any way for me to tell how far he had gone in the darkness.

There was a burst of light, far brighter than Jason's lighter. It was a flashlight, pointed right at us. For a second I could see even less than when it had been just darkness, but then whoever was holding the flashlight lowered it down and I could make out who it was—a lifeguard. I could tell by the red bathing suit he wore. In fact, it was the lifeguard from earlier, the one I had seen in the changing room—I couldn't really make out his face but I could tell because of his tattoo.

"What are you doing here?" said the lifeguard, shining his flashlight at us. He was tall, taller than either of us, and he was soaking wet from head to toe.

I could see the water oozing down his skin slower than it should have been. The sight of it made something in my stomach churn.

"Nothing!" said Jason, springing up from the tube and standing up straight like he was a marine or something. He dropped the lighter as he did, which went out the moment it hit the ground. For a second I could make out the soil. It was a strange mix of purple beneath green, I had never seen dirt that color before, and it smelled strange too, like the way a skinned knee smells before you put antiseptic on it.

"We went down the slide," I said. I always knew when you got in trouble, it was best to come clean immediately, and somehow I knew that lying right here and now would be an incredibly bad idea.

"Don't tell him that," hissed Jason. I guess he thought there was still a chance that the lifeguard didn't know what we had done—and for a second I felt a flash of anger at him, that he thought he could pull the wool over literally everybody's eyes, everywhere. I choked it down, though, because the lifeguard had locked eyes with me. I couldn't see his face but I could feel him looking at me and I couldn't move.

The lifeguard stepped forward; the water seemed to cling to his skin and the ground at the same time. It was pulling at his skin, tearing whole stretches of it off at a time, like when you have a sunburn and the skin finally starts to peel, leaving splotches of pink under the red and maybe a few new moles. But the skin underneath his skin wasn't pink, it looked like it was the same strange color of the ground we were standing on. Even as his skin was sliding off I could still make out the tattoo on his arm, except now it looked more like it was something on his arm. It moved, writhing around like it was alive, all up and down his arm and his chest and even further still. It wasn't—it wasn't as terrible as it sounds. I was frightened—I had the same feeling in my stomach I would get on a roller coaster or when Jason would convince me to do something that he knew I was going to hate. But at that moment I understood why people did that sort of thing.

"What the hell?" shouted Jason, scrambling onto the ground, grabbing at his lighter. He opened it up again and flicked it on before he started waving it back and forth in front of the lifeguard. "Stay away you freak!" he shouted, and when that didn't have any effect he finally threw it at him; it bounced off of his chest and landed on the ground with a clunk. The lifeguard continued walking towards us as if Jason hadn't done anything.

Jason stepped between the two of us; I guess he thought he was going to fight him. Before he could do anything I put my hand on his shoulder; when he still didn't respond I locked my arms around his and pulled him to the ground. I had always been bigger than him, even if he didn't like to admit it.

"Don't move," I said, looking down at Jason. He didn't say anything, he just kept looking at me and then back at the lifeguard, his mouth slightly open like he was trying to think of something to say but finally he didn't have anything to add so he stayed silent.

"We've been waiting for you," he hummed, his voice deep, emanating from the back his throat; I felt the sound in my eardrums, a heavy buzzing that traveled down my spine to my stomach and lower. "We've seen you. Watching us. You're almost ready. Aren't you ready?"

"I think so," I said, looking him in the eyes. They had gone completely black, but every now and then a thin layer of what I guess was skin would slide across his eyes. His eyes made me think of . . . not nothing but nothingness, what the world must look like when you're miles below the surface of the ocean. It's darker than space down there you know, at least in space you can see the stars.

"What about him?" I said, looking back at Jason. He was back in the inner tube, his arms wrapped around his chest, and he was shaking a little bit. His eyes locked with mine and I could see that he was crying. I don't think I had ever seen him cry before, not even that time he had convinced his little brother to jump off of the roof and he had broken his leg.

"What are you doing?" hissed Jason, looking up at me. I didn't answer him. He reached up to grab me, and I pushed him down again.

"It's okay," I said. "You just have to trust me."

"You can leave him," said the lifeguard. "Leave him if you want. Eat him. See what he tastes like. Whatever you want."

"I want him," I said. "I want him. I don't care what it means, I want him."

"He can't really be yours," said the lifeguard. "You know that. But you can have him. And make no one else have him. Because that's what having him is. Is that what you want?"

"What are you talking about?" said Jason; he didn't try to get up this time, I guess he had learned his lesson.

"You know what I'm talking about," I said. "I've lost enough friends. I'm not going to lose you."

They never found Jason. It was assumed that he was a runaway. Nobody really had an explanation for why he had left his car at the park if that was true, but I guess that was the easiest explanation. Lisa didn't understand at all what had happened. She said she came out of the slide and then a second later I came out of the slide but then Jason never did.

After about a couple of weeks or so people stopped talking about it. The park was closed for the season by then anyway, so there wasn't really anything for people to talk about. Pretty much everybody had forgotten about it the next year—they all lined up to ride the rides—that included the Black Vortex, which had

Chris Pearce

finally opened to the public. I did too—after I applied for a job to be a lifeguard there.

Employment at the park had so many perks, I just couldn't pass it up.

And besides—how else was I going to see Jason?

BIOGRAPHY: *Chris Pearce is allegedly an aspiring writer and student of the occult. He lives in an undisclosed location somewhere in the central United States. When not pouring over forbidden tomes of blasphemous lore, he spends his time preparing for Halloween or working a rather mundane nine to five job.*

Enclosures

SUMIKO SAULSON

There are many kinds of enclosures. A house is a building, which encloses within the treasures of its occupants. These treasures are not merely physical trinkets, the ornamentation and decoration we acquire throughout the day to day business of going through what we deem living, but memories. All of these accumulate to create residential fortresses we call homes. Bodies are merely flesh, encasing emotion and intellect, experience and education we collectively think of as spirit.

There are many kinds of enclosures I have coveted over the course of my twenty-eight years. I have lusted for comely flesh. I have been envious of the economic prowess of successful others. I have an acquisitive nature. I have always wanted things that weren't my own.

My grandfather warned me, "Be careful what you wish for." I took his curmudgeonly counsels as the trite and confused ramblings of a worn-out old man. There was nothing he had to say that I hadn't heard before. During the visit, I politely pretended to listen to his advice with glazed over eyes, eyes that were otherwise bright and eager. His were jaundiced and bleary. When he spoke, his desiccated lips stuck to the ochre tinted surface of his decade-old, coffee-and-pipe-tobacco stained dentures. For appearances, I resisted nodding out during his endless lectures, holding myself at attention by sheer force of will, as the yellowed crust formed in the cavernous pocket of his sagging tear duct.

He was the esteemed Reginald Moore. I, though less esteemed, am named after him, with a pretentious-sounding moniker Reginald Henry Moore III. Perhaps I would have heeded his advice, but hubris is the gift of the young. I imagined I knew everything about how the world actually worked. I thought him a doddering old fool, sitting alone in his five bedroom three bathroom craftsman-style home on Clear Lake. His solitary bedroom was surrounded by rooms converted into voluminous libraries filled with musty old tomes and yellowing World War II era periodicals.

Bulging and precariously sagging bookshelves lined the guest bedroom I slept in. I feared for my life in case of an earthquake. Mount Konocti had not erupted in more than ten thousand years, but was prone to periodic tremors. I often rode out my fear of being crushed to death beneath his rickety bookshelves in order to spend a night in the isolated estate in order to impress the old man.

The books were interesting. He seemed to have dabbled in mysticism some time ago, back when Kennedy was in office. The strange thing was that some of these books had been inscribed with the name Reginald Henry Moore even though they dated back to the Hoover administration, more than a decade before my grandfather's birth. Strange noises accompanied the musty odors in the room, and I often spotted odd greenish lights on the surface of the lake at night. I wouldn't have bothered with my regular visits to his home in Clear Lake, California if I hadn't been on the short list of potential heirs to his larger estate, which included a ranch and winery off the Russian River in Sonoma.

My frequent visits with the man gave him the wrong impression, however. Evidently, he decided I was interested in the two story house in Clear Lake. Perched on stilts above a winding staircase that descended to a modest private pier on the lakefront, the home was beautiful.

He left it to me in his will when he died.

However, Clear Lake was ninety miles from San Francisco and sixty miles from Santa Rosa.

It was far too far away from the exciting nightlife I had been enjoying as a young man in my twenties. If the will didn't prevent such an action I would have immediately placed it on the market. The cool half million my real estate agent sought for the property would barely leave me with enough money to buy a one bedroom condominium in the city.

I began to dream up ways to stay in my urban environment. I was lucky I had a job at the post office. I made a decent wage and had a comfortable benefits package. My relationship with a girl named Leslie Parsons had been casual so far, but the thought of extra income in this difficult economy tempted me to suggest domestic partnership. I wasn't interested in marriage, but living in the most expensive city in the country made a man practical.

Sumiko Saulson

Don't think that I don't know what you are thinking right now; that I am a rogue and a scoundrel. Perhaps you think that I never cared for the elder Reginald Moore. Maybe you, having met the sweet but plain looking Miss Parsons believe my interest in her was purely opportunistic. Leslie, after all, was gainfully employed as a dental hygienist, and could afford to pay her own way. You are mistaken. I am not a cruel man by any means. I am merely a practical one. I loved Miss Parsons in my own way. I often miss her these days.

I wish I had pursued a genuine relationship with her. Perhaps, over time, I would have grown to love and even marry her. If I hadn't spent so much time down by the lake, pursuing my own petty ambitions, things might have been different. We could have been happy.

Instead, I wound up married to a house on the lake and the ghost of the old man whose name I bear.

The strangeness at the lake began the first week after the funeral. I'd inherited the house on Clear Lake and all that was within it. It had been strictly stipulated that I could not sell the property or live anywhere else for a period of one year. I was young, and ambitious, and I believed that I would eventually be in the position to sell. I asked for and received a transfer to a postal route in Ukiah, only an hour away. The three hour drive to San Francisco took a toll on my social life, and I rarely saw old friends. Still, sacrifices had to be made sometimes. I was approaching thirty, and I thought I should be practical.

I also believed I was too old for the shivers, night terrors, and childhood fears of the dead. Perhaps it was the loneliness of the vast, empty space, but I began to feel at ill ease. There was an oppressive emptiness in the home. The vacant space left was just waiting for strange imaginings.

I spent late nights alone by the fireplace reading from my grandfather's remarkably well preserved group of old periodicals. I became hyperaware of every stray cool breeze and creak of settling floorboards. Occasionally, I became comfortable, relaxed in the illusion of peaceful solitude, lulled by the sound of crickets. These moments were brief, soon interrupted by the sounds of teeming wildlife. A city boy, I found myself as easily disturbed by a raccoon rummaging through the garbage as a mountain lion roaming through the brush. If these weren't bad enough, the occasional tremors terrified me with the volcano so nearby.

I was literally jumping at shadows.

It was in this susceptible frame of mind that I first came in contact with the other occupant of my lonely estate. The presence was easily discernible from the natural inhabitants of the area, although in retrospect, I feel I should not assume its occurrence was other than natural. The term preternatural is used to describe those things that exist beyond the natural order of things. Supernatural describes things we simply do not yet understand. I don't know if it is unnatural.

When I say it, I should say 'he' . . .

He did not exist outside of the house, as a part of the eerie symphony of hauntingly peaceful sounds that were comforting to natives but disturbing to my untrained urban ear. He did not exist in the library, among the yellowing volumes of ancient pages bound in moldering linen thread and concealed within stale leather binders.

I found him one day in the bathroom, staring back at me from behind a silver-lined mirror, soap scum obscuring its crystal-cut edges. He stared back at me from the mirror. At first, I believed I was imagining things. My bright hazel eyes appeared murky and morose beyond the usual darkening associated with my moods. Their irises mimicked the muddy brown hue of my grandfather's. Likewise, they were encircled in hazy gray haloes, an optical illusion of some sort.

As the day wore on into evening, I became increasingly convinced that my grandfather was in the room with me somehow. I felt him not as a presence that might leap unannounced from a dark corner, but as an unwanted invader beneath my skin.

I started to believe that I was losing my mind.

I'd done nothing wrong, surely. I had no reason for a guilty conscience, when the old man died of natural causes. I wasn't responsible for his passing and he'd survived to a ripe old age. Perhaps I felt a twinge of remorse over the many times I feigned attention when he spoke to me. I could have been kinder, more interested. I might have a mild case of regret about the lack of real concern I felt for the man. After all, my grandfather seemed to truly care for me. There weren't many others who had. My parents and I were not close. They'd left the country many years ago, taking their wealth with them. They said I was spoiled and self-centered. Maybe I was.

Convinced that it was all in my imagination, I went about my day. I was in the kitchen, when I was once again overcome by the sense that I was not alone. The anxiety and foreboding increased as I sorted through his cabinets in search of a pot. I found an intricately formed old copper tea kettle whose handle was shaped like winding grape vines in an orchard. The old man kept loose tea leaves in a series of small metal cylinders on the kitchen counter, each labeled. He had an old fashioned metal steeping ball, the kind that could be filled with tea leaves and then dropped into a pot of hot water. I had just finished the task of brewing a pot of ginger tea when my fingers began to tremble of their own accord.

Perplexed by the involuntary body movements, I began to press my hands down flat upon the cold gray marble countertop in order to prevent the digits from moving. No matter how hard I pressed, they continued with their involuntary dance. Soon, my arms and wrists were tired and aching from the exertion.

The pot issued forth a loud pitched whistle and I jumped in alarm, conking the top of my head against the cabinets above me. I winced and let out a yelp of pain. Catching my breath, I spun around on my heel and then carefully turned down the gas burner on the stove. I spent a few moments nursing my aching head as the tea kettle cooled.

By the time I began preparing my tea I had developed a sudden, very agitated sounding persistent cough. Every cough increased the pressure at the base of my skull, and the pain from the earlier head bump began to reform into a headache. The hacking worsened, and was shortly accompanied by a reflexive spasm of the jaw. I'd never experienced these sorts of unwanted body movements before. Panic set in. Had I misjudged my grandfather? Had the old man in a fit of vengeance, poisoned the tea?

I carefully set down the teacup, afraid to take another sip. I was certain I was going to die. What happened next was even more unexpected and equally, if not more, terrifying.

I felt I might leap from my skin when an outside presence forced open my mouth to speak. At first it felt like a jaw spasm, but the movements of lip and tongue and the beginnings of unmistakable vocalization horrified me. A voice was coming out of my body, and although it resembled mine, it was not my own. I recognized the pronunciation immediately, and I knew it was my grandfather.

"I hope you're enjoying the estate," Reginald hissed, his sibilant vocalization no longer hindered by dentures, or muffled by aging flesh. The voice was forcibly torn from my own throat. I felt my chest tighten with anxiety and my pulse began to quicken. I was overcome by an urge to run screaming from the room, but where would I run to? My grandfather somehow possessed my body. How could you escape something that was inside of your very skin?

"Out, demon!" I screamed back, alarmed.

My protests were to no avail. I attempted to leave the room, but I couldn't move my own feet. The occupying force held me steady in place, refusing to allow me the luxury of turning my head to one side to look away from it.

"You know I am no demon," my grandfather sarcastically retorted. Even in death, he was insufferably pompous. "Things might be simpler if I had been a demon. Then, I would have no need for flesh. But I, like you, am a spiritual traveler. It's an inherited condition. Unfortunately for you, you won't be living long enough to learn how to exercise your powers.”

What did he mean by inherited? I was a passenger in my own body, as the pushy old man strode my feet into his kitchen. He chuckled under my breath, lending his lilting tone to my voice as he described in some detail his experiences as an entity who occupied the flesh of others.

“I'm much older than you think,” the old man explained, pouring himself a fresh cup of ginger tea. “Yours is the third body I've occupied. I was your grandfather's grandfather before I took his flesh. I was a young man in the early eighteenth century. Believe it or not, I was your age when *Gulliver's Travels* was published back in 1726.”

“Fascinating,” I told the old man in my body. “I bet my grandfather was as amused by your endless jabbering as I am now.”

The old man cut me off without a thought, as though I had said nothing. He simply continued his lecture as though I were an unruly student. “Traveling was all the rage for young men of my era and background. We left our homes in Europe to sail the seas, in search of exotic locales in Asia and Africa. Some of us traveled as I did, by caravan, to locations near but not less enticing. I took the spice roads into the Near East, traveling with merchants who variously sold spices, clothing dyes, and fancy cloth. It was during these travels that I became well acquainted with any number of popular opiates and additionally, the theories regarding astral projection.”

“You've been reading too many old horror stories,”

I told myself in irritation. "You sound like a character from W. W. Jacobs' *The Monkey's Paw*."

"That certainly is a modern tale," the old man chuckled. "I rather enjoyed it. I wish I could say I wrote anything anywhere near as imaginative, but as you can see by my bookshelves, all I have written were dry academic articles and fanciful travelogues encouraging bored young men to sail the seven seas in search of adventure."

"I need ask you to leave my body," I cried in frustration. I'm not sure why I argued with the foreign invader in my body. Perhaps I had some strange notion that the parasite could be reasoned with. It did not seem reasonable, refusing as it did to allow me to control myself. It took me through the motions of bathing and tooth brushing before it adjourned to bed.

"How lovely it is, having teeth again," the old man said as he brushed.

It was just before dawn when I awoke quite naturally to the gradual illumination of the pink-tinged gray clouds in the morning sky. I felt no tinge of the unwanted presence around me, and momentarily, believed it had all been a terrible nightmare. I was overcome by sense of relief so pervasive that it filtered into all aspects of my being. I walked through the house rolling up shades, binding curtains with sashes and throwing open the windows. Fresh air entered the rooms, cleaning away the dank and dusty scents from the corners. Drops of sunshine entered the room, illuminating the dark corners. I felt as though my very soul was cleansed.

It was in this carefree and happy state that I stepped out the back door and entered into my garden.

I was smiling when I entered the tin walled gardening shed and picked out a pair of gloves, a weeding hoe, and pruning shears. My grin only broadened as I sat in the dirt, tending to the garden. Half an hour passed before it occurred to me that gardening was nowhere among my ordinary set of leisure activities. I frowned. When had I suddenly developed an interest in gardening? As if in answer to my unspoken question, my jaw burst open in a series of braying guffaws.

"I bet you didn't know I was here," Reginald chuckled in my mind, sending me leaping up from my seat. My lips didn't move this time, so I thought that perhaps I'd just imagined it. "You probably thought you developed some new talents through osmosis as you slept," it taunted. "You always were the arrogant one, ignoring my good advice."

By the time my body was finished gardening, my mood and spirits had dampened considerably. I began to believe I was having some kind of a break down, and I was losing my mind. A sense of malaise overtook me.

In my despair, I began to daydream of my kind and ordinary Leslie. She had been such a loyal and dependable person. I remembered how she'd visited me with soups and lozenges when I'd been sick two months ago with the flu. She'd been heartbroken when I decided to move so far away. She called me daily now that we were far apart. How I missed her today.

"You won't miss her for long," the ominous voice issuing forth from my strained vocal chords mocked. "Soon, you won't feel anything at all, except what I allow you to feel."

The next three days were a series of ongoing and increasingly futile battles to regain control of my own body. Reginald seemed to wait until I was exhausted, physically and mentally, to take over completely and run me like a marionette all through the house. When I resisted, he used the physical exertion of my own efforts to purposely tire me. Soon, I realized that my only hope at winning this battle was to cease struggling against him and to allow myself to become rested enough to resist.

I was in this meditative mode, disciplining myself not to resist, when I first found myself terrifyingly untethered from my own body. I floated through the air to a destination one to two feet above my head. It was frightening, this sense of liberation from my own flesh. I felt anxious that I would never return to it if I did not immediately reenter, and so I shoved myself back into my body. I was sweating and delirious, trapped in my own skin, staring into the mirror while Reginald went through the motions of shaving.

Every day, I found myself spending more and more time outside of my body. When I ventured back in, I was lectured by the caustic first Reginald Moore. He assured me that soon, my detachment would be permanent. I would become a bodiless, wandering spirit like all of the others before me. I might haunt him briefly, but like my grandfather before me, and his grandfather before that, I would give up one day and simply vanish.

When I was able to focus on other things, my attention went to sweet Leslie. Absence in this case did indeed make the heart grow fonder. Her virtues began to outshine any flaws in my memories of her. I focused on her so much that I believe, almost superstitiously now, that it was my thoughts that brought her knocking on my door on the seventh day of my disembodiment. It was not, of course. It was the elder Reginald's failure to respond to her calls and text messages. Still, it was wonderful to see her face.

"Can you hear me?" I asked her, my wandering spirit chattering restlessly in her ear. My grandfather batted away my persistent attempts to reenter my body, my former lifelong domicile. It was useless. I, the previous resident, had been illegally evicted.

How I wished that I could communicate with my poor, dear Leslie.

But my grandfather was right when he said be careful what you wish for.

I imagine that it was my avid concentration on Leslie that caused me to become sucked into her body. The magnetism that pulled me inward was nearly irresistible, a force of nature, like a tornado, spinning me into a vortex somewhere in the center of her soul where she longed for me.

The moment I arrived at her center, the volcano roused in seeming disagreement, and the earth shook in trembling complaint. Hearing its plea and warning, I wished to quickly exit her body. It was too late. I was bound to her flesh.

Now I sit in Leslie's body, trying desperately to refrain from exerting my own will upon her. How would I be able to bear it, if I had to subject this innocent woman to the fear and disillusionment I experienced when my grandfather operated me against my will? A million times a day I wished I could extinguish myself, but it was not anything I could control.

So I sit here instead, in the wee hours of the night,

typing a manuscript with the sleeping body of my beloved Leslie. I worry that she will become conscious, and aware of my usurping her power. I trouble myself with thoughts of how difficult it will be for me to allow her free will, especially when she may make choices that I disapprove of, like taking another lover.

If I were my grandfather, I would have taken her against her will. Her body would now be my full time residence, and she would be ousted from her tenancy. But I am not him. I can't bear to do it. So I live here, hiding my presence. I hide here, hoping I will remain undetected, and not the instrument that will send my unfortunate love into a state of unrelenting psychosis.

Woe, Violent Water

LILY CHILDS

I have fingers that creep," she said. "From the line of your spine to that place on your neck where I could break you, shake you, steal your soul."

Exhaustion stopped the Elders from doling out more punishment to the wild waif they'd gathered into their bosom, but they listened to the words crackle from her husky throat. They would not forget.

"Enid." A young mother clapped hands over her baby's ears; the child wailed into the eternal sunset. "Your voice could curdle butter, girl."

"It does," the girl said. "And it shall again." She squatted on the barren earth, shifted the skirts they'd lent her, and relieved herself in a great gush. "Do not speak my name. It is mine, not yours to spill."

They forbade Enid to dance, and would not let her sing.

Dragging themselves across dustbowls toward ever-distant mountains, the Woebegones regarded the girl's ceaseless energy.

Whilst they lost muscle from bone, and organs failed from malnutrition and thirst, Enid thrived.

Her company was not fruitless, however. Disappearing for hours into nowhere, her return always yielded gifts of sweet water. Together with the fittest of the group, she shared it out in small doses.

"T'will be enough to keep us alive," the Elders agreed. They offered no thanks to their benefactor, sending prayers instead to the unearthly provider in the sky. Enid said nothing more about this. She would gain her reward when she buried the Woebegones' dead.

Boots ruptured, clothes tattered, they moved on, half the number that had started out on the great journey. They awoke one morning to thick fog, a cold potage that soaked their garments.

"T'is a sign," someone said. But of what, they could not agree. Murmurs of salvation countered wailing omens of a hell arisen from the depths. All for the sake of a little mist.

Enid climbed off a boy and whispered in his ear.

"There's a change in land nearby, that's all. It's no great portent."

Enamoured yet fearful of what he had just given himself up to, the breasts he had suckled, the boy shivered as his body succumbed to an all-pervading chill. He stared into the murk of this new morning. No day would ever be the same.

"Enid," he called.

She didn't call back.

The group set about collecting the moisture to drink. Women wrung out sodden blankets, hats and clothing, not questioning whether the filth of travel, of creeping uncleanliness could ever be boiled out of the black water that emerged. They filtered it carefully, hopefully.

The mist rose.

The sun set.

The light did not change.

"We must travel overnight," said the Elders. They did not argue, for the Woebegones kept books of punishments due. No-one wanted their names on those pages to be associated with Enid by pen, her misdemeanours recorded with ink and spit.

They trudged onwards, belongings clattering as nocturnal bells on their backs. Human asses. Heads down. Eyes half-closed.

"Stop!"

They didn't stop, accustomed to Enid's outbursts.

"Drown then," she said, loud enough to falter the most stubborn of steps. She stood before the leading pack, signalling, waving, her arms clad in tattered-edged sleeves, wings of leather. "You cannot cross here."

A woman collapsed to her knees, then down again to hit her head upon stony ground. The babe strapped to her chest was crushed by the fall. It didn't cry. Instant death. By the time its mother regained her spirits, the child had been baptised in the flowing river and buried beside it.

After resting for two days upon the riverside's lush land, the Woebegones fell into two camps—those that wished to settle right there and those who believed the distant mountains offered better survival choices. The Elders commanded a bridge be built. The younger people refused. Despite a declaration that such dissent would be neither tolerated nor go unpunished, the young stood strong. When the Woebegones' Punisher took a whip to three men's backs, it only strengthened their resolve. And when the Punisher was found dead the next morning with a rope of human gut tied around his throat, the split was finally made.

Enid was blamed. For causing ructions, for debasing the Woebegones' young men, for murder. And worse.

"We cannot suffer a witch to live."

"But she saved us, Borthwick—brought us water, gave us sustenance."

"And all the while she blossomed at our expense," the leader cried. "How do you think she fared so well whilst the rest of us were dying? What do you think she did with our corpses?"

Seeds of doubt swiftly sown.

She had eaten their flesh, sucked the souls from their mouths. The cloaks and skins she wore were not the hides of animals but those of the Woebegones themselves. All rumours, all plausible grains of truth.

As the mountain-goers constructed a simple bridge and the valley dwellers made huts of stone and mud, Enid was shackled and caged. Everyone ignored her pleas and rants, whispering instead of her madness as she howled through the nights, disturbing their sleep.

The day came for the community to select their chosen paths. Having come to a temporary peace, the Elders travelling on to the mountains cast a blessing over the river valley.

One of their number would remain behind, Borthwick declared, to act as their intermediary with God. Feet shuffled whilst voices stayed silent. The Elders controlled them still, burdening them with rigid beliefs. The young watched the old traverse the bridge on foot, pulling with them the groups' remaining carts.

They reached the other side and waited as their leader traipsed back to the centre of the bridge. Both groups looked on, expecting another blessing. Borthwick turned to his appointed deputy on the valley side—his brother—and nodded. Gasps arose from both camps as the deputy returned to the bridge with a naked, bleeding Enid. Her beguiling face a miasma of bruises, one shoulder dislocated. Her right arm hung a full hand's length farther down than the left.

Women, both sides of the bridge, covered their eyes in disgust and pity. Some of the men looked down in shame.

"Just let her go," said a carpenter from the valley. "It's what we agreed. She should not suffer this humiliation."

"I agreed nothing." Borthwick stepped towards Enid, who stood, head held high despite her injuries. He took a knife from his cloak. Its dull blade twinkled at Enid's throat.

He cut.

Tress, by tress, Enid's ink-black hair fell into the fast flow of the river.

"You are no longer Delilah, no more the temptress sent to weaken our men."

Enid shot him a look, defiant to the end.

"Foul bastard, you cannot even recite your own bible tales with accuracy." She spat in his open mouth. "I am no more Delilah than I am Samson; cutting off my hair will never sever my strength, even in death."

Borthwick pushed her to the cusp of the bridge. Her toes clawed the edge.

"You will die for your sins, girl."

"And what of your sins? Where was your

repentance as you fucked me front and back while your wife lay sleeping?"

The Elder's mouth closed tight, the girl's spittle still poison on his tongue as Enid cursed the Woebegones, valley-side, mountain-side; cursed their children, cursed the bridge. He brought the blade back to her throat. Before he could cast her into the river she called to the men on its east and west banks, capturing them all with her gaze.

"I carry your child, and yours. All here in my womb, together. I take your future into death. You will all suffer my pain."

***

"Power's out again."

Curtis slammed his keys on the kitchen worktop. Third day in a row it had cut out; half the staff sent home from the store without pay. The freezers were fucked.

Sarah stroked her belly; they couldn't afford for him to lose wages. The baby was already overdue; so was the rent.

"What do you think's causing it?"

"That new unit Mervin put in. They're saying he's fiddled with the supply down at the bridge, diverted it."

The baby kicked. Sarah belched.

"What an idiot. Of all the things to screw with . . . "

Everyone steered clear of the River Need. It ebbed and flowed with enough ferocity to claim a half dozen fisherman a year where the water eddied and sucked. Sarah's brother had drowned there the previous winter. No fisherman, Shaun had died of a broken heart, a love letter still in his pocket. The last conversation Sarah had shared with him was of despair; he was in love with a girl from the valley over the bridge. Sarah questioned who even lived out there anymore, and Shaun agreed; said whenever he went looking for her he never found her. But she always found *him*.

And only after begging for her name had she finally told him, "Call me Enid, like the river."

"I've never met anyone like her," Shaun had said. "She's like some forest spirit, dancing one minute, climbing trees the next."

Sarah hadn't wanted to hear about the sex but he'd told her anyway. It was unique, utter bliss. Shaun had made an art of his carnal skills, getting in trouble over it, running away from it. This Enid must truly be something else. But after they found Shaun's body swinging from the Need Bridge, from a rope of his own intestines, the girl—and any evidence she even existed—was nowhere to be found.

Sarah was right. The valley houses were long gone, torn down after decades of dercliction. Settlers had occupied the site for almost four hundred years, but settled they weren't. The area was bad news. It regularly flooded. Cholera had wiped out whole communities if they weren't already poisoned by the arsenic which naturally occurred in the earth, permeating their crops, crippling their immunity.

After Shaun's death Sarah started crossing the Need Bridge on an almost daily basis, looking for the girl no-one else had heard of and had certainly never seen. No easy conquest; Enid was the real thing. Shaun had kept her to himself.

"The cops are useless, Curt," Sarah told her

husband. "They've given up. But she killed him—I know it."

Curt didn't believe it; he thought Shaun had needed help, mental health-type help. It was all imagined. But then he wasn't an expert in such things. He was a warehouseman in a store owned by a thief.

He watched his wife slink into a top that no longer fit. Her belly button protruded against the thin fabric. It repulsed him. Guilt spread through his wiry veins, but it didn't change how he felt. He flipped his back to Sarah.

"Going out again?"

"Uh huh."

They hardly spoke these days.

"You know what?" said Sarah. "Why don't you come with me to the bridge?" Curtis flinched. "No worries then. I'm going to the library first anyway. You stay here and reheat the brisket from yesterday."

Choke on it.

Curt nodded but didn't look at her, not even when he kissed her goodbye.

The road to the library was as long as the road to the bridge. Once ensconced, Sarah studied a series of booklets covering the valley's history—fact and myth. Recent excavations showed the area had been inhabited on and off for millennia, but in the 1640s a community of English settlers constructed the first known bridge over the river from stone and wood. Over time, dozens of badly built bridges replaced the first. The current characterless 1970s beast was already riddled with cracks and had been decaying for years. With no local investment in infrastructure, the bridge was maintained by the town's utilities supplier instead—for a profit.

Woe, Violent Water

Sarah read further pamphlets about the strange Woebegone community, borrowed a few more, then set off to the Need Bridge. Halfway across, the skies turned a bruised yellow. Gusts roared through the trees on either side of the river. Heading toward the protection of the valley, Sarah clutched her pregnant bulk. The camber was deeper than she'd realised; the bridge less solid. She slipped and stumbled, tripping in sneakers with holes in the soles. Freezing rain stabbed her back; vicious ice daggers. Cursing the tempest with words swallowed by the wind she slid sideways as a gush of warm water filled her shoes. Cruel contractions immediately clenched her womb—no gentle ease into childbirth. She bit down against the pain, bit her cheek, bit her tongue. Her mouth filled with blood.

Respite.

She stood again as a new bout of rain hit the bridge. Laced with sleet, it whipped up to slice her face. The River Need below churned against the foundations. Grit and earth slid from its banks, muddying the waters, easing the river's flood path onto the land. With sudden clarity, Sarah realised she had to get off the bridge or risk giving birth on a fluid median between valleys. Not a religious woman, deeper intuition told her there was something intrinsically dangerous for a life delivered over violent water. This was no twinkly birthing pool. In response, her womb spasmed again, stealing her breath away.

"Let me help you."

The contraction eased.

Sarah squinted toward the valley. There, beneath the umbrella of a towering tree stood a girl. Tall, lithe, her mouth formed words Sarah couldn't hear. The young woman's tattered dress fluttered heavily around her as though made of leather. She raised an arm and beckoned, thin fingers unfurled like skeletal ferns, curling again, unfurling.

Enid.

Sarah gripped the trembling bridge wall; waves thundered against old brick, matching the pulsing pressure at her groin. When it next subsided the girl had reached the bridge. Bare toes pointed at the tarmac, she withdrew her foot as though unable to tread farther.

"Come," she said, her voice a leaf on the wind. "I can save your child."

Am I losing the baby?

Sarah clasped her arms around her belly; all she knew of this girl, this ghost—all the rumours, the slaughter, the breaking of her brother's heart—meant she should turn and run without looking back, yet when she raised her head she saw not madness or revenge in Enid's eyes, only hope.

She hesitated, then stumbled on toward the final curve.

Enid reached out her hand once more. Sarah took it.

***

The bracken camp was barely visible for what it was. On the slow journey through the woods Sarah had given it no regard. It resembled the rest of the wild, unmanaged forest, a mossy mess of fallen branches and leaves, wrapped around with killer brambles. Enid deftly avoided the spines as she tugged on a twine of ivy. A door of vegetable matter, just large enough for a pregnant woman to crawl through, opened to reveal a shelter. Enid scuttled in.

"Come, come."

On hands and knees, Sarah entered the organic cave, collapsing onto sweet-smelling rushes as the most violent of contractions clenched.

What the hell was she thinking? She needed drugs. She needed a fucking epidural.

Sarah opened her eyes; skeletal fingers probed between her legs.

"Hey—what are you doing?"

"Feeling. From your posture, I feared the babe breached." Enid ran her other hand over Sarah's belly, pressing hard. "He has turned," she said. "He is ready."

Ignoring Enid's assumption it would be a boy, Sarah rolled onto her back and raised her legs, as recommended by the town's elderly midwife.

"No!" Enid flipped her over and up into a squat, baby bulk weighing heavy against Sarah's thighs. "You people give birth like you fuck, on your back. You need to shit this baby out."

There was no time to argue. Though the baby was ready, Sarah's body was not. Enid massaged and washed her; somehow, somewhere boiling up water to douse her with. In the still moments, Enid held a wooden cup to Sarah's mouth, instructing her to sip, not gulp. The noxious liquid dulled the pain yet increased her strength. Ripped and bleeding, Sarah gave one last push. Curtis's child slipped into the waiting hands of a living ghost.

With the baby clutched to her breast, Enid bent to bite the cord. Sarah fell onto her side, exhausted, exhilarated. Enid moved away, wiping the blood from the wiggling baby's skin but not from her own mouth. Her lips bubbled red as she sang a soft lullaby in a strange tongue. When the baby let forth its first cry, she threw back her head and howled. Sarah held out her arms, the sound of Enid's primal call piercing her soul just as the icy rain outside had stabbed her shoulders.

"Give me my child, Enid."

Sarah pulled herself up on weak legs. She shuddered as the drug she'd been given began to withdraw.

"I thank you for carrying him, Sarah. You do your brother's work well. I am grateful."

The ground, so solid as she'd lain there, became fluid beneath Sarah's feet. She tripped.

"Give me my son."

Enid rushed at her, wedging the baby in between them. The leather skins slapped against Sarah's thighs, her arms. Nose to nose, Sarah stared deep into Enid's eyes. There she saw wandering, fertility . . . strife. Deeper still, tribal men, white men, women, children.

"They *hurt* me."

Enid trod backward, caressing the baby boy in her arms. Sarah remained still.

"Who are you?"

"I am of this place. I wasn't born—I became."

The girl's insane.

"How long have you been here?"

Enid glanced at Sarah's rucksack. It had tumbled over to release the library books, the pamphlets; Shaun's letter.

"For all time," she said. "I am the daughter of the River Need, of her banks, her swells and her tides. I welcomed many incomers to this land, saved and guided them. In return they tortured and cast me out."

Sarah edged forward, her baby's screaming breath within tasting distance.

"I've read about you," she said, dismissing her former belief that Shaun's Enid was nothing more than a disenchanted girl obsessed with local legends. "What was the name of the Englishman that condemned you?"

Enid withdrew, snatching the baby out of sight.

"Obadiah Borthwick," she spat. "A grandfather of yours."

The name jarred—everyone was allegedly descended from the Borthwicks around these parts, in legitimate or other ways. A cult, neither Pilgrim nor Puritan, Sarah hadn't realised the extent of the Woebegone brothers' tyranny until she read the full history that afternoon. It wasn't the sanitised version townsfolk were taught in school.

She shifted forward.

"I'm so sorry they hurt you."

Enid's neck click, click, clicked in a half circle. She looked at Sarah, her body facing a different direction.

"They hurt, but I do not die, Sarah," she said. "I fail to live for a while because of this or because of that. And so I sleep." She turned and handed the baby over to his birth mother. The child immediately opened his mouth in search of Sarah's tit for sustenance and comfort. Sarah fell back with the ecstasy of his suckling, only vaguely conscious of the longing in Enid's eyes.

"Thank you."

"You must name him for your brother."

"I will," Sarah said. She stroked the baby's fine golden hair—like hers, like Curtis' thinning curls; like Shaun's. "I'm so sorry you couldn't meet your uncle, little one. He would have loved you."

"Loved him?"

Enid roared toward her and snatched the baby. Kicking Sarah as she tried to crawl on lazy legs, Enid backed out of the shelter, Sarah's son wailing for America.

"No." Sarah reached the makeshift door and shouted through the gap into the darkness of the woodland. "Bring my baby back. Please."

The morning's storm raged higher now, bending the treetops. Branches and leaves snapped and flew, obscuring any path Enid might have taken. Sarah moved faster, blood and oxygen working again but with it, post-partum pain. She winced. Rapid, shallow breaths abated the agony as she fought through. The river was close; she could hear it and then . . . a primal howl matched by her baby's cries permeated the air. Sarah knew exactly where her son was.

Enid stood by the bridge; calm, smiling up at the sky. The water raged at her back. Fluid fingers stretched toward then fell away from her, not daring to touch. She had her thumb in the baby's mouth. He sucked greedily one moment and screamed out his frustration the next; sucked again. Screamed.

"Let me help," Sarah echoed Enid's earlier offer.

The girl's head turned sharply.

"I ask you again," she said. "Loved him? This is not your brother's nephew to be fawned over and failed by a community that knows nothing of love, of humanity."

"No, no—you're right. Our town isn't the best place to bring up a child." Old fashioned, poor facilities, a plummeting population. Maybe it *was* time for her and Curtis to give up on tainted pioneer pride and move somewhere more progressive.

Enid's thick eyebrows frowned. "You misunderstand," she said. "I repeat, this is not your brother's nephew. It *is* your brother, it *is* Shaun." Enid turned her back on Sarah, still talking, and ran onto the bridge.

You couldn't walk there before.

" . . . not your baby."

"What?" Sarah moved toward the bridge, reached for the rail and quickly withdrew her hand.

"Like diving into mud, isn't it?" Enid shouted. "It looks real then when you touch it, touch the bridge, it ripples like water. Try to cross, and it repels you."

"I . . . I don't understand."

"There's nothing to understand, Sarah. Shaun gave his life to be reborn after I lost our own child." She rubbed her hand over her belly, where it lingered. Sarah struggled to deal with the news; she'd had no idea. "It could only be you; your family blood, my spirit. I've been watching over you since you fell pregnant, the day Shaun died."

Sarah recalled the initial 24-hour guttural expulsion, which kept her in bed with a bucket at her side. She'd put it down to grief and a hangover. Weeks and weeks of it later, when her breasts hurt so bad, she'd finally caught on. She and Curtis hardly ever did it anymore, but thinking back, the night before the sickness started had ended with a tearful, drunken fumble for them both. As far as Sarah was concerned, she'd fallen asleep; Curtis couldn't even remember going to bed.

Enid grinned, hearing Sarah's thoughts.

"We were all there, Sarah. You, me . . . Shaun working his seed into that worm of a prick your man is so proud of."

"That's ridiculous. Shaun was dead."

"Who's to say what magic happens in those hours after our hearts stop beating? Don't trust your scientists' lies."

Enid edged closer to the bridge wall, the baby held out before her. "What of me—am I dead? How do you explain what *I* am?" She tucked the baby under her arm, its head nestled into her armpit. She leapt up onto the wall.

"No!"

Sarah lurched forward, going nowhere. Her scream faded into the violent winds which in turn carried the warped clang of nuts and bolts, the twist of metal and the crack of tarmac. The entire bridge shifted. Enid clung on with bare feet then threw herself, baby and all, into the raging river that bore her name.

Sarah looked on, unable to move or speak until finally the bridge gave way. She scrambled backwards, feet slipping in the spreading mud.

At Enid's tree, Sarah slowed her pace and reached out to steady herself on the gnarled trunk which groaned with creeping ivy. Her fingers, caught in the warp and weft of nature's weave were tangled in strips of paper-thin skin, a sinuous twine of flesh-like string. The childless mother threw back her head to keen, arms raised to the sky, arms that were covered in tattered-edged sleeves of hide which hung down from her shoulders.

Wings of leather, they fluttered heavily in the breeze.

BIOGRAPHY: *Lily Childs has an unhealthy obsession with misunderstood demons. They make her write bad things about real people, people who think they deserve better. With over sixty published tales from the darkest Gothic horror to twisted British crime, morbid fairy tales to savage ghost stories, Lily has just finished her first novel—a terrifying supernatural asylum thriller set in the south of England, where she lives with her artist husband, daughter and black cat, Scarlet.*

The Cruel

HARPER HULL

The first time it happened was the day David Smith fell over his own feet on the way out of chemistry class. Mark Holland was right behind him and, as David tumbled over and landed hard on his left shoulder, Mark made a sound. It was a horrible, whining drone of a sound, somewhere between an old air raid siren and an angry goat. Mark stood over the fallen boy making the ugly noise, gradually getting louder, until Mrs. the chcmistry came over, put a hand on his shoulder and, with a quite exasperated look on her face, told him to stop. Mark went quiet and walked away down the corridor as the teacher helped David get to his feet.

The next day David and Mark were both present during lunch break when the school bully Francis White decided to smash up a lower year kid, Gary Barnshaw, for beating him at marbles. It was out amongst the trees at the rear of the school, a veritable marbling assault course of roots and muddy channels. Francis had the smaller, younger lad in a headlock and, after easily taking him to ground, began punching him in the face with his free hand. Marbles spilled from Gary's blazer pockets as he struggled to get free and rolled in all directions.

As usual in these situations, the chant of "Fight! Fight! Fight!" started up and children, boys and girls, came running from all over to witness the beating. In what seemed like absolute harmony, Mark and David opened their mouths and spill the horrible sound.

'Nyeeeeeeeeeeerrrrrrrrrrrrrrrrrrrrrrr!'

Francis now had a scarlet fist as Gary's nose was cut and bloody, but the bigger boy kept on pummeling away the sound was taken up by more of the children crowded around. Louder and louder it got, until it seemed everyone standing was taking part, and as Gary lay bloody and crying in the dirt and Francis, finally letting him go, scooped up as many loosed marbles as he could find, a large figure pushed through the circle of droning children and began shouting.

"That is ENOUGH!" roared Evans, the bearded, stout deputy headmaster. "Francis White, my office NOW! Gary, get yourself to the nurse, boy. The rest of you, BE QUIET! Stop that infernal racket and get back inside, bell goes in two minutes. Stop it, NOW!"

The noise stopped, just like that.

The children slowly walked back towards the red-bricked school buildings.

Mr. Evans helped Gary up, gave him a handkerchief from his jacket pocket and shook his head, wondering what new ridiculous trend this group droning thing was.

***

Over the next few days *the lamentation*, as the noise was named by Mr. Helby—the English literature teacher—during a discussion in the staff room, occurred more and more.

It became a regular part of practically every break and lunchtime. Each successive day it increased in volume as more and more of the children joined the terrible chorus.

Mrs. Colback, the elderly school secretary, quit her job because of it, saying it reminded her of when the Germans were sending doodlebugs into the skies and raining death down upon the city.

Teachers at one end of the school complex would hear the 'nyeeeeeeerrr!' sound rise way off at the other end and rush across to help their fellow staff calm the situation. It was always the same form of trigger; someone had dropped something, fallen over, started a fight, broken an item, and the hideous, broken Klaxon-like dirge would emanate from the pupils in the vicinity.

On Friday, during lunch, all of the teachers were eating together in the dining hall at the staff table. Even Mr. Talbot, the headmaster, had made a rare appearance to dine with his colleagues. He usually just stayed in his office during lunch and ate a Cornish pasty, a bag of cheese and onion crisps and a Scotch egg, all washed down with a carton of Ribena. The hall was full with blue-blazered pupils and the low, incoherent buzz of multiple conversations filled the space. The air was filled with the aromas of the various food items being offered by the dinner ladies that day—beef sausages, chicken curry, grilled turbot—all battling to dominate the sense of smell, creating a whirling, pungent atmosphere of oils, tang and spice.

"Well," said Mr. Talbot, slicing into a sausage and

piling mash onto his fork, "let's see if this monstrous din rises up today. If it does then this is a good place to address all of the children at once before the weekend, and I have ordered Miss Honeydew to photocopy a letter I composed to send home to the parents."

"I'm sure it's just a silly trend," Miss Winter suggested, "just like when they were wearing those beer bottle caps on their shoes or when all the boys were tucking their ties into their shirts, it'll become boring to them soon enough and they'll wait for the next ridiculous gimmick to come along."

Mr. Evans rubbed his beard and shook his head. "No, not a trend, this one, Beverley. It's something else entirely. It almost seems to be—for want of a less dramatic—contagious. It started with that Holland boy and now half the bloody school are doing it."

"I think it's all about the empathy of the child's soul," Mr. Helby said, pushing a piece of fish around his plate absentmindedly, "this sound, this *lamentation*, they're somehow passing the feelings of sadness and sympathy between themselves and expressing those feelings with the basest of noises. It's quite remarkable, actually."

"No offense, Mr. Helby, but that's poppycock! I was there when Mark Holland started this whole nonsense and, I assure you, there was no sympathy involved, it was a horrible and mocking thing. *The lamentation?* More like *the cruel.*" Mrs. Dodd sat back after her little outburst, not even realizing she had leaned quite so far forward whilst talking, and felt the quick heat of a flush in her cheeks. "Anyway, if you will excuse me, I do need to pop across to the chemist before lunch is over, and pick up a prescription." She stood, gathered her plate and cutlery and dropped them into a plastic bin on her way out of the hall, handbag swinging from the crook of an elbow.

"See what you did, Andrew?" said Mr. Evans, pointing a fork with a piece of chicken pierced on the tines at his colleague. "Poor woman couldn't get out of here fast enough. Prescription my arse. She was absolutely traumatized that day with the Holland lad, and you calling it a good thing is not going to help. I agree with her, too, it's a bloody disease is what it is."

"Language, Timothy!" Mr. Talbot lowered his head and surveyed the table over the top of his spectacles. "There are children around us, in case you had forgotten."

A loud clatter sounded across the hall as one of the dinner ladies dropped a big, empty metal serving dish to the tiled floor. All the teachers inhaled sharply and held their breath for a moment; the sound they dreaded immediately started to rise as child after child stood and began to wail.

Table by table the students stood and joined the cacophony, staring and pointing in the direction of the unfortunate dinner lady who stood silent and still, horrified.

Mr. Talbot took in the scene for a short while, utterly bemused, before pushing himself up from the table and shouting at the children to stop it and sit down. He couldn't make his voice heard over the awful noise even when shouting. "You lot! Don't just sit there, help me with them!"

Mr. Talbot slammed both fists into the tabletop as he berated his teaching staff at the top of his lungs.

Everyone quickly rose and dispersed around the room, clapping their hands and yelling for silence.

***

Eileen Dodd sat in the small café down the road from the school, drinking a large mug of tea and chain-smoking a pack of Benson & Hedges, trying to calm down. Andrew Helby was an infuriating buffoon on the best of days but his attempts to explain away that bloody horrible noise as an act of good had really rattled her cage.

She blew smoke from her nose with a big huff, shaking her head, knowing she shouldn't let herself get so wound up by the man.

There was a rumble as one of the town's signature cream and maroon double-decker buses passed by in the street and Eileen placed a hand against the window, felt the vibrations in the glass.

Right, Eileen, finish this tea and get back to it, no more being mardy over Helby, he's always going to be an annoying idiot just like a dog is always going to bark when the postman comes, not worth the stress.

She put her cigarette out in a ceramic ashtray with a series of stabbing motions and gulped the last of the tea. As she stood up to leave, a great crashing noise came from down the road, a terrible screech, glass breaking, people screaming, causing everyone both in the café and on the street to turn their heads towards the commotion. It had felt like the whole building shook.

"That sounded like it came from the school!" said a waitress, peering through the window, and Eileen was out of the door in a flash, joining a number of people who were already hurrying up the road towards the source of the commotion.

As she neared the corner, a new sound joined the screams and moans, overpowering them; that infernal drone, *the cruel*. A heavy sense of dread soured Eileen's belly as she rounded the corner and the deep red brick of the school buildings leant a hard backdrop to the scene ahead. The black and grey undercarriage of the bus she had seen just a minute earlier was exposed and facing in her direction, the bus having tipped over onto its side. The two left side wheels that were now up in the air span around, going nowhere. There was glass all over the street, shards glinting in the sunlight, whilst the heads and shoulders of several passengers emerged from the broken windows of the bus, some of them bloodied, some waving their hands for help as they struggled to pull themselves up and out of the toppled vehicle.

Groans, screams and cries came from inside the bus where, Eileen imagined, most of the people on board would be piled up against the side of the vehicle that now lay against the street itself.

The poor people upstairs would have hit a lot harder than those down below, she thought.

Worse than all of this, though, was what greeted Eileen as she moved around the back of the bus, towards the terrible noise; it was so loud she actually placed her hands over her ears.

A river of blue filled the road, every single pupil from the school it seemed standing in columns, mouths wide open as they howled. At the very front, nearest to the crash, stood the teachers. Talbot, Winter, Helby, even tough Mr. Evans, every last one of them. Right arms outstretched, index fingers pointing forwards, eyes wide, *the cruel* issued forth from the adults far louder and harsher than anything the children were capable of.

She noticed with a quick horror that made her sweat and feel cold all at the same time that the anxious and curious bystanders who had rushed to the scene with her were, one by one, moving towards the back of the bus and lining up with the children and teachers, raising their arms and joining in with the terrible hell howl.

Old ladies with blue rinses out shopping for soup, shopkeepers in aprons and baker's jackets, young families out for lunch in the local eateries, even a solitary policeman who had been riding by on his bicycle, all took their place in the chorus of hate.

Eileen knew she had to get as far away as she could, and turned to run as fast as she could; her feet disobeyed her intentions and stayed stuck to the ground as she tried to turn, resulting in a horrible, twisting face plant.

Before she could even acknowledge the loose teeth in her jaws and the blood pouring from her smashed nose she was crawling towards the abominable choir, hand over hand and elbow over elbow.

She felt her wrecked mouth open wide to its fullest extent and all hope was lost.

BIOGRAPHY: *Harper has been writing unsettling stories across many genres for the last few years. He has had stories appear in collections with such great tale tellers such as George RR Martin, John Shirley, Joe R. Lansdale, Nancy Collins, Brian Keene and Tim Curran. He currently has his first solo collection of short stories ready for publication and two novels in progress.*

Red Scream with Little Smile

PAUL EDMONDS

Garland has always been a cultural mousetrap. Things creep in, usually when they're used-up and on clearance, but nothing ever leaves. Walk downtown and you'll see the past on full display, the beatup cars and the fanny packs and the greasy Elvis haircuts, all of it just swirling around, blocking out the contemporary like some weird nuclear winter. It happens when a place is left holding the short straw of geography—so much gets lost in transit that it locks in whatever it can. Recycles the old days like air in a sealed room. And that's just what happened in the spring of 1996, when the students of Garland High decided to send up a call to Melinda Barrett.

It was a PBS special that pulled her memory from the clouds of time. *The Decline of the Brown River Valley*. The documentary, which played over two nights in early May, targeted the cluster of small towns that comprised a thirty mile stretch of hopelessness, which began in the north-central part of the state and petered off at the Berkshire Mountains to the west. It ruffled a lot of feathers in Garland, but there was no disputing the salient points: An alarming number of high school dropouts; the scourge of domestic violence; a teenage pregnancy rate that could rival the most prolific puppy mill.

Most damning was the bleak report of the Valley's manufacturing industry, a once-bustling juggernaut that had devolved into a disgrace of low wages and dangerous working conditions. Singled out was the Barrett Tool Company, one of the few factories that had trudged on after the Great War.

Interspersed between current shots of the building's crumbling edifice were stills of the factory during its golden age—an idyllic blue-collar paradise of smiling workers and gleaming machines. At the center of the glowing, old-timey images, was Melinda Barrett, beautiful and stern-faced among her fawning employees. Melinda Barrett, who'd inherited her husband's half of the business in the twenties, rescued Garland from the slavering jaws of the Great Depression. Melinda Barrett, who drowned at age thirty-five, was found downriver, spread out on a rock, birds fighting over her eyes.

The doc pried opened her casket, but it was Alan Trembley, sociology teacher at Garland High School, who kicked it over, that sent Melinda's corpse skidding across his classroom floor. Trembley had been hit hard by the documentary. He captured all four hours on videotape, and over the course of a week, made his students watch every depressing minute. He would stop the tape frequently to contradict the filmmakers and wring his hands like a damsel in some silent movie. But despite the animated commentary, interest quickly waned, and by Friday most of his class had checked out, nodding off and drooling onto their desks.

Until one girl, Freda Castine, was plucked from her semi-coma by something she glimpsed on the small Magnavox TV.

"What's that?" she said, wiping spittle off her chin.

Trembley paused the video, tapped the screen with the remote. "This?"

It was a black and white picture, a wide-angle snap of the Millers River, sparkling in the day's last light. In the background, photobombing the pleasant scene, was the Barrett Tool Company, black against the setting sun. In the foreground were a dozen teenagers crowded along the scrubby bank, several more clinging to the riveted support beams of the Exchange Street Bridge. They had funny haircuts, were decked out in high-waisted trousers and pleated skirts and baggy cardigan sweaters. Their mouths were open wide, their chests puffed up, as if they were trying to blow the massive brick eyesore into the next county.

"Yeah," Freda said. 'What are they doing?"

Her sudden interest roused the rest of the class. They sat up, rubbing the sleep from their eyes.

Trembley grinned. "Scream Night."

"Scream Night?" Freda said. "Never heard of it."

"Tradition's been dead for a while," Trembley said, and sat on the edge of his desk. "Was popular in the thirties and early forties when this school was just eight rooms and an outhouse."

Freda squinted, gave the picture a closer study. "What were they screaming at?"

Trembley rewound the tape, froze on a portrait of Melinda Barrett. Her thin lips were set in a tight frown, her haired pulled back into a tidy businesswoman's bun. She had a rose pinned to her blouse, so big it could have been a strange third breast. She looked like the kind of woman who could handle your finances, or revamp your assembly line, or maybe shoot off your balls.

"This little lady."

"The tool chick?" Jim Fournier, nicely stoned, hair sticking up in chunks and spikes. "What'd she do, steal their mascot or something?"

"You're an idiot," Freda said, but she was smiling. She'd been best friends with Jim since first grade, along with Billy LaFond, who was home that day recovering from knee surgery.

"Nothing so reasonable," Trembley said, and folded his arms. "They were trying to raise her from the grave."

The class leaned forward, all at once, as if it'd been choreographed.

"Zombie style," Freda said excitedly.

"Well, no," Trembley said. "It was her spirit they were attempting to summon. They believed that if they made enough noise, Melinda Barrett would show herself." He sniffed. "And if she did, then a good summer would follow."

"Like when a groundhog sees his shadow," Jim said, licking his lips. "Early spring and all that."

"Similar theory, I guess."

Freda fidgeted in her seat. "Why would seeing some dead lady mean a good summer?"

"She was like a patron saint to this town,"

Trembley said. "Her husband, Sydney, started the business in 1913, and from day one Melinda campaigned for the employees. Sydney rarely listened, though. He was a stubborn man. Same with Aldo Brighenti, his partner. The bottom line was all they cared about."

"Damn," Freda said. "The Brighentis owned the factory way back then?"

"Half of it, they did. But then Sydney passed—stroke—and Melinda took over his share of the factory. She made some big changes. Saw to it that her people were treated fairly. Paid them well. It caused a lot of friction with Brighenti." Trembley scratched his bushy beard. "After Melinda died unexpectedly, things went downhill. Brighenti put things back the way they'd been before. Slashed wages, tossed safety out the window. I'm sure a lot of those kids felt the effects at home. Maybe they figured it couldn't hurt to send out a little prayer to the woman—or at least their version of a prayer."

"Did anyone ever see her?" Jim asked.

"I'm sure a few of those screamers saw something they *thought* was a ghost. Reflection off the water, a wink of light from some girl's sparkly bracelet."

"But you don't believe any of it was real?" Freda said, sounding a little dejected.

"Sorry," Trembley said. "I don't."

"Maybe they *did* see something, though," Jim said. "A mass hallucination. Like Haley's Comet."

Freda glared at him. "That really happened, dummy."

Trembley shrugged his shoulders. "Want to know what I think? They were just having fun. Being kids.

And if they passed around a few stories, so what? Whole thing was harmless enough. Helped them forget their problems for a while."

"Why'd they stop doing it, then?" Freda said.

"Part of it was the war. Making a joke of death wasn't very funny once Garland boys started coming home in caskets. But mostly, I think it was just the town itself. The factories started closing, optimism became a scarce commodity. Wishing for a good summer—a good anything—must have seemed pointless."

The class chewed on this for a moment, and then Trembley resumed the video. The narrator's flat voice filled the room. Students drifted off again, one by one, like lights going out in a prison block.

Except Freda, who watched the dispiriting images glide across the screen. Current snaps of her dying town. The soaped-up windows, the jalopy cars. The dirty river, broiling with trash and swaths of yellow foam. And Barrett Tool, all crumbling brick and crashed-in windows. Workers out on the lawn by the water—a patchwork of lunch buckets and tired, apple-doll faces.

She could use a good summer, something to look forward to.

Hell, they all could.

***

Billy sat in bed, knee propped up, puzzling over his calculus textbook. He turned some numbers in his head, couldn't make them fit. After a moment he closed the book and dashed it across the room.

He fell back on his pillows, feeling frustrated and lonely. His surgical follow-up had not gone well.

Another month of bed rest. And right smack in the meaty part of spring. There'd be no pickup baseball games for him. No smoking cigs and guzzling Pabst with Jim and Freda, down by the railroad tracks. All because he wanted to save three bucks, sneak into the Friday night football game by scaling the visitors' bleachers.

The bedroom door opened a crack. His mother's big blue eye winked at him.

"Everything alright?"

"Fine, Ma. Dropped my book is all."

She came in, and a sharp odor followed her. Something that looked like vomit was splashed across the front of her Garth Brooks T-shirt. She was holding her bandaged hand. A few red drops had soaked through the gauze. The tip of her index finger looked purple and swollen, like a tick about to pop.

She picked up the textbook with her good hand and brought it over to Billy. He took it and set it aside.

"Maybe I could hire a tutor."

"We can't afford that." Billy forced a smile. "I'll be fine. Just have to concentrate."

The big front door slammed shut downstairs. There was a scurry of footsteps, some commotion in the hall, and then Freda and Jim were in the room. Freda unshouldered her bulging backpack, wiped sweat from her forehead with the sleeve of her hoodie. She took a breath, wrinkled her nose, and glanced in the direction of the kitchen.

Jim, as always, looked cool and unperturbed, caught somewhere between awareness and oblivion.

"Dude," Freda said, turning to Billy. "Have you heard of this thing called Scream Night?"

Billy's mom slid between Freda and Jim. "Don't mind me."

"Oh, hi," Freda said. "Sorry."

"Whoa," Jim said, pointing at her injured hand. "What happened?"

"She got hurt at work," Billy said.

"Again?" Freda said.

Billy's mom raised her hand, adjusted the gauze. "It's not that bad. My fault, really. I wasn't paying attention."

"Right," Billy said, sitting up, triggering an avalanche of magazines and wrapped fruit strips. "You always stick up for them."

"They've been good to us."

"Yeah, just great. We're living in the lap of luxury, all thanks to Barrett Tool."

An alarm sounded in the kitchen. A ribbon of black smoke drifted into the room. Billy's mom cursed and ran off, slamming the door behind her.

"So?" Freda said, sitting on the end of the bed.

"So what?" Billy said, unwrapping a fruit strip and tearing into it like a wild dog.

"Do you know about Scream Night?"

"Think so," he said through a mouthful of strawberry-banana gruel. "Melinda Barrett?"

"Yeah, that's right," Freda said, bouncing up and down. "Wow, Trembley's really gotten to you."

"Best buds," Jim added, and chuckled.

Billy grunted. Mr. Trembley had turned him onto Garland town history. The old hippie had called to check on him after his knee surgery, and they'd ended up shooting the breeze for two hours. The next day Freda and Jim came over with a stack of dusty books to accompany his usual folder of homework assignments. Billy ate up the monster tomes—all of them from Trembley's personal collection—until he could almost smell the horseshit on the stone-paved streets, the industrial stink from the leather tanneries and furniture factories that used to line Upper Main Street.

"What do you know about it?" Freda said, drawing her legs up Indian-style.

"Not a whole lot," Billy said. "Started after she died, obviously. Supposed to bring good luck or something. Lame, if you ask me."

"Yeah, yeah. We know all that. What else?"

"I don't know," Billy said, and nibbled his fruit strip. "They would do it down by the river. She drowned, Melinda Barrett. Fell into the Millers at a carnival, or something. Why are you so interested? Was Trembley talking about it?"

"Yes. Well, it was in that documentary. Not Scream Night, but there was this picture, a bunch of old-fashioned kids hanging around the water. I asked Trembley about it, and he told us the story."

"The documentary, sure," Billy said. He hadn't seen it. The only television in the apartment was in the living room, and his mother would sooner sell a kidney than miss her nightly shows. Trembley had promised to lend him the tape.

"So, what else?" Freda said.

"Guess the factory workers took it hard. She treated them real good, like family." He looked over at the closed door, listened to the scrape of pots and pans, the strained sounds of his overworked mother trying to salvage another cheap supper. "Not like now."

"And?" Freda pressed.

"God, I feel like I'm on the witness stand. I read somewhere she was partially deaf. That's what did her in, I think. Got knocked into the Millers by a runaway horse, couldn't hear the people yelling at her to move."

"Yeah, that makes sense," Freda added, chewing on the end of her thumb. "That's why they'd scream, to warn her."

"How could a dead lady hear anything?" Jim said, taking a pair of Mickey Mouse ears off a bookshelf and pulling them onto his big head. "Once you're in the ground, that's it."

"It's symbolic," Freda said.

"Right," Jim said absently, examining himself in the dresser mirror. "Symbolic."

"Well, guess what?" Freda said, patting Billy's foot. "I'm bringing it back. Already been spreading the word."

Billy tossed his empty wrapper onto the floor. "What for?"

"Because this town could use some good luck. Don't you think?"

"But it's not real," Billy said. "Never was. Might as well rub a rabbit's foot, or get yourself a four-leaf clover."

"Ah," Freda said, wagging a finger at him. "Been thinking about that. In that picture we saw there were twenty, thirty kids. I bet they weren't loud enough. Not with so few of them. But imagine if a hundred of us got together, going all out, top of our lungs. We might actually see something. How cool would that be?"

"Shit, man," Jim said, his shoulders sagging. "I never thought it could really happen." He took off the mouse ears and let them fall to the floor. "I'll have nightmares."

"You're both insane," Billy said. "Sincerely, how did I get stuck with you two?"

"Well, it's happening," Freda said. "Next Friday."

Billy laid back, stared at the ceiling. "Great. You can tell me all about it."

"Oh yeah," Jim said. He squeezed onto the bed beside Freda. "How'd it go today?"

"Another month."

"Sorry, bud," Freda said. "Here, these might cheer you up." She hefted her backpack onto the bed, and Jim helped her unload several musty volumes. "From Trembley. That documentary has him full of piss and vinegar. He wants you to read these."

Billy grabbed one and flipped through the pages. Motes of dust tickled his nose.

"Great," he said. "Who needs a social life when you've got books?"

***

By the time Freda turned onto Exchange Street, the sun was already setting behind Barrett Tool. She was late, had gotten roped into helping her mother fold a couple tons of laundry, but stopped for a moment anyway to admire the bright orange halo encircling the building, the rich colors splashed across the Millers. She was struck by how pretty the town could look sometimes, with all its grittiness stripped away.

She reached the bridge, slid down the rocky riverbank, and damn, the turnout was even greater than she'd hoped for. She got her hundred kids, plus about fifty more. They were mingling in loose groups, passing joints, bottles of booze. Some had slipped off their shoes and were splashing around in the water. Everyone had paper roses pinned to their shirts.

She looked around for Jim, tried to pick out his corkscrew hair, but couldn't find him.

Marcia Spokes, another student from Trembley's soc class, emerged from a thicket of bodies. She spotted Freda, took a rose from a canvas sling she was wearing, and pinned it on her.

"What's this?" Freda said.

"I made them," Marcia said. Her breath was all rum and cigarettes. "So we could be like Melinda. Had to guess at the color, since all the pictures were in black and white. But roses are usually red, aren't they?"

"Sure are," Freda said, fiddling with the delicate tissue paper.

Someone started clapping. Soon the whole assembly was applauding and chanting Freda's name. She took a little bow, then walked toward the river, stopping to hit a huge spliff rolled in a couple cigar wrappers. She hopped onto a big rock and raised her hands. Things got quiet. She scanned the crowd. Glowing cigarettes dotted the gloom like red fireflies. An army of flashlights lighted the underside of the bridge, its generations of lurid graffiti. No Jim.

"Sorry, Jimbo," Freda said, and turned to face the factory. The river rushed by, misting her skin. She threw her head back, and like some mad orchestra whose conductor had just dropped her wand, they all began to scream.

***

Jim stood outside the Friend's Café, looking across Main Street at the puke-green bridge. He saw a few shadowy figures disappear underneath its hulking skeleton, and he felt as depressed as he ever would, picturing the good time he was missing. He'd bet anything *their* fathers weren't drunks, didn't need to be retrieved from some scummy downtown barroom like a child who'd pissed himself at a birthday party. He shook his head, spat onto the sidewalk, then pushed through the saloon-style doors.

The old man was in back, spread out on a pool table. Jim saw that he actually had pissed his pants; there was a big wet spot on the front of his jeans in the shape of a fried egg. He slapped his dad's grizzled cheek, got him conscious enough to lead him out into the front room, holding him up under the arms like a big rag doll.

The pair was almost at the exit when they were shoved aside by a couple men in twill pants and grease-stained T-shirts. Jim spun on his heels and fell on his ass; his father shot forward, as if from a cannon. Daddy-O landed underneath the Old West doors—which were still swinging from the men's hasty exit—half in and half out, snoring like a grizzly bear full of sleeping pills.

More patrons were leaving the bar, walking across the old man's back like it was the world's lumpiest welcome mat. One fellow came down on his father's hand with a chunky work boot, and the sound Jim heard was like someone biting into crunchy cereal. He got to his hands and knees, and just managed to scoot out of the path of a big mama in baggy jeans and a Barrett Tool trucker hat. She was staring straight ahead, a dumb little smile on her round, sweaty face.

Jim crawled underneath the doors, grabbed his dad and dragged him onto the sidewalk. He sat him up against their rust-covered van and peeked over the hood. Men and women were shuffling down the street, all of them with queer grins spread across their lips. They staggered out of bars and apartment houses, the VFW hall on the corner, turning right when they reached the end of the block, towards Upper Main Street.

Jim sat on the van's creaky bumper, out of breath and eminently confused. He turned his head at a noise across the way, by the bridge—the shriek of what sounded like a hundred and half screaming voices.

***

Billy glanced out the open window. He could see pieces of the Exchange Street Bridge through gaps between the faded downtown buildings. He'd promised Freda he would listen, but there was no way he'd be able to hear them, no matter how loud they got.

He turned back to his book, scribbled a date on a composition pad. He was putting together some notes for a letter he planned to write Mr. Trembley. They'd been doing that lately, trading thoughts on what they read. And with Scream Night on his mind, Billy had dug up some curious items—things that made him question the events surrounding Melinda Barrett's freak drowning.

She hadn't died at a carnival but rather a summer picnic for Barrett Tool employees and their families. There'd been big barbeque pits, rides—including a Ferris wheel that'd run at the 1931 Colonial Exposition in Paris—and a travelling animal circus. Billy had come across all this in a book of historic newspaper articles, as well as an accompanying photo of Melinda Barrett and Aldo Brighenti posing with a gorgeous American

Quarter horse. Gorgeous except for one detail: a missing ear. A gnarled hunk of cartilage stuck out from the side of the horse's lopsided head like a big brown thumb. The caption underneath the pic was darkly concise: *The last image of tool baroness Melinda Barrett, moments before her death.* The article didn't say if the one-eared horse had been the one to kick Mrs. Barrett into the Millers, but Billy thought it was a safe bet.

He went on to find a set of court documents in another book Trembley had lent him, *A Record of Local Manufactories, 1850-1950.* It was a motion that Aldo Brighenti had filed with the Massachusetts Superior Court, claiming the illegal transfer of Sydney Barrett's half of the business to Melinda upon his death. This was in September of 1932, less than a year before she was carried downriver. Billy searched, but there'd been nothing among the hundreds of other documents to indicate an outcome.

He got to thinking about the party again, the bizarre nature of Melinda Barrett's demise. More than two hundred people had been on the lawn behind Barrett Tool that day, but only Melinda was struck down when that rogue equine went on its rampage. Plus he thought it was strange how Brighenti had simply absorbed Barrett's share of the factory after her death. On a whim, Billy consulted his set of supermarket encyclopedias. He discovered that American Quarters were docile creatures, unlikely to commit random acts of violence. That is, he theorized, unless they were trained to. He took another look at the picture of Melinda and Aldo Brighenti, tried to find something in the guy's appearance that suggested foreknowledge of his partner's impending doom. Billy stared at that photo for a long time, until it all melted into a gray smear, then gave up.

He knew it was weak detective work. The closest he'd ever come to solving a mystery were the games of *Clue* he played with Freda and Jim. Still, he wanted Trembley's opinion.

The sound of the kitchen door startled him, and he dropped the book in his lap, squishing his balls. He groaned and pushed the book aside. Noises in the hall, the creak of rickety stairs. He peered out the window and saw his mother walking down the driveway. She was in her robe and fuzzy slippers. The bandage on her hand had come loose; it trailed behind her, blowing in the breeze.

"Ma," he called, but she kept going, slid behind the wheel of her dented Dodge. Billy could see her grinning through the windshield. The expression was cold and mean—it made him think of a villain in some spy flick, a split second before hitting the death switch.

He yelled again, but his mother was already backing out. She ran over a mailbox, lurched forward, and scraped the side of a parked minivan before turning the corner.

Billy blinked away the ghosts of the Dodge's tail lights, watched the empty street. He wondered if she'd mixed up her prescriptions and taken some loopy cocktail of painkillers and antibiotics.

He sat back and pondered his mother's strange exit, wondered if he should call the cops. He began flipping absently through his book, browsing the grainy pictures. After a few pages he stopped, went back. He pulled his bedside lamp closer.

Red Scream with Little Smile

It was a picture of Aldo Brighenti's retirement party. 1942, according to the simple caption, at his vacation home in Edenville, New York. It looked like a gala affair. There were steaming buffet tables, clutches of balloons, enough bunting and crepe paper to choke an elephant. Brighenti was handing a set of keys to a younger man, a fellow who looked too much like the old taskmaster not to be his son. And behind them, hitched to a tree and looking about two days from the grave, was a horse, missing one ear and appearing to grin as he worked on a big pile of apples.

***

Freda rubbed her throat, surveyed her defeated troops. They'd gone at it for ten minutes, looking more and more embarrassed for each other as their screams got weaker, finally calling it quits after Marcia Spokes got a bloody nose, panicked and pulled her boyfriend into the river, nearly killing them both.

Now everyone was just hanging around, draining what was left of their beers and wine coolers. A group of guys were lighting their paper roses and tossing them into the river, seeing how far they'd go before the foamy water doused the flames.

Freda watched, liking the way the paper burned colorful in the gathering darkness. It made her feel less foolish somehow. Most of the little torches didn't last long, though, going out within a couple seconds of hitting the water. Except one. It held its place, the small blue and orange flame licking the cool air. Freda figured it'd gotten marooned on a jutting rock, would eventually burn off like all the rest.

Only it didn't. The fire grew, and now she could see that the flame wasn't on the water but crawling up the side of the Barrett Tool factory, across the river. Shapes started to materialize in its windows, floor by floor; clumsy, flailing things that looked like drunken shadows. Glass exploded from the side of the building, sparkled in the last scraps of light, rained onto the unkempt lawn below.

Freda backed away from the water. Her classmates were scrambling up the embankment onto Exchange Street. Someone clipped her shoulder and sent her into one of the metal struts. She grabbed on and swung around so she was facing the underside of the bridge. A dropped flashlight illuminated the defaced beams, the drifts of empty bottles, the anemic bushes growing up through the rocky soil. Freda saw these things clearly. Saw them and also the woman lingering near the water. She pulsed weakly at the periphery of the light, like a television screen getting ready to die. But not before she raised a hand, flashed Freda a little smile.

***

Meanwhile:

Timothy Brighenti, fourth-generation toolmaker, answers a knock at his well-appointed Pleasant Street home. He's surprised to see the smiling, oil-streaked face of Clyde Chaisson, one of his day shift foremen. Clyde nods politely, then hammers Brighenti to death with a Barrett Ballpeen # 4. Well, not quite. The tool falls apart halfway through the job, and Clyde has to finish things by putting the sharp end of the hilt through his boss's eye.

Walking down the gravel driveway afterward, his shirt sticky with blood and brains, Clyde thinks about leaving town, starting over. Somewhere beyond the smoke and the flames, the cinders falling into the rushing water.

BIOGRAPHY: *Paul Edmonds lives in Massachusetts. His fiction has recently appeared in* The Literary Hatchet, *and anthologies from Rainstorm Press and Horrified Press. He has a website, which he updates on a semi-regular basis: pauledmonds.net.*

Maybelle

MERE JOYCE

The worn carpet is stained with a hundred spilled drinks, a thousand muddy boots, an entire town history all of its own. I smile as the floor creaks under my weight, the quiet whine of the boards a satisfactory greeting. Most of the other libraries in town have been remodelled, freshly designed for a new generation of users. But I like this old branch best. The dust is warm, the high rows and dank overhead lighting familiar. My childhood took place here.

"I hate this library, Aunt Henny," Bennett mutters, as we exit the elevator and head past a wall of romance books.

I give my nephew my best look of indignant surprise. "This is my favourite library," I say sternly.

"Why couldn't we go to the one downtown?" Bennett asks, his pre-adolescent face brimming with distaste. He runs his fingers along the book spines as we walk. The resulting sound is like the music of a paper orchestra. "It's way nicer."

"But this one is way closer," I remind him.

"You know you could learn to drive," he says, glancing at my lower half. "People without any legs can drive. And you've still got one."

"Well technically I have two." I reposition my crutch as we curve up the main aisle between the stacks. "It's just a foot I'm missing."

"Yeah, well, even less of an excuse," Bennett says. He veers towards an aisle, the sign on the end cap labelling it as the fantasy section.

"Fantasy, eh? I see you've got your aunt's tastes."

"Who, you?" Bennett barely manages the exclamation of surprise before he disappears between the rows. "You never read anything besides craft books."

"I used to," I say, joining him in the narrow aisle. "I used to come to this library and check out books from this very section."

Bennett's sceptical of my declaration. I'd laugh at his suspicious gaze, if I wasn't oddly unsettled moving among the shelves of my youth, the stories I used to read for hours on end whispering reminders of my past.

"So why'd you stop?"

I tilt my head to one side as I peer at the assortment of colourful covers lined up in author-alphabetical order.

"Don't know," I say, reaching up to a shelf and stroking the spine of a few books at random. "Just decided I liked reality better, I guess."

It's a lie, or at least half of one. I stopped reading fantasy fifteen years ago, after the fire took my foot and scarred great portions of the remaining skin on my left side. But I can't remember why the fire made me cling to reality, when my reality had become so grotesque.

My fingers clutch at a book, pulling it from the shelf. The title, Blood and Honour, is not exactly original nor is the cover illustration of a sword-yielding warrior a very inspired piece of art. It looks like an abysmal read, but still I open the cover and begin rifling through the pages.

"I think I read this when I was younger," I say as Bennett glances over to see what I'm looking at.

"Any good?" he asks, his own hands flipping through the pages of a potential read.

"I never finished it," I say slowly, my voice its own unanswered question. I stop at a chapter, my fingers running over the inked words until I feel a bulk under the paper. I pass a chapter or two more, and with the turn of a certain page, the book falls open and my eyes drift to something wedged in the crack of the spine.

I let out a strangled laugh.

"I can't believe it," I murmur, as I reach forward to grab the object.

"What is it?" Bennett steps close to me as I hold up a small bird, paper-thin but actually made from sewn together scraps of fabric. Its wings are spread in flight, its head raised up to the right.

"This is mine," I say, turning the bird over, studying the floral fabrics joined to the checkered ones, the tiny black-threaded eyes and yellow-threaded beak.

"Really?" Bennett grabs the bird. It fits nicely in his palm. "Did you make it?"

The answer takes several seconds to form. "No," I say uncertainly, feeling my way through the cobwebs of memory. "I didn't make it . . . I found it." A slow grin spreads across my face as I recall the past so recently uncovered. "In our old house, there was a loose bit of baseboard in my room. Behind it, I found this bird. Maybelle, I called it. It—she—was special. She was like a treasure."

"Cool," Bennett nods, impressed with my story but bored with my bird. He hands her back to me and returns to his task, and I return Blood and Honour to its spot on the shelf, Maybelle no longer gracing its pages.

"It is pretty cool," I say smugly to myself. I pocket the bird and glance up at my nephew. "I'm going to sit by the elevator. Don't take too long, okay? Your dad's moving in this afternoon, and we've got to help."

Bennett glowers. "Don't remind me," he mumbles. He's as angry with his mother as I am about Kaleb moving back into the house. She promised it wouldn't happen again, and we were both fools to believe her.

I give Bennett a sympathetic smile before I make my way towards the row of seats by the elevator, pulling a knitting book out of my tote bag once I sit down. I start reading the pattern for a sweater I'd like to knit, but within the space of two or three sentences, my thoughts drift back to my bird.

I lower the book to my lap and fish Maybelle out of my pocket. As I study the delicate needlework still even and tight, I let myself wander through half-formed recollections of our days together. I try to remember how we parted ways, but I'm soon distracted by a stinging pain in my left foot. I flex my toes in discomfort, and only then do I realize my left foot cannot be hurting, because my left foot became dead flesh when it was amputated fifteen years ago. I look down at the stump above my ankle, confused. I haven't had phantom pain this intense since right after the fire. I haven't had any phantom pain in years.

I swallow and concentrate on the blank space where my foot should be, the sting gradually dissolving into the stuffy air of the library.

"What do you make of that, Maybelle?" I squeeze my fist, expecting the woven softness of patchwork, but feel only my nails digging in against the flesh of my palm. I drop my gaze to the knitting book, where the bird has fallen from my grasp and landed on the page. I cup my hand around her wings, just as my eye catches something in the text. My fingers still pressing Maybelle to the glossy paper, I pause to consider the knitting instructions.

I read a handful of words before the world around me shifts.

Without warning I'm pitched forward, the room rocking as if the entire library is nothing more than a small boat in a big storm. The book drops from my lap, and I roll off my seat. I land painlessly on my side, the fall cushioned by something soft. When I push myself onto my hands and knees, I see it's something green, the colour of grass.

"What the . . . " I look around the library, only to discover I'm not in the library anymore. Around me, the grass-green expands in all directions, and I get the distinct impression I'm in a peculiar kind of meadow. Overhead stretches a makeshift sky of blue, no cloud in sight to spoil the vibrant effect. But it's all wrong. The grass, the sky. I grip the green beneath my hand, my fingers sliding into evenly spaced holes within the softness. The ground beneath and the sky above are made of knitted yarn.

I scan the horizon, taking in the sight of the endless soft landscape like something from an incomplete picture book. When I try to stand, the ground is too soft, as if there's nothing underneath the knitted blanket of green. I slouch into a cross-legged position instead, vaguely aware of two ankles, two heels, two arches curving up towards ten wriggling toes. My foot is back, my skin unscarred and full of blood, veins, and feeling.

Grasping the beautifully warm flesh of my left foot, I stare dumbfounded at my surreal surroundings until a sound attracts my attention.

It's a sweet, singing whistle. Birdsong.

"Maybelle," I mutter with quiet satisfaction, and only after I've said it do I wonder how I know it's the bird. I glance to where the knitting book fell in the tumble between the library and this meadow. The book is beside me, only it's no longer the same book I dropped. I grab it, pulling it onto my lap again. The patchwork bird isn't lying on the page, but when I focus on the text, the trilling birdsong tingles against my fingertips where they grip the book's covers.

The words make no sense. There are no letters, no sentences in English or any other language I've ever encountered. Except, I have encountered it. As I take in the unfamiliar sight of the black symbols scrawled haphazardly over the page, I'm overcome with the certainty of what to do next.

When I was eleven, there was a morning spent studying for a geography test before school. I used Maybelle as a bookmark while I hurried to get ready, and before I left, I opened my textbook again, desperate to absorb just one more fact. I read a sentence in my room, and then I found myself spinning into someplace else. I caught my breath, looked around, and found I was by mountains like the ones in my book, only the formations were made of snow with rocky caps threatening to crush them.

It was like someone, something, had translated the words of the book, but the language got twisted along the way. I sat before the mountains in awe, until I heard the birdsong, grabbed the book, read the unreal text and found myself back at my desk as if nothing had happened.

How did I ever forget? My own magic portal, a best friend to transport me to new realities.

I read the foreign words of the book in the meadow, even if I can't understand what they are, can't actually identify them as words at all. And when I read, Maybelle's song becomes louder, shriller, my whole body shivering with its vibrations. The sickening motion of summersaulting through a murky sea jerks my limbs and chokes my throat as I'm flung back into the library.

Within an instant I've returned to my seat, the knitting book still in my hands, and the small bird lying in the middle of the page. I pick her up, clench her in my fist, and giggle like a child.

"What's so funny?" Bennett asks, walking up the aisle with a book in one hand.

"Nothing," I reply, but it's a struggle not to hold Maybelle out in the air and cover her with kisses of delight.

***

Mere Joyce

I never found out where Maybelle came from. I assumed she was a toy sewn decades before we moved into the house, a plain explanation which satiated any desire for history I may have had. I never wondered why, when I found her, she didn't have so much as a speck of dust on her mismatched feathers. I never questioned why I settled on the name Maybelle. I never pondered who had created her, never asked myself why he or she stuck Maybelle behind a baseboard in the first place.

These details were unimportant to me then, and they're still unimportant now. Sitting in the living room after we've returned from the library and finished dragging Kaleb's things back into the house, I'm more interested in discovering how Maybelle ended up pressed between the pages of a mediocre book.

"Hey Stump, stop hogging the popcorn," Kaleb says.

"Don't call her that," my sister Cleo snaps, and Kaleb's smirk quickly hardens.

"She likes it," he sneers, and sadly, I can't deny that at one time I did. Kaleb used to call me Stump with the happy gleam of an inside joke I loved being a part of. I grit my teeth against the vicious way he's twisted the once endearing nickname.

Kaleb came into our lives when I was eight—my sister fifteen—his dark hair and dark eyes and bright, unshadowed smile irresistible to us both. The injury changed him. Six years into dating Cleo, an illegal tackle on the lacrosse field ruined Kaleb's back, along with his dreams of playing lacrosse in the national league.

The first six years with Kaleb were wondrous for my sister and for me. But it's been a long time since those days of wonder. Now, Kaleb does little more than hate. He hates my sister and his son because they're able to do the things he cannot. He hates me because I'm like him, without the constant waves of bitter self-pity.

"Here," I say, handing over the popcorn bowl. I meet Kaleb's smug gaze, refusing to allow him the pleasure of power over my nerves.

I sit back against the sofa, slipping my hand into the pocket of my cardigan and pressing my fingers against Maybelle's sides.

As Bennett's choice of movie rambles on in the background, I work to piece together my memories of Maybelle. I recall the nights I would flip through my geography book, picking the prettiest locations and travelling to strange copies of them. The translation was never perfect. White-cliffed beaches would turn into expanses of rock framed by enormous, frozen waves. Forests would fly while elongated birds stayed rooted to the ground. But it was good enough for me. Better, in fact. It was mine.

Eventually I moved into history books, biographies. I wanted to visit famous people long dead, but the bird couldn't translate bodies correctly, either. They were always featureless, their limbs wavy and misshapen. Still, I loved seeing what they would be like. Guessing at the mistakes became part of the fun.

I relax against Cleo's sofa, the putrid scents—dirt and old sweat—mingling with the buttery aroma of popcorn.

A thought niggles at the back of my mind, a vision

blurred and dark . . . The day I decided to test what would happen if I used Maybelle to enter a fictional world. I try to pull the unclear memory into focus, but it refuses to sharpen. My fingers tingle against the bird's stitched feathers, and a cold sweat dampens my forehead. I tune out my surroundings, focus on the memory until it's so close a single blink of the eye could bring it to the surface or push it away.

"Hey Stump, do you want the popcorn back or not?"

Kaleb's voice explodes into black spots behind my eyes. Pain shoots down the left side of my face, my chest and arm, my hip, my leg, my foot.

I gasp, scream. The blackness obscures my vision until I can't see anything, and I collapse, sliding off the couch and curling into a ball on the floor. Blindly, I claw at the bottom of my leg, trying to grasp my foot, trying to curb the searing ache as the memory cascades over me.

Blood and Honour. A fantasy about mystical creatures and handsome knights. I chose the climactic scene, imagined I could watch the hero battling the fire-breathing dragon. I didn't consider how the translation might fail, how anything could go wrong.

All those years ago, I found myself transported to a place full of raging fire with living swords hacking through the air and a faceless beast advancing towards me, the shaking force of its footsteps bringing a wall of fire down on top of my body. With my last inklings of pain-drenched sanity, I heard Maybelle's birdsong, and screamed the not-words to plunge back into reality.

I was already unconscious when I returned to my

room. My parents found me, and they blamed the old house's electrical system because they didn't know how else to explain the massive burns. They must have eventually returned the undamaged copy of Blood and Honour to the library, Maybelle tucked unseen among the pages.

I feel the pain I could never recall after waking in the hospital. The burning of my flesh, the scorching torture destroying my foot.

"Henny, what's the matter?" Cleo says worriedly. I hear rustling around me as my hands continue to grab wildly at the air.

Air. No limb, just air.

"What the hell is this?" Kaleb says.

"She's obviously in pain," Cleo snaps. "Kaleb, let me go!"

"She's just trying to get attention," Kaleb replies coldly. Someone kneels beside me. I'm sobbing now, certain of what happened to my foot, wondering how it ever escaped my memory.

"Henny, you okay?" It's Bennett whispering into my ear, and I struggle to nod, struggle to shake off the blackness concealing my vision. When at last the living room blinks back into sight, Bennett helps me sit up, and then runs to fetch a warm cloth for my face.

Kaleb studies me, trying to decide if my pain was real. I don't look at him, but I hold my head up so he knows I'm not being meek.

"You're such a drama queen," he says after a minute, shaking his head. Even from the corner of my eye, I can see his stare is dark, unnerving. He wants to give me something real to cry about. I take a long, steady breath, and slip my hand back into my pocket.

I grip the patchwork bird until I'm sure my knuckles are white.

Maybelle's translation caused my leg to burn, and now, fifteen years later, I think she's trying to make amends for the damage she caused. In her world, I have two feet. I can walk without crutch or imbalance.

But it's not my injury she's concerned with.

I move my head just enough to glimpse Kaleb's moody stare. If I can be repaired by Maybelle's magic, maybe he can, too.

***

I wake early the next morning and wait impatiently for the clock to strike nine so I can catch the bus to the library. I don't stop to revel in the nostalgia of the old building, nor do I pause to look at anything I think might make a good personal read. I head directly into the stacks, gathering books on geography, astronomy, and history, before I go to the basement and collect fiction novels set on beaches, in futuristic cities, even altogether different dimensions.

Maybelle gives me back my foot, if only for the short times I live in the worlds of her creation. But if she can temporarily heal my wounds, then surely she can offer Kaleb the same kind of respite from his damaged spine. If I find a place, a large field where he can run, jump, bend himself without tear or fracture, I can let him borrow Maybelle's powers for a few moments of unrestrained relief. And if his injury disappears in the midst of Maybelle's perfect, magical world, maybe his permanent scowl will disappear, too.

I check out a dozen books, my tote bag heavy and awkward as I make my way back to the bus station. I struggle home, dragging the books up the stairs to my room so I can start marking the descriptions I think are best suited to Kaleb's tastes.

I search until all of the books are open and spread across my room like a sea of musty pages. By the time I hear ugly footsteps outside my door, I've reached a state of excited giddiness, a light-hearted sensation which plummets when the door is thrown open.

"Hey, Stump." Kaleb stomps in without knocking. He grins at me, and then peers at the books on my floor. "What the hell are you doing?"

"Something for you," I say, wishing I hadn't mentioned anything to him until I was ready for his arrival. I asked Kaleb to come to my room hours from now, but as usual he hasn't listened to my request. He walks into the room trailing mud from the backyard, one hand rubbing the stubble on his chin.

"Well, what do you want? I've got things to do," he mutters, glancing briefly at my face before fixing his eyes on my leg. I wonder if he remembers the nights when he consoled me about my foot, when my girlhood self snuggled securely in against his side.

I walk among the books, working to make a quick decision. "I have a gift for you. Something to help your back."

"A miracle cure?" Kaleb asks, and I look up at his softened tone, only to see him sneer at my hopeful glance. "I wouldn't trust an idiot with a miracle. You can't do shit-all for my back."

"Kaleb." I breathe his name in frustration. How can it be possible for the progression of time to change someone so drastically? How can one injury steal away an entire personality?

I pick up one of the books, skim over the selected

page. It describes a cottage in an English pasture. It's not perfect, but it'll do for now.

"I have a gift. And, yeah, it's kind of a miracle," I say, holding the book out in front of me. "Read this book, and you'll see."

"So you are a total idiot," Kaleb scoffs, turning back towards the door.

"It gives me back my foot," I blurt out. The reasoning is stupid, but I haven't had time to think up a plausible explanation. "If you read this, your back will be better."

His shoulders tense at my words. "I've had enough," he says, stepping away until I grab his arm.

"Kaleb!" I shout his name, my heart hammering against my ribs, my fingers trembling with furious agitation. "Just listen to me."

"Don't you touch me." Kaleb swings around and pushes me away. I topple backwards, tripping over the books and stumble sideways until I fall onto my bed.

"I'm trying to help you," I tell him, the words hissing through my clenched teeth. "I'm trying to give you a way out, a way to get back what you've lost."

Kaleb stands before the bed, his once lean and muscled arms doughy across his chest. "Help me? Like you're not an even bigger waste than I am."

"Kaleb." I struggle upright, and immediately he pushes me back down, his hard grip on my shoulder leaving behind a pulsing ache. I wince in discomfort, and raise my eyes to see him looming above me with a wolfish grin. There never used to be a wolf inside Kaleb. One must have slipped in alongside the metal rods in his spine.

He licks his lips, but when I curl my knees up to block my body from his view, he only laughs.

"Who would want rotted meat like you? I've already had your sister, and that's bad enough." He turns away from the bed, missing the way my features shade with stony resolve.

I get up fast, as if I have two feet to stand on, and I reach for a book near the bed. It's a science fiction novel, one I chose for a beautiful passage describing a crystalline pool where peaceful men and women bathe under a blanket of emerald stars. But I saw more of this book before I spotted the lovely scene, and now I want to locate a passage of a wholly different nature.

"Kaleb." This time his name is a growl on my lips. I lift the novel, and am surprised to notice Maybelle's beak peeking out top near the back of the book. I don't remember taking her out of my pocket, but as I open to the page she's marking, I find the passage I was after.

Kaleb is already at the door, and he makes no effort to acknowledge my voice. I hobble across the small room, book in one hand, the other outstretched and poised to grab. I pull at Kaleb's arm with enough force to rock him backwards, and I pin him to the wall.

"You're going to regret this," he says. I push my knee in against his jeans so he knows how serious I am.

"Read the passage," I say, holding the book before him. He snatches the novel out of my grasp.

"What passage?" he asks, his lips sliced into a blood red smirk. He thinks I'm clueless of the gruesome plans forming in his head. He has no idea how much grislier are the ones in my own.

"This one, right here. Read." I point to the passage,

careful not to touch the paper, and I step back as Kaleb begins, his voice flat with suppressed rage.

"Thunder bellowed as the black lake engulfed them, the once serene pools now alight with hellfire and eternal screams as the Underworld claimed them all."

Invisible flames race up my side, but I steel myself against the pain, refusing to succumb to its agony. I don't want to miss this. I watch as Kaleb reads the words, and catch the first glimpse of his shocked expression before he disappears from the room, the book dropping to the floor.

I kneel down to look at the page, grasping Maybelle safely between my fingers before I study the passage, the sentence, the words Kaleb had been reading when the pain returned and his voice vanished.

Hellfire and eternal screams as the Underworld claimed them all.

I don't have to wonder if Kaleb was transported, if the translation made the horrific passage even worse. I know he's there. I know it's more terrifying than I can comprehend. And I know he can't get back without Maybelle's birdsong to guide his way.

I stare at the page for a long, silent moment, remembering the nightmare of my own trip into a world probably half as frightening as this one. I wanted to help Kaleb, give him something to look forward to so he could perhaps look forward to the rest of his life as well. But I was as stupid as he claimed to think I could change the person he's become. I've told my sister to accept it a million times, and I have to accept it as well. The old Kaleb is gone, and we'll never get him back.

I slip the fabric bird into my pocket as I take one final look at the passage of Kaleb's portal. If the old Kaleb is gone, the least I can do for my family is make sure the new one is, too.

I press my fingers against the cursed words, and then I close the book.

BIOGRAPHY: *Mere Joyce is a Canadian author of short stories and novels. As both a writer and a librarian, she understands the importance of reading, and the impact the right story can have. She's never seen a bird like Maybelle, but through the power of books she's still been transported to many new worlds, some darker than others.*

The Deeper I Go the Deeper I Fear

NATALIE CARROLL

I never believed in whimsical tales as a kid. You know the type about mythical creatures lurking in the depths.

I never experienced real fear either.

But that all came to an end when my parents decided to go on holiday to the sea, and to my dismay I had to go along.

The cabin we rented was old, dusty and there were cobwebs everywhere. Walking through the cabin, we left behind our footprints in thick layers of dust. Upon our inspection of the derelict little vacation house, I admit I found something homey about it. Of course, there was no TV, no game console nothing of which my life had been built around. Not even a bar of signal could be obtained. But it seemed familiar somehow.

I made my way to my chosen room where only a lamp and a bed decorated the space. This was where I wanted to hole up for the duration of the trip, *if* I had any say in the matter. I didn't, of course, but at least my parents left me alone that first night of our holiday.

The following morning, a blaze of streaming gold shined through the cracks in my darkened curtains.

"Come on Jakey," my sister said as she jumped up and down. "Get up!" She tugged at my covers

I groaned at the thought of getting up.

"Get out of my room." I mumbled.

She sauntered off eventually, but by then I knew I wouldn't get back to sleep.

I got up, got dressed, and made my way down to the dock where my family already waited on the boat. We set sail, to heaven knows where. Family time, I assume. The sun blazed down, colouring my pale skin red. The wind ran its way through my hair. Fish jumped along the side of the boat, which glided through the ocean waves. We came to a halt; the perfect spot for fishing. My father pulled up a chair on the deck, and cast his line. I suspect he was trying to teach Little Miss Sunshine how to fish.

"Look, Jakey! Look at the fish," she said in an excited high-pitched voice.

As reluctant as I was, I unfolded my arms and rolled my eyes.

Eventually, I dragged myself over to where she stood pointing at a school of fish. As soon as I peered over the side, however, the fish scattered.

"Where did all the fishies go?" she asked.

I leaned over the side, to see if a predator roamed the waters, but I couldn't see anything of the sort. My father shouted out that he'd caught something. I turned my attention to him, watched him trying to reel in his catch, but he lost his grip and fell backward. I dove for the rod, grabbed the sleek metal before it could disappear into the depths, and tried to reel the fish in myself.

Whatever had taken the bait was unnaturally strong, a real fighter.

"Dad, throw me your knife," I shouted, hoping I could cut the line before the rod was lost.

He threw me his Swiss army knife, but time had run out. The next thing I knew I was being pulled into the water, rod still in hand. My mother shouted my name, my father tried to grab a hold of me, while my sister just screamed her head off. Salt water obscured my vision, burning my eyes. I didn't really get a full picture of what I saw below the surface but it was big. The shadow flitted past, heading for the murky depths where no man could follow.

It moved like a snake, yet bobbed up and down at the same time.

A frenzy of fear shot down my spine, right to the very marrow.

But fear mingled with fascination.

Suspended by the water, I stared after the retreating creature in my spellbound state.

***

I woke in a daze.

Questions ran through my mind, questions I had no answers to.

It took me a while to figure out my surroundings, longer than I care to admit. I lay on a hard surface, and wore different clothes.

Odd, I thought.

I pushed myself onto my side and surveyed the room. Clinical white walls greeted me. Stainless steel barriers kept me prisoner on the bed; plastic tubes and surgical needles penetrated my body.

How long have I have I been here? Days? Weeks even?

My stomach grumbled. It was a sound only a dying whale could make.

I groaned, reached to the tubes and needles, and ripped them out my flesh.

An incessant beeping sounded, coming from nowhere and everywhere. A flurry of white–clad women rushed into the room. Nurses, I guessed. Hands suddenly pushed me back against the bed, trying to hold me down. I tried to fight back, but weakness kept me from succeeding.

A tall man wearing a white coat came into my room.

"What happened?" I asked, still delirious and fearful.

"An accident" he said. "You almost drowned."

The man went on to tell me how I came to be in the hospital, everything from the moment I fell overboard.

"When can I go home?" I asked when he finished.

The man glanced at his charts. "Tonight, if all your tests are clear."

Good news, at least.

He left swiftly thereafter.

***

My mother greeted me with a bone-crushing hug, accompanied by her salty tears and misinterpreted whaling speech when I returned home. My father kept patting me on my shoulder, avoiding eye–contact. My sister, however, bounded around me like a puppy; wanting to know *everything* she'd missed.

The Deeper I Go the Deeper I Fear

I excused myself from their presence, saying I was tired. And I was, to be honest, but I just needed to get away from all the attention at that point.

I couldn't sleep, though. The bed was uncomfortable, and my skin felt raw against my scratchy polyester sheets. Still, I lay there and watched the world through the window, watched day grow into night. I snuck out when the cabin grew quiet, and eventually found myself walking across the pebble beach within that chilly wind that blew from the sea.

Suddenly I found myself walking towards the water; closer and closer something out there beckoned me back to the depths. I tried to tell my legs to stop moving, but the message didn't seem to get through. I felt possessed.

Step by step the ring line where the water hit my shirt changed, higher and higher. My heart pounded in my chest. I dove towards my watery grave.

Beneath the surface of the murky waters, the icy water stabbed at my skin, freezing me to my core. However, that feeling soon faded when the cold had become a foreboding kind of numbness. At that point all of my extremities felt swollen, clumsy, stiff and useless, dulling the sensation of touch.

My heart rate gradually slowed.

At some point I had come to realise that I was not alone, and whatever lurked in the water was not friendly. I couldn't do much about it now, seeing as my time was quickly coming to an end. My lungs were burning from disuse already. At any giving moment my life could be shortened.

Everything around me turned black soon thereafter.

Death approached.

***

My eyes fluttered open, throat raw and lungs aching. I lay on a hard surface in an unfamiliar cabin. Feeling dizzy I tried to sit up and was met by a shabby-looking man.

"Wh . . . where am I?" I asked as I tried to look around my surroundings.

"You'll be safe here," said he said.

My vision was a bit hazy.

"How did I get here?" I asked.

"I was out fishing and I caught you instead. Just in time, too."

"What do you mean by *just in time.*"

The man looked concerned as he regarded me. "Do you not know lad?"

"Know what?"

"Legends have it that this is the place where the last living kelpie resides," he said.

"A kelpie? Is that what those are?" I asked, pointing towards the pieces of paper strewn about a table's surface nearby. Sketches of unnatural creatures covered the entirety of the pages with words scrawled beside the illustrations.

"Yes, they are malicious creatures."

"What is a kelpie?" I asked.

"A kelpie . . . well, they are a mystical creatures. Legends describe them as powerful horses that roam the oceans. It is said that they have the strength of a hundred men."

"So how would you know what it would look like?" I asked.

"It would disguise itself as black or white horse. Sometimes it would even shift its shape into disguising itself as a pony. It would be identified by its constantly dripping mane." The man drew a chair closer and took a seat. "It is said that its skin was silky smooth just like a seal, but it is cold as death when touched."

"So what the big deal then?" I asked. "You see them, you run. It's kind of obvious."

"The trick for a kelpie is to look innocent, that's what makes them so deadly. Sometimes they can transform themselves into a beautiful woman. A watery grave awaits those who fall for their seductions, though. These malicious creatures are masters at creating illusions."

"How do you kill them?" I asked.

"It can only be killed by being shot with a silver bullet."

Having played along with this charade long enough. "Firstly, thank you for saving my life. Secondly, no offense, but how do you know kelpies even exist? Like you said, it's just a legend."

"It is real. I saw it with my own eyes, but . . . I got there a little too late," he said.

"What happened?" I asked.

"There is a story about five children who came in contact with the creature. They didn't know what it was, but children being children, decided to pet the creature that had turned itself into a horse. At first, nothing seemed out of place, but when they tried to pull their hands away things quickly took a turn for the worst. Their hands rebounded like elastic, returning to the kelpie's skin. However, there was one child who didn't pet the horse that day. So the horse took a step forward towards the boy. The boy stepped back. Again, the horse stepped closer, and the boy retreated.

Frustrated, the kelpie leaped towards the boy and revealed its true identity," the man said.

"The boy was frozen with fear, giving the kelpie time to devour him whole. The kelpie then dove back into the sea and never returned . . . until now. All that was left of my little boy was his teddy bear, and ever since then I have been seeking revenge."

The man stood and walked to a shiny wooden chest situated on the table. He opened the chest, and cradled within the red velvet bedding was a silver gun with swirls patterns on it.

"Inside of this are five silver pullets," he said, handing me the revolver.

Confused and panicking, I asked: "Why are you giving me this?"

"Chances are it will come back, and you need to be prepared if it happens. As long as you are around it won't quit trying to lure you to your death."

I reluctantly took the gun from him, staring at the unique design.

"There's something you should know, though," he continued, "In order for those around you to survive you must sacrifice yourself."

A knock at the door interrupted our strange conversation.

"I'm coming!" he called over his shoulder, before turning back to me. "You should take that for protection and see if you ever come into contact with the kelpie again." He gestured to the gun.

I nodded and hid it in the back of my trousers, covering it with my T-shirt. Only when he was sure the gun wouldn't peek out did he open the door.

My mother rushed in and swept me off my feet,

squeezing me until I couldn't breathe. My father however, didn't even move from the car.

"Thank you," my mother said.

"No problem. The name's Ethan Blurgerson." The man held out his hand out to shake hers.

Pleasantries were exchanged, before we went on our way again. I still couldn't quite comprehend what had happened when I was pushed into the family car.

The moment the door closed, all I heard was my father's voice, lecturing me on how irresponsible I was; how inconsiderate and selfish. I tuned him out and stared out the window.

It went on and on until we got back to the cabin, and continued even after I'd shut my bedroom door in his face.

I took the gun from the back of my trousers and studied it as I lay down on the bed. Twisting and turning the weapon, I wondered whether this would be my salvation or downfall. My eyes grew weaker as exhaustion took over. I hid the gun under my pillow, dragged the duvet over me, and closed my eyes.

Whatever peaceful sleep I might have gotten was interrupted when there was a knock at the window. I tried to ignore it and get back to sleep, but it came again. The tapping grew louder, more desperate.

I grabbed the gun, climbed out of bed, and headed towards the window. But when I pulled back the curtains there was nothing except a strand of seaweed on the sill.

I heard it again, a gentle *tap-tap-tap* that grew more intense. This time, however, the sound came from my little sister's room. Without thinking, I rushed to my bedroom door, shouting frantically: "We need to get ourselves into the car and drive as far away as possible!"

"Its two o'clock in the bloody morning! What are you talking about?" My father stumbled out of the main bedroom, clearly annoyed.

"Come on we have to go," I shouted.

My mother suddenly screamed, and my father and I rushed to her aid.

"What's the matter?"

"There's a horse at my window," she cried out. "But it seemed . . . wrong. I don't know how to explain it."

"Whatever you do don't look at the window," I said. I rushed to her side of the bed, creating a barrier between her and the window.

"Dad, take mum to the car. I'll meet you there."

My father nodded.

I couldn't stick around with my parents when my little sister was all by herself.

"Oh my God, Charlotte," I whispered to myself, before I sprinted to her room. "Charlotte!" I screamed, turning the corner to her room. "Stop," I shouted, arriving just in time to see her reaching through the open window to pet the horse. "Don't pet the horse."

"Why?" she asked, pulling her hand away from the window.

"It's dangerous, come away from there."

"No it isn't." Charlotte didn't seem too sure, though.

The horse, or rather the kelpie in its shifted form, suddenly snatched Charlotte's collar, and dragged her out of the window.

There's nothing in this world that breaks a person more than hearing your little sister scream, I can tell you that much. I run to the window and jump out the window and feel the lush grass turn to gravel underfoot, while I set chase after them.

"Whatever you do, don't go into the water with it," I shouted after them, hoping she heard me, and would heed my warning.

Somewhere along the way, the kelpie dropped her. I ran up to her side, pulled her behind me and aimed my weapon at the creature who was threatening my family. I went to pull the trigger, to end this thing's miserably homicidal life once and for all, but the gun locked. It freaking locked!

My parents arrived a moment later, ignoring my suggestion to wait in the car. Good thing too, it seemed.

"Take her," I said, shoving Charlotte towards them—towards safety.

Seeing as the gun didn't work, I needed to distract the kelpie another way. I waved and ran in the opposite of my parents. When there was a bit of distance between me and the creature, I picked up some stones and threw them at it. Piss the kelpie off enough and it'll forget all about Charlotte . . . I hoped.

I ran up to a hill, the kelpie following close behind.

The hill, it turned out, was a cliff that overlooked the ocean. I skid to a stop at the edge, and looked back to see the beast catching up quickly. Seeing me cornered, it took its sweet time to close in. When it was just a few feet away, however, the kelpie revealed its true form by shifting in front of me.

With a neck like a giraffe, long and thick, and a head shaped like that of a crocodile—almost as leathery as one too. Its mane feathery and glowing.

And hazel eyes with purple irises that felt somewhat familiar.

Instead of seeing innocence in its true form, all I saw was the evil that feasted off of my fear.

I realised then that I was staring my fate in the face.

With my heart beating in my throat, I decided not to go down without a fight. Bravery consumed me. It tried to reach me with its giraffe-like neck. Without thinking about the consequences, I jumped onto the kelpie's neck, twisted and turned it, hoping to either scare it off or downright kill it. Unable to reach me or shake me off, the kelpie rushed towards the edge of the cliff and dove into the sea below. I held on for dear life. It's all I could do, really.

The deeper I went the deeper I feared.

My lungs were collapsing from the pressure of the water. I knew then I had to risk my life to save it from this monster from the deep.

I swung around just enough to put the gun I still held to its head, and got pinged back into place by its elastic skin.

My finger twitched into position, and I said a little prayer for good luck—hoping the gun would actually work underwater.

I pulled the trigger.

The water rippled as the bullet hit the malicious beast's head. Its elastic skin lost its hold on me, and the next thing I knew it fell down to the dark depths. Wasting no more time I used all the strength I had left to kick myself back to the surface.

The work was tiring, the water's icy fingers working its way to numb my muscles and slow my heartbeat. I didn't stop kicking, though. I wanted to live.

The Deeper I Go the Deeper I Fear

Once I broke through the water, I gasped for air, and slowly positioned myself so I could float.

I kept moving my arms in a circular motion and my legs back and forth to keep my blood circulating, while I look around for that dreadful monstrosity.

It took me a while longer to come to grips with the fact that I had escaped its jaws of death, that watery grave the strange man had warned me about.

Or did I?

In the distance I saw the familiar form of that sleek, unnatural body. Those hazel eyes with the purple irises glowed maliciously in the moonlight.

This wasn't over yet.

I turned around in the water and started swimming, fighting against the strong current. Each time I glanced back the dark figure was gaining speed, getting closer. Its pearl teeth gleamed within its jaws.

I push myself harder and swim faster, until I reach the shore.

I crawl out of the water, tired from the night's activity, and see the kelpie still pursuing its prey.

There's no time to waste. I run as fast as my legs could possibly carry me and dove behind a cluster of large rocks just beyond the beach.

The kelpie's hooves sunk into the sand, coming closer to my hiding place.

I held my breath, fearful of what might happen if I was found by the creature. I hear it sniff and snort. Its long neck came into view, bloodthirsty eyes searching.

I leaned back, out of sight.

The kelpie was so close I could touch it.

My lungs were burning for air by now, but I'd rather suffocate on land than get anywhere near its lair.

Natalie Carroll

Its nostrils flared, before it suddenly retreated.

I peered over the rock and watched it return to the sea, waited until it was far on the horizon, before I finally let out a shaky exhale and filled my lungs again.

I never thought legends had any truth to them . . . But I'm a believer now.

BIOGRAPHY: *Natalie is 20 years old. She loves to write about anything and everything she can. She also loves doing just about any sports.*

The Pigmalion Pigs

MARK ALLAN GUNNELLS

Joe came back into the living room to find Tasha stretched out on the sofa, watching a cooking competition show on TV. Joe lifted her legs, dropped onto the cushion, and settled his wife's feet on his lap.

"Julie get to sleep okay?" Tasha asked, wiggling her toes.

Joe recognized this as her nonverbal way of asking for a foot rub so he started kneading her soles, causing her to purr softly. "Yeah, she was out before I even got halfway through the book."

"What did you read her tonight?"

"Something called *The Mouse and the Motorcycle.*"

"That sounds fun."

"She liked it when I made the engine revving sounds."

"I think it's so wonderful that you read to her every night. That way, when she's old enough to read herself, she'll already have an appreciation for books."

"Exactly. Then I won't have to worry about her

spending hour after hour staring blankly at stupid reality TV shows."

Tasha tore her eyes away from the screen then playfully kicked at her husband. "Hey, that's not nice. This is quality entertainment. Look, that chef has to cook with a potato masher duct taped to his hand."

"I stand corrected. I didn't realize how intellectual this show is."

The two shared a laugh. This type of teasing was familiar territory between them, Tasha's love of television and Joe's aversion to the medium. Ironic, considering he worked for the local NBC affiliate, WYFF 4, albeit in the marketing department.

"You know," Joe said during the commercial break, when he knew he had a better chance of getting his wife's full attention, "I was thinking about my favorite book when I was Julie's age."

"*Encyclopedia Brown*?"

"No, it was called *The Pigmalion Pigs*."

"I don't think I've ever heard of that one. Then again, I didn't grow up in a household that had many books in it. Lots of alcohol, but not so much with the books."

"It was about this family of pigs. Percy and Pricilla Pigmalion, and their children Peter and Patty. Patty Pigmalion was kind of shy and bookish, but one day she got invited to this big party that everyone in school was going to and she was worried about looking like a big nerd. Her family banded together and gave her a makeover; a fancy new dress, make-up, stunning hairdo, the whole nine yards."

"Ah, thus the Pygmalion part."

"Yes, though I wasn't familiar with that term at the

time. The book actually had a great message about being yourself, because when she got to the party all the other kids were put off by her new look and said they had liked her the way she was. So she changed into some sweats, scrubbed off the makeup and mussed up her hair, and everybody had a great time."

"That's sweet."

"Yeah, I bet Julie would really get a kick out of it. I wonder if it's still in print."

Leaning forward, he snagged the iPad from the coffee table and opened Amazon. In the search engine he typed "Pigmalion Pigs."

DID YOU MEAN: *Pygmalion Pigs*?

Joe frowned, certain he'd used the correct spelling for the book, but he clicked the link and sat for a moment staring at the cover image that appeared.

It was just as he remembered from his childhood. Percy, Priscilla, and Peter standing around little Patty who was resplendent in a sparkly blue dress, her hair swept up onto of her head with a string of pearls resting atop the bun like a tiara, and bright red lipstick on her snout. Exactly the way he saw it in his memory . . .

. . . except for the title at the top.

The Pygmalion Pigs.

"They changed it."

"What?" Tasha asked, having gotten immersed in her program again.

"They changed the spelling of the book's title."

He held up the tablet for her to see. "It looks right to me."

"It is right, and that's why it's wrong. Originally they spelled it with an 'i' after the 'p', not a 'y'."

"That's misspelled," she said.

"I know, but they were playing off the word pig. Get it?"

"Of course I get it, but what I'm saying is, maybe they started to worry that it wasn't setting a good example for kids, having a misspelling right in the title like that."

Joe glanced back at the image on the screen. "I guess that could be it."

"What's wrong? You've suddenly got your down-in-the-dumps face."

"I don't know, it's just . . . I mean, it's silly, but seeing that they altered the title is like seeing your favorite childhood playground turned into a parking lot or your childhood home demolished."

Tasha giggled, sat up and gave him a peck on the cheek. "I love you, but you can be all kinds of melodramatic sometimes."

Joe found himself laughing as well. "In any case, with an 'i' or a 'y', I think Julie will love it."

And Joe clicked ORDER NOW.

***

It was after six when Joe got home from the station. He stepped inside, sat his briefcase in the foyer, loosened his tie, and went down the hallway, through the swinging door, and into the kitchen.

Tasha stood at the stove, working on supper. Julie sat in her booster seat at the table, coloring. Actually she merely scribbled all over the page with a red crayon. When she saw her father standing there, she squealed, dropping the crayon and holding her arms out. Joe picked her up and kissed her on the top of the head. He knew he was biased, but he thought she was the most adorable four-year old in the world.

"Hey, honey," Tasha said, not looking up from the boiling pot on the burner. Joe wasn't sure what she was making, but it smelled delicious. "How was your day?"

"Can't complain. How about you?"

"Upstairs toilet was clogged. Took me an hour and a drain snake to fix it. Turns out Julie flushed one of her dolls."

"You wouldn't do a thing like that . . . would you?" he said to the girl, scrunching up his face in mock seriousness. Julie giggled and buried her face in his chest.

"A package came for you today," Tasha said, pointing toward the counter. "It's from Amazon."

"Awesome, it must be my little surprise for Julie."

"For me," the girl said, her little hands gripping Joe's shoulders.

"That's right, for you."

"Are you sure she deserves a treat after clogging the toilet?" Tasha asked.

"I'll bc good, Mommy, I promise."

Tasha looked at the girl with a titled head. "I don't know, I noticed someone had toys strewn all over the living room."

"I go clean them up right now," the girl said, squirming to get down. Joe placed her on the floor and she took off like a wind-up toy, pushing through the door and making a beeline for the living room.

"Jesus," Joe said. "She's so excited, I'm afraid it will be a huge disappointment when she discovers her surprise is just a book."

Tasha returned to the stove. "She loves story time with Daddy. She'll be absolutely delighted."

Joe stepped to the counter and picked up the package, opening it and letting the thin oversized book slide out into his hands. That familiar cover, but the not-quite-right title. "You want to hear something strange?"

"The stranger, the better."

"I got online at work to research this book."

"That is strange," Tasha said. "Using your work time to research a children's story."

"That's not the strange part. I wanted to find out when exactly they altered the title's spelling."

"And what did you find out?"

"Nothing."

"What do you mean?"

"I mean every single reference I found about the book has Pygmalion spelled with a 'y', and I can't find anything about the title ever being changed. In fact, I found some images of old copies that are spelled with a 'y', none with an 'i'."

"Hmm," she said, tasting the stew that bubbled in the pot.

"That's all you have to say? Hmm?"

"What do you want me to say? You just remembered it wrong."

"No, I didn't. That was my favorite book from the time I was four until I was in second grade. I still had the thing when I finally moved out of my parents' house at twenty-one. I'm telling you it was Pigmalion with an 'i'."

"Honey, I'm not doubting your mental prowess, but you were a kid, and with the story being about pigs, you probably just got that all jumbled up in your memory."

"I remember that cover vividly."

Tasha stood with her head titled again, the same skeptical look she always gave Julie when she thought the girl was being less than honest. "What then? You think someone methodically went through the net and rewrote the history of a children's book?"

Joe laughed, although the sound was somewhat forced. "I know, it's just weird is all."

"Memory is weird. Growing up, I heard people tell the story of how my sister Violet got her big toe cut off in a bicycle chain when she was six so often that I truly believed I remembered being there and seeing it happen, even though I wasn't born for another year."

"I know you're right," Joe said, though a tingle of unease still lingered in his gut.

"I always am. Now go wash up, supper will be ready in about ten minutes."

Joe kissed his wife then slid the book back into the package so Julie wouldn't see it on his way upstairs.

***

Julie cuddled under the comforter, her head dimpling the plush pillow. Joe sat on the edge of the bed by her feet, the book open in his lap. He read to her in a soft tone, changing his voice for the various characters. He thought his daughter was enjoying the story; she giggled in all the appropriate places and the expression on her face could only be described as enraptured.

For that matter, Joe was pretty enraptured himself. Despite the simplicity of the story, he found himself really enjoying it. He realized most of this was pure nostalgia, but he thought the story was full of charm and warmth and humor, and he was so glad to be able to share this part of his own childhood with Julie.

He turned to the final page. Patty had just arrived at the party, which was attended by a menagerie of animal children—dogs and cats and horses and cows and squirrels and porcupines. Something seemed a bit off about the illustration, but Joe wasn't really focused on the picture. He read along.

"'A hush fell over the room as everyone froze, staring at Patty. She felt like she was under a microscope. Finally Gina Giraffe stepped forward, bending down her long neck to look Patty over. Then Gina exclaimed, "Oh Patty, I simply *love* your new look!" Everyone at the party exploded into cheers. Patty felt like crying as the wave of acceptance washed over—'"

"Daddy, why'd you stop?"

Joe looked up at his daughter then let his gaze dropped back to the page, rereading the words over and over, expecting them to rearrange themselves into something that made sense. Yet they stubbornly remained the same.

"Daddy!" Julie said again, sitting up. "Finish the story."

He stuttered for a moment before finally finishing the rest. "'Patty felt like crying as the wave of acceptance washed over her. Finally she was one of the gang, no longer an outcast or a freak. With a smile on her snout, she joined the party and had a great time.'"

"Yay!" Julie exclaimed. "I'm glad everybody likes her now that she's like them."

Joe closed the book, staring down at the cover and the title that was misspelled by being spelled correctly.

"You know, you don't have to be like everybody else for them to like you. You can be your own person, and that's good enough."

Julie shrugged and settled back onto the pillow. "Thank you for the story, Daddy. It was good."

"Yeah, you get some sleep, sweetie."

Joe kissed his daughter on the forehead, turned out the lamp by her bed, leaving the nightlight plugged into an outlet across the room glowing softly. He stepped out into the hall and closed the door halfway then walked back to the living room. He felt detached, not quite in his body, as if his soul were attached by a tether, bobbing along just above and behind him.

Tasha sat cross-legged on the floor between the sofa and coffee table, working on one of her thousand-piece puzzles. She collected puzzles but rarely worked on them, stacking them up in the hall closet to form teetering towers. Normally he would have wondered if she'd pulled one out tonight just to prove some point about how she wasn't addicted to TV and could stop at any time, but his mind was on other matters at the moment.

"They rewrote it," he said, tossing the book on the table, causing the puzzle pieces to jump and a few to fall onto the carpet.

Tasha gave him an annoyed look and started picking up the fallen pieces. "What?"

"The book, it has a different ending. Now instead of the kids telling her she didn't have to change for them, they are all happy she changed, makes it seem like that was the only way she'd be able to fit in."

Tasha picked up the book and started flipping through it. "That's a terrible message to send kids."

"And it's not the original ending," he said, taking a seat on the sofa. "I know you think I'm just misremembering the spelling of the title, but I am positive how that book ended and this is different."

After placing the book back on the table, Tasha looked up at her husband with one eyebrow raised and a small smile curling the corners of her mouth.

"What's that look for?" he asked.

"Nothing. It's just that . . . well, you're starting to sound a little bit like one of those nutty conspiracy theorists."

"Are you saying I don't know how my favorite childhood story ends? One of my first memories is of my mother sitting by my bed reading the damn thing to me."

Tasha held up her hands in surrender, but there was steel in her eyes when she said, "Hey, don't yell at me, I'm just saying you're getting a little obsessive over this."

Joe opened his mouth to say he wasn't yelling when he realized that his voice was louder and more strident than he'd intended. He took a deep breath before resuming. "I'm sorry. This whole thing is just really weird."

"Do you think it's possible your mother didn't like the ending and made up one she thought had a better message, and that's the one you remember?"

Joe shook his head. "No, after I learned to read, I started reading it myself. Read it so much the pages started falling out and my mother had to tape them back in."

Tasha shrugged, reminding him of little Julie who had picked up a lot of her mother's body language.

"Maybe they thought the original ending was too old-fashioned and they changed it to be more in line with the times. Call it Breakfast Club Syndrome."

"Breakfast Club Syndrome?"

"Yeah, remember in the movie *The Breakfast Club*, Ally Sheedy's goth character had to completely change her look in order to get Emilio Estevez."

Joe laughed, and it felt good. "You have a very interesting way of looking at the world, you know that?"

"So I've been told. Now if you'll excuse me, I have about 997 pieces of this puzzle that I still have to put together. Want to help?"

"I could . . . or we could watch *Project Runway*."

"Well, if you're going to twist my arm," Tasha said, already swiping the pieces back into the box.

***

When Joe came home the next evening, Tasha was waiting in the foyer with her arms crossed over her chest, her lips a stern slash of red. He'd been expecting this.

"Evening, sweetie," he said with a forced smile.

"Where have you been? I've been calling and texting you for the last two hours."

"Sorry, I turned my cell off."

"I called the station, and Jeff said that you left early today."

"Don't worry, I wasn't having an affair or anything."

"Just tell me where you were."

"I went to the library then stopped by all the used bookstores in town to see if I could find any old copies of *The Pigmalion Pigs*."

Tasha paused a moment then said, "I'd rather you were having an affair."

"You're funny."

"I'm not joking. You're obsessed with this thing. It's starting to seem OCD or something."

"I simply wanted to see what I could find."

"And?"

"Well, I located two copies of the book that were published in the 60s. Both spelled Pygmalion with a 'y' and had the ending where the kids love Patty's new look."

"Then that settles it, you were mistaken."

"I guess," Joe said, beating his briefcase against his leg.

Tasha rolled her eyes. "What more proof do you need?"

"I don't know, but I'm positive that the copy I had when I was a kid was different."

"Maybe you're losing your mind."

Joe sputtered a laugh. "That's entirely possible. What's for dinner?"

"Spaghetti. The garlic bread is almost done."

"Okay, I'm going to do a couple of emails for work then I'll set the table."

Tasha's expression softened slightly and she gave him a peck on the cheek.

He headed into the living room where Julie sat on the floor playing with her Barbie dolls. She had arranged them in a circle.

"Hey munchkin," he said, reaching down to pinch one of her plump cheeks. "You and your dolls having a party?"

"Yes, Daddy. You wanna be invited?"

"Thanks, but this looks like an all girls kind of shindig. I'll just be over on the sofa if your friends get rowdy and you need a bouncer."

Julie giggled as if she understood what her father was talking about then turned back to her dolls.

Joe took a seat and pulled the iPad from his briefcase. Instead of going to his email, he opened a search engine and typed "Pigmalion Pigs name change." Several articles appeared, but one in particular caught his interest, because it was from a website entitled Proof of Other Realities. Joe clicked the link and started reading.

"The children's book The Pygmalion Pigs *is considered by many to be compelling evidence of the existence of alternate realities. This website recently conducted an informal poll and found that 4 out of 10 people remember the book's title being spelled* The Pigmalion Pigs. *Some even stated that they remember the story unfolding differently. And yet there is no evidence that the book ever appeared in any other form than it does now, with the title spelled* The Pygmalion Pigs. *Some of those polled said they dug up their childhood copies and were surprised to find the spelling was even changed on those. What is most fascinating about this case is that it not only suggests the existence of parallel universes, but it suggests that we can shift from one to the other throughout our lives."*

Joe was still reading when the tablet was suddenly snatched from his hands. Tasha looked at the screen then turned her withering gaze on him. "I knew you weren't doing work emails."

"I was. I mean, I was going to, I just—"

"Get out of this house."

"What?"

"Didn't you tell me once that your parents still have a bunch of your childhood toys boxed up in their basement?"

"Yeah, I think so."

"Then there's a chance that book is there as well. Hop in your car and head over there."

"Now? That's crazy."

"Yes, which is exactly how you've been acting. This is just going to continue eating at your mind until you do this. Please, for your sake and mine, go."

Joe made a show of debating the issue with himself before rising from the couch and kissing his wife. "Thanks, sweetie, I won't be long."

***

"Well, to what do I owe the pleasure of an unexpected visit from my baby boy?" Joe's mother said as she greeted him at the door.

"Mom, I called you fifteen minutes ago and told you I was on my way."

She stood aside and let him into the den, where his father sat in a recliner, watching TV. He glanced over and raised a hand to his son then returned his focus to the tube.

"Yes," his mother said, "but it's very unusual for you to come calling so late, and just to go rummaging through some old boxes."

"I told you, I really think Julie will get a kick out of some of my old picture books from when I was a kid."

"And you had to rush right over? It couldn't wait?"

"I wanted to get to it before it slipped my mind."

The two of them walked through the archway into

the kitchen, leaving his father bathed in the glow of the TV.

"Have you eaten?" his mother asked, opened the oven door and peered inside. The familiar aroma of roast wafted on the air. "I can fix you a plate."

"Tasha is keeping some spaghetti warm for me. Besides, this will only take a few minutes."

"Okay, you be careful. It's probably crawling with spiders down there."

As Joe opened the door to the basement and started down the narrow stairs, he couldn't help but smile. His mother had few fears, at sixty she went skydiving for the first time, but she couldn't abide spiders.

The basement was a small square with a concrete floor, the air musty and full of dust. Spider webs dangled from the low ceiling like old forgotten party decorations. To the right were the washer and dryer, straight ahead stood an old work bench that his father used to tinker with home repairs. Currently a toaster was strewn across the top in several pieces. Stacked against the wall to the left were about a dozen cardboard boxes.

Working by the harsh light of the overhead florescent tubes, Joe began opening the boxes one by one. He found old dresses that had belonged to his mother, a box of his father's bowling trophies from when he was in a league, broken knickknacks and chipped china, faded photos and old birthday cards.

He'd gone through half the boxes when he finally hit pay dirt.

He pulled back the flaps of a ripped box with water stains on the top and the first thing he saw was He-

Man and Luke Skywalker tangled together in a somewhat obscene knot of plastic and sculpted muscle. He tossed them aside and began pawing through more of his past, action figures and matchbox cars and toy guns and yoyos. At the very bottom of the box were several pictures books, some Seuss and *Amelia Bedelia* and *Babar*. All these he discarded, they could be incinerated for all he cared. He was interested in only one book, and it had to be—

He moved aside a copy of *Dandelion* and caught a glimpse of Patty in her new dress. Joe snatched up the book, an idiot grin spread across his face. The book was tattered and discolored, several of the pages falling out to sift down like autumn leaves. He glanced at the front cover, preparing for vindication as he read the title.

The Pygmalion Pigs.

The grin withering to a tense frown, Joe quickly flipped to the last page of the book. The image showed all the animals at the party cheering and laughing and dancing, with Patty in her new dress at the center.

"No, no, no, this is all wrong."

Joe experienced a moment of vertigo, a woozy lightheadedness overcoming him, and his voice echoed in his own ears. He reached out to the wall to steady himself . . .

. . . but gasped and jerked his hand back when he realized the wall was no longer in front of him. Instead he saw a reflection of the room, as if the bricks had become a mirror. He stared at his own face, a dumbfounded expression making him look like one of the mentally handicapped children that lived in the group home on Wellington Street. He crouched there, frozen, for a moment, and then watched himself sneeze, lose his balance, and fall over onto his bottom.

And yet he hadn't sneezed, he hadn't lost his balance, he hadn't fallen over. It was only his reflection who had done that.

Joe bolted to his feet, and so did his reflection. Only at a slower pace. "What the hell is going on?" he and his doppelgänger said at the same time, creating that curious doubling effect again.

Joe reached up and scratched his chin as the reflection ran his fingers through his hair. "Am I dreaming?" the double said, closing his eyes. His voice had the same timbre and inflection as Joe's own. A perfect imitation.

"This isn't real," Joe said with a laugh as brittle as cracked ice. "Maybe Tasha's right, maybe I'm losing my mind."

The doppelgänger's eyes snapped open. "Tasha? What do you know about Tasha?"

"She's my wife," Joe said, thinking: *Why am I talking to myself?*

The reflection looked down at the book in his hands. "I don't understand what's happening. I just wanted to come find this book, to see if the title was spelled the way I remembered it."

Joe glanced down at the book in his own hands. "Pygmalion with a 'y'?"

"No, that's the way it *should be*, that's the way I remember it, but every copy including this one has Pigmalion spelled with an 'i'."

"That's the way I remember it, but on every copy here it's spelled with a 'y'."

Joe found himself thinking of the article he'd read

earlier, all that nonsense about parallel universes and alternate realities. At least it had seemed like nonsense at the time, but now that he was staring at the mirror image of himself, he started to wonder. And he could tell by the look in the doppelgänger's eyes that he was wondering the same thing.

"Maybe we should switch," the double said.

Joe frowned. "What?"

"Books, maybe we should switch books. You have the one I remember from childhood, I have the one you remember. Maybe we should just switch back."

"Can we do that? Is it possible?"

"I don't know how any of this is possible. Maybe because we're in the exact same place at the exact same time for the exact same reason. Maybe that opened some kind of, I don't know, *window* or something."

Taking shuffling, hesitant steps, Joe approached the line of boxes that separated this basement from the identical one that existed across some unknowable gulf of time and space. His hand trembled as he held out the book, his double doing the same. Would they encounter resistance, an invisible wall? Would the air ripple like water or sizzle with electricity?

Joe didn't experience any of that, but he did notice a low hum in his ears. Not the buzz of an electrical current, but more like a hive of bees. Vertigo overcame him again and he swayed on his feet. The room seemed to spin. He thought he was falling . . .

. . . but then the spell passed and he was standing in his parents' basement, staring at the blank wall. No doppelgänger, no reflection of the room. Just the wall.

"We didn't even get to switch bo—" he started, but then glanced at the cover.

The Pigmalion Pigs.

Quickly he flipped to the last page, where Gina Giraffe tells Patty Pigmalion that she didn't have to change for anyone, that everyone at the party had liked her just the way she was.

"Yes! Now I can prove to Tasha that I'm not crazy."

Without bothering to place the items he'd unpacked back in the boxes, he started up the staircase. Halfway to the top he became aware of the roaring sound of rain hitting the roof, and when he came up into the dark kitchen lightning flared bright through the windows. The air held the acrid stench of something burnt. Apparently his mother had cooked the roast a little too long.

He turned to head through the archway and almost collided with his father. "Oh, sorry, Pop."

"Find what you were looking for down there?" the man asked with an amiable smile.

Joe held up the book. "Sure did."

"Want to split a frozen pizza?"

"No thanks, Tasha's waiting."

His father's fuzzy eyebrows rose up. "You're eating with Tasha and Julie tonight?"

Joe opened his mouth to ask why his father sounded so surprised when thunder rocked the house. "Jesus, this storm just rolled in out of nowhere."

"You feeling all right, son? It's been raining all day."

A chill spread all over Joe's skin, and he found himself staring at the book again, and the sight of the title now restored to coincide with his memory made him shiver. "Um, I need to go, Pop." He went into the den, which was quiet and empty. "Tell Mom I love her and I'll call tomorrow."

Hand on the doorknob, he glanced back to see his father frozen in the center of the room, his body shaking as tears rolled down his face.

"Pop, what's wrong?"

"Do you think you're funny?" the old man said in a deep, husky voice that Joe had never heard before. As if his father's body was now inhabited by a stranger.

"What are you talking about?"

"Son, I know you've been having a rough time lately, but that is no excuse for you to be so cruel."

"I really don't know—"

"Just get out of here," his father said then turned to the right and disappeared down the hall that led to the bedrooms. Joe considered going after him, but he had a sinking feeling that he needed to get home as soon as possible.

The rain came down in a torrent, impacting the earth with such force that each drop splashed back up like a mini-explosion. As if to compliment this image, thunder crashed loud enough to cause the windows of the house to rattle, and lighting illuminated the sky in an atomic flash.

Joe was drenched within thirty seconds of stepping outside, but still he paused on the front walk, staring at the spot where he'd parked his Honda Fit when he first arrived. The car was gone, and in its place was a beat-up Pontiac Sunfire with a bent antenna.

He didn't understand what was happening. At least, he didn't want to understand. Reaching into his pocket for his keys, he discovered not the fob for the Fit but instead a plain metal key with Pontiac written on it.

The urgency to get home reaching a fever pitch, he

jumped in the unfamiliar car, tossing the wet book on the passenger's seat, and backed quickly out into the street. The drive back to his house usually took half an hour, but despite the horrible weather conditions, Joe made the trip in half that time.

***

He skidded to a stop at the curb, not bothering to pull into the garage. The control for the automatic door wasn't hooked to the visor in this car anyway. Not bothering to close the car door but taking the time to grab the copy of *The Pigmalion Pigs*, he splashed through a puddle deep enough to drown a Chihuahua, and bounded to the door.

Once he was on the porch and out of the relentless rain, he fumbled with his keys, shifting through them to find the one for the front door. He noticed he had fewer keys than usual, and the house key was not among them. He went through them four times to be sure. With a growl of frustration, he pounded on the door with a fist.

"Tasha! Tasha, open up, it's me! I must have lost my key!"

The storm was moving on, the rain slackening and the thunder and lightning fading, but twilight had descended, lending the neighborhood a shadowy gloom that filled him with a sense of foreboding.

Five minutes after he started knocking, the porch light buzzed to life and the door opened. Just a crack, and the security chain was still attached. Tasha's face, strained and pensive, peered out from the opening. "What do you want, Joe?"

"What do you think I want? I want to come in and get out of these wet clothes. I lost my key."

"Are you drunk?"

"No, I'm not drunk, I was just over at my folks' house looking for this," he said, holding up the waterlogged book.

"Jesus, Joe, are you still going on about that book? You need to see a shrink."

"Look at the spelling, Tash. Pigmalion with an 'i'."

"Yes, just the way it has always been. Now maybe you'll stop with all this nonsense about how it used to be spelled with a 'y'."

Joe let his arms drop, as well as his mental defenses. Realization finally sunk in. Crazy as it sounded, he and the doppelgänger had exchanged more than just books.

"Maybe I'll read this to Julie tonight," he said.

Tasha barked a harsh laugh, glaring at him with a coldness he'd never witnessed before. "You know good and well you don't have her again until next weekend."

"Have her? No, this isn't right. This is where I belong. Let me come in and we can talk."

"Found a job yet?" Tasha asked.

"What? A job? WYFF—"

"The station laid you off almost a year ago. It's time you gave up on this idea that they're going to ask you back. Those unemployment checks aren't going to keep coming forever. Grow up, find another job, maybe then you can get your own place and move out of your father's house."

"Wait, I live with Pop?"

Tasha sighed and let her head hang down as if she hadn't the energy to hold it up any longer. "Go home and sleep it off, Joe. I swear to you, if you pull something like this again, I'll contact my lawyer and you'll lose the one weekend a month you get with Julie."

Before Joe could respond, the door slammed in his face. The porch light went out, leaving him clothed in darkness.

He remained on the porch for another five minutes before turning and starting back to the car. The rain had tapered to just a light misting, but the saturated ground squelched under his feet and his hair dripped cold droplets down his face.

As he pulled away from the curb, he mused on how much his life had changed since he'd left the house earlier, barely more than an hour ago. Life hadn't been perfect, but whose was? Not perfect, but certainly wonderful. Now he was unemployed, separated or possibly divorced, able to see his daughter only one weekend a month, living with his father, and all signs pointed to his mother being dead. All because of that damn book.

Gripping the steering wheel tighter, Joe pressed the gas pedal and rocketed through the streets. Determination made him fearless as he sped past stop signs, took turns at breakneck speeds, once clipping a mailbox but not stopping to see how much damage was done. He had to get back to his parents' house quickly. He would go down to the basement and sit amongst the boxes and stare at that wall, *The Pigmalion Pigs* in his hands, until the other him showed up and they could switch places again.

As he sped around a sharp curve, the book slid off the passenger's seat and fell into the floorboard, flipping open to the final page. The happy ending where Patty gets to be herself and everyone accepts her as she is.

Mark Allan Gunnells

The doppelgänger will never show up again.

Of course not. Why would he? The trade had left him ensconced in a life where he had a loving wife and daughter, two living parents, a thriving career. Earlier Joe had thought that life hadn't been perfect, but it certainly seemed so compared to this one.

So he would sit in that basement and stare at the wall and wait for the opportunity to steal his life back. Weeks, months, years—however long it took.

However long.

BIOGRAPHY: *Mark Allan Gunnells loves to tell stories, has been doing so since the age of ten. Over the past ten years he has published several novels with a variety of small press publishers and has enjoyed every minute of it. He lives in Greer, SC, with his fiancé Craig Metcalf.*

Chemical Oasis

TOMMY B. SMITH

The **glowing speck** on Michael's tongue made everything right in the delicious beauty of paradise. He swallowed it down.

"Thank you," he said.

"You're welcome, Michael." Lucille's dazzling smile was as white as her uniform.

Michael smiled back. He was so happy.

It was strange then that the ultimate pinnacle of bliss hovered out of reach. Even while a tiny point of brilliance outshone everything else, a quiet shadow held its breath in the back of his mind as if waiting for a punchline.

Michael was happy. Wasn't that enough?

The face. That was it. It was an ugly face that emerged from amid the trees of the dead forest. It still bothered him.

Lucille had placed cool fingers against his cheek, had gently turned his head from the high window to face her milky features framed by dark brown hair. Her round brown eyes probed him.

"Come on now, Michael. Don't look out the window."

Michael nodded. She smiled. He returned the smile as he always did, but for the first time since he could remember, it was forced.

From the third-floor window his gaze had drifted to the shimmering river and beyond to the forest, where he had seen the face. The vision clung to his thoughts like a leech. The joy was seeping away, leaving a troubling chill in its stead.

His imagination wouldn't rest. Despite Lucille's warning, he had to look one more time. He hoped he wouldn't see the face again.

He stood at the window and stared down to the forest, gray and dead. He could envision the face against it.

A hand touched his shoulder. He jolted around with a startled cry. His hand struck Lucille's and the pill flew.

"Michael!" she exclaimed. "What did I tell you?"

"I'm sorry," he said quickly. "I—thought I saw something."

"I told you not to look out the window," Lucille said under her breath. She was on the floor now, searching for the pill.

"There's something out there," Michael said.

Lucille raised her head. Her hair was mussed, and her lips were flat, unsmiling. She stared through Michael.

"I told you not to look out the window," she said. "Why did you disobey me?"

She stood and held out her hand, opening it to reveal the pill in her palm. "Here. Take this."

The hallway had dimmed. Michael considered Lucille's tone, which had changed as well. He studied her face. His eyes trailed downward, where he noticed a faint yellow smudge on her uniform's collar.

"Take the pill, Michael," Lucille spoke.

Michael stared at her. Strange thoughts converged in his mind.

"No," he said.

"No?" Lucille turned her head. "I need some help with this one!"

Footsteps answered her.

Michael tensed, seeing several white-uniformed figures running up the corridor toward them.

"I'm sorry, Michael, but we're going to have to do this by force," Lucille said.

The others rustled past her toward Michael.

Michael was confronted by a tall, powerfully-built man with a shaven head, and a dark-haired man who was shorter, but equally fit.

The bald man seized Michael's arm. "Don't make this any harder than it has to be," he said. The thick, powerful fingers squeezed Michael's arm just above the elbow.

Michael jerked his arm back, and the other man ran forward to assist in detaining him.

He fought, yanking his arm away and throwing a misguided punch. The bald man flung powerful arms around him, pinning his arms to his sides. The other man slipped from his sight. Lucille came forward with the pill between two fingers.

"Relax, Michael," she said. "It will be over soon."

Michael cracked his head into the bald man's forehead. The man reeled, and Michael was free until arms locked onto him from behind. It was the other man, the one he could no longer see. Michael twisted to free himself and punched the man in the face. The man shouted, enraged, and hurled a hard fist into Michael's ribs. The bald man joined in, striking him across the face. Michael tumbled backward. His tailbone crunched against the bottom edge of a window.

The men advanced. With an impulsive spring of his legs, Michael propelled himself back. Glass shattered. He was plummeting downward. He fought to gain a grip on himself for all it would even matter, because he was already striking a liquid surface, and an oily murk consumed him.

It burned. His head was spinning. He thrashed and fought for the surface. The world, in mere minutes, had become a blur.

Through his confusion he managed to crawl from the awful slurry and collapsed on the bank. His skin was burning. A tingling sensation flittered through his brain. His senses scattered.

Water splashed across his reddening skin. He didn't move. He didn't react when the second bucketful of water struck him either, or when the ropes encircled him and rough hands cinched them into an expert knot.

When Michael came to, he was more than aware of the ropes' painful tightness against his blistered skin. He struggled for a moment, still confused, while his eyes locked on the first visible image of a dirty building and its surrounding moat of rancid brown liquid.

His heart thudded an accelerating machine-gun rhythm. He continued to strain, but it only made the affair more agonizing. The ropes allowed no movement. When he glimpsed his captor, he recoiled, surprised and a bit disgusted.

Seeing his reaction, the man with the horrible face chuckled. He strode into Michael's full line of vision, and scarred features came into view. The ugly face was attached to a tall, wiry body wrapped in a tan trench coat.

"Are you finished now, Mike?" he said.

Michael felt a spark of his frustration return. He swirled his tongue around in his mouth. Grit coated the inside of it.

"What did you call me?" Michael said after a couple of minutes. He had to speak slowly so the words wouldn't be slurred outside of comprehension.

"I called you by your name."

Michael shook his head at the words, which didn't seem to make much sense, and focused instead on his surroundings. It was dark around, but he could make out the withered, dead trees.

The dead forest.

He gasped.

"What's going on?" was all Michael could think to ask.

"You tell me," the ugly man said. *James.* That was his name, Michael realized. Agent James Mitchell.

Michael's skin crawled. The coarse ground was unpleasant against his skin, but far worse was that river, that dirty chemical moat. He had fallen out of the window, directly into it.

"The river," Michael said. "It burns so much."

"You're telling me?" James replied. "I know better than anybody. Look at my face. That isn't enough of a reminder?"

"That's what happened to you?"

"You know that's what happened to me. That stuff kills. It's poison. It's the byproduct of the Synthesizer. It's killed the trees and land for some distance around. You're lucky I was able to pull you out quick enough and throw some water on you."

James rattled out a sigh. He stared across the moat to the tall, dark-brown building it encircled.

"The others are still in there," James said. "They probably don't have any idea. You don't, and you've only been in there a few days."

"It was so beautiful," Michael said. "But so—"

"Wrong?" James finished. "Look at it, Mike."

"It just looks like an old building," Mike said.

"It's a factory of lies." James gestured to the dead forest around them, the thin, decayed tree trunks with lifeless limbs and the dry gray dirt that buried the dead trees' feeble roots. "But this is real. You and me, here and now. That's real. Look at me." He came closer, and leaned down close.

Mike flinched.

"Look at my face," James said. "Yeah. I know. But you know what? It's part of who I am now and I can deal with it." He straightened. "This has gone too far, Mike. This isn't just an investigation anymore. It's war. We have to do something. The Synthesizer is destroying everything, and everybody inside that place serves it either because they're on the payroll or on the stuff, as you were."

The sense of familiarity was returning to Michael—Mike, as James had called him—and the others, before they had lost themselves to the Synthesizer and its wonderful magic.

"So you aren't going to try anything crazy, right?" James said.

Mike didn't reply.

James came close with a curved knife in his hand.

"All right," James said. "Hold still."

James slashed the ropes with quick efficiency, and Mike climbed to his feet. His limbs were stiff and sore. His arms, he saw, were covered in red blisters. He imagined his face was in a similar shape, but he could at least be thankful he didn't look like James.

"What do we do now?" he asked.

"Funny, you asking me such a thing," James said.

"Why?" Mike asked.

"We have a plan," James answered. "Y*our* plan, only you don't seem to remember it now. I'm thrilled you should ask me to remind you. Come on."

James led him through the forest. Mike stumbled over a large rock, but James kept walking. Mike hurried to kccp up.

James stopped and gestured down to a bare patch of ashy dirt.

Mike blinked. "There isn't anything there," he said.

Without answering, James crouched and began pushing dirt with his hands. He paused after a half-minute's effort. "Are you going to help me with this, or what?"

Mike came over to assist. Even between the two of them, the process of pushing and digging became exhausting.

"What are we doing?" Mike asked.

James answered with some vague muttering Mike couldn't really even understand. He shook his head, and went back to digging.

When they uncovered the wooden crates, James drew a sharp breath. He pried open the top of one crate and hefted a lengthy, black item from it.

It was an automatic rifle. The crates were filled with firearms.

"We buried them." Mike recalled at last.

"You always were paranoid and suspicious, Mike," James said. "But for once it paid off. The manufacturing of AX-633 could only benefit everyone, they said. Cure us all of pain, fear, and misery." He shoved a clip into the gun. "And you were right, whether you remember it or not, when you said it was too good to be true. There's only one miracle cure for life, and that's death. The death of freedom? Or the death of everything, in the end?" He motioned to the trees and the dead, nutrient-sapped soil. "But the end isn't here yet. There's still time. Here, catch." He threw the rifle to Mike, who caught it in both hands, but almost lost his balance in the process. James picked up another rifle, loaded it, and began stocking his jacket with ammunition clips.

Mike looked over the rifle uneasily. It was too familiar.

"You told me you'd be back in a week," James said. "I was starting to wonder."

"I was only inside for a week?"

"That's it."

"It seems like forever. I can hardly remember anything from before that."

"Of course. What's worse, you're probably better off than a lot of the others in there. Some of them have been in there for a long time. They don't know who they are or what they're doing."

James paused, studying his rifle. He raised it and fired. Flames erupted from the barrel and the shot tore through a narrow tree-trunk.

"Just testing," James said. He glanced back at Mike. "Are you ready?"

"For what?"

"Think. Look deep into that brain of yours, Mike. I think you know, on some level, don't you?"

Mike stood in silence. The longer he stood there, looking at James's ugly face, the deeper he sank into realization.

"We have to go back in," he whispered.

"We have to do it, Mike," James said. "If we walk away and file some stupid report, it'll be stonewalled like all of the others before, and we'll never get another chance. There is no other way."

Mike swallowed. His eyes fell back to the rifle in his hands.

"Ready?" James asked him. Mike kept looking at the rifle. His stomach felt like it was full of lead, but he nodded.

"Then let's go," James said, and turned to walk.

They made their way for the entrance.

Mike searched his mind and found the way, a hidden bridge across the moat which he activated. They waited for the metal bridge to extend, and when it locked into place, they crossed it to the large door.

Mike knew the entry code also, he discovered. He punched the correct combination of numbers into the keypad, and the door popped open.

They slipped in.

A gray-haired, white-uniformed denizen froze. The older man turned to run, and called out for security.

James opened fire and riddled the man's back with bullets. He flopped forward to the ground, blood soaking the back of his uniform.

Mike shouted, surprised, before the security officers in brown uniforms rushed in.

James squeezed the trigger of his raised weapon and released a flurry of bullets.

Mike, torn between the past and present, flinched at the gunfire, but a steel clamp squeezed his brain. There was no place for indecision here. Impulse guided his hands. He gripped the weapon and gripped its trigger. Bodies fell. Mike killed because there was no alternative, and he found it almost second-nature.

One was backed into a corner, pressed against a wall with eyes stretched wide open. He wore a torn and dirty navy blue shirt, and jeans.

"He's one of us," James said, pointing. "Leave him. When the drug wears off he'll see the truth. So will others." He glanced at Mike. "With our help they'll remember, I hope. Let's go. We can't stop now."

As if in response, a man in a brown uniform charged into the room, rifle readied and swinging toward James and Mike. James fired, and Mike was quick to join in. The man's body shook in an involuntary bullet-dance and his rifle struck the floor at his feet. He soon followed it, slumping across the white, shiny floor, his blood running free.

"Where is it?" James asked him.

He was talking about the Synthesizer. Mike strained to scour his clogged memory.

"The sixth floor," he said. "There's an elevator that way."

"Good," James said with a nod. They moved on, weapons ready.

Mike still struggled with his memories, but hesitation was unaffordable. As he and James pushed through the building, both fired at anything that moved in a white or brown uniform.

"The elevator," Mike said. "It's that way." He pointed ahead.

Mike kept watch, his rifle primed, while James hit the elevator's single button. When the *ding* sounded, Mike turned and took aim along with James, as the door opened.

The elevator was empty. James stepped in, and Mike after him. The doors slid shut.

"It only goes up to five," James said, studying the buttons.

"The sixth floor is only available by stairway," Mike said, thinking carefully. "We take the elevator to five, and take the stairs at the opposite end up to six."

James punched the button for 5.

The elevator rose.

Mike's heart pounded. His hands were sweating, which made the rifle uncomfortably slick in his grip. During the elevator's ascent, he took a moment to wipe his palms on his pants and returned a tight grip to the weapon.

The elevator's *ding* halted them at the fourth floor. The door opened, and they fired. A man in a white uniform sprawled to the floor, dead. The doors closed again.

The two exchanged glances. At the fifth floor the carriage stopped its ascent.

Ding.

The doors opened, and they came out with guns blazing. Screams and gunfire filled the room. A crowd parted, some falling beneath the gunfire and some fleeing.

White and brown uniforms went red, and the blood of liberation struck the walls and floor. James went for the browns first. Michael made quick sense and followed suit; security was apt to be the best-equipped for combat.

Their combined efforts eliminated the immediate security threat in less than a minute. The white uniforms, while not as dangerous, still posed a threat. They were the next targets, although a few had been downed already.

To Mike there came a familiar glimpse and a face that seemed from a faraway dream.

"Michael, why?" Lucille cried right before his bullets quieted her voice forever.

Mike stared down at Lucille's blood-washed body as if paralyzed. He tried to sort through the emotions that buffeted him, to make some sense of them, but there was no time. Another gunshot rang out. Mike turned with his weapon to fire, but saw James standing there and the last white-uniformed body falling.

His gun smoking, James looked to Mike and asked, "What else is on the sixth floor? How well-guarded is it?"

"Just the Synthesizer," he said after a moment of pause. "The last wave of security is stationed on this floor."

"Then I shouldn't have any problems?" James asked.

"Not from here. There are only a few who go up to the Synthesizer for maintenance and routine inspection. Most work on separate units throughout the building, all of which receive regular input from the Synthesizer."

"Got it." James looked around at the disoriented bunch who lingered, and motioned with his gun. "Can you get the rest of them outside? I'm going up to the top."

Before Mike could answer, James was gone.

For the survivors of the onslaught, those huddled against walls and in corners, the pills' effects were wearing thin. Once the Synthesizer was destroyed, there would be no more specks of shining merciful oblivion to swallow, and no chemical oasis in this dead region.

The people looked around, confusion setting in. Some of them stared at Mike and the weapon in his hand. Others looked at the bodies that covered the floor with a slow-dawning horror infiltrating their minds and eyes.

"I know you don't understand what's happening," Mike said. "I barely do myself. But listen, I need you all to follow me, right now."

Mike backed away. He motioned, and some of the people followed, while others deliberated.

"Come on! If you can understand what I'm saying to you, I need you to help me get everyone out. Your lives all depend on it. Follow me!"

Mike backed toward the elevator. Some of the people pushed in, crowding it.

"Some of you will have to take the stairs," Mike said. "Do any of you remember where the stairs are?"

Numerous people nodded. "Use the stairs," Mike reiterated. "Go down to the ground floor and I'll meet you at the front door."

The elevator doors closed, and moved down. Mike was uncomfortable in the hot, crowded carriage. When it reached the first floor, he kept his weapon ready. When the doors reopened, to Mike's relief, no further opposition waited for them beyond. He pushed his way between the people around him and moved out, heading for the front door and the metal bridge that spanned the chemical moat.

Outside, the people watched the building. One man sat down and looked across the moat. A woman stifled a sob.

The top of the building erupted into a fiery explosion, drawing all eyes. For minutes, they watched it burn until James came back to them from across the bridge.

"That's it," James said. He walked on by, and the people watched him pass, heading for the ruined trees. He paused mid-way. "Mike?" he called.

"I'm coming." Mike walked slowly, but he could not ignore their faces.

"Look at them," Mike said to James.

"Give them time," James said, but kept his gaze fixed on the dead forest. "They need time, Mike."

Mike turned to look back. They still looked to him, lost and afraid.

One spoke with some trepidation. "What will we do?"

Mike pondered the question. No easy answer came.

"I don't know," he said at last and trailed after James into the gray ghost of a forest.

BIOGRAPHY: *Tommy B. Smith is a writer of dark fiction and the author of* Poisonous *and* Pieces of Chaos. *His work has appeared in numerous publications over the years to include* Every Day Fiction, Night to Dawn, Blood Moon Rising, *and a variety of other magazines and anthologies. His presence infests Fort Smith, Arkansas, where he resides with his wife and cats. More information can be found on his website at http://www.tommybsmith.com.*

Hush

SERGIO PEREIRA

Just push it harder. "

"I'm trying to. It's stuck."

"You're being *dof*. Hold the crowbar tighter and push it. Don't pull it, dumbass."

Clink.

A puff of dust spoiled the air with a horrible taste akin to that of a licked five cent coin. The rusty bolt popped off with aplomb and the grate that covered the old ventilation shaft loosened, uncovering the square opening in the wall. "Why didn't you just say that from the start, Heino?"

Heino rolled his eyes at his skinny companion. "Go stand over there and see if anyone is coming. I'll call the girls."

"But what about me? Who'll stand watch while I climb in?"

"Darren," Heino let out an exhausted sigh, "we've spoken about this already: Lauren, Justine and I will take a quick look around while you keep watch out here. I'll snap some pictures on my phone and we'll be out in no time."

"Why can't we bribe the security guards like everyone else? Then we can all go in."

The veins on Heino's neck bulged and his eyes blackened. "Didn't you hear what Hannes said the other day? He said the guards want a hundred bucks per person. There's no way in hell that I'm going to pay that much to go into some abandoned hospital. My tax money already pays for the guards to sit around all day and do nothing. So stop arguing and stick to the original plan."

Darren frowned. "Ag man, sometimes I feel like you just keep me around to be your own personal car guard."

Any idiot could figure out Heino's plan was to get the girls alone. Darren didn't quite get the message, though, regardless of how blatant and forceful it was.

Darren tiptoed to the edge of the building.

Despite being forced into guard alert he had the glow of someone about to be involved in something not-quite-so legal.

This was something he could tell people about. Something exciting.

Like a schoolchild crossing the road, Darren looked left, right and then left again. The darkness cloaked him, as he sought a discreet way to let Heino know the coast was clear. Eventually throwing caution to the wind, Darren shouted, "All clear, *charna.*"

Heino yanked the grate to the floor, making a loud ruckus he instantly regretted. He dusted his hands off on his camo pants and hustled for the micro flashlight from his back pocket. He tapped the flashlight's button twice, shining two beams of light into the sweet dead of the African summer night. What an evening it was, too. Neither hot nor cold, perfectly comfortable. Complementing the temperature, the nightfall hushed with only the sounds of empty crisp packets crinkling in the deserted parking lot and the echoes of police sirens in the faraway distance . . . and the murmur of a muffled giggle. Followed by a loud guffaw.

"Hey. Keep it down," Heino scolded, as much as one can with a whisper. The giggles persisted even as the footsteps quickened. "*Jirre*. You women can never keep quiet, can you?"

"What are you so worried about?" the blonde woman in the black pencil skirt said.

A second woman stepped out from behind her. She pulled back her long red hair and quipped, "It's not like we'll get arrested or anything . . . "

"*Ja*, but I don't particularly feel like paying off a guard because your mouth has no mute button, Justine."

"He's such a cheapskate, Lauren," Justine said, much to her blonde friend's obvious amusement.

Heino kept his mouth shut, and motioned to the dark opening in the wall. "Ladies first."

"Through the ventilation shaft?" Justine asked. "Are you mad? That thing hasn't been cleaned for decades. *Nee fok*, man. There could be mould and . . . spiders." She shivered as she mouthed the last word.

"S-s-spiders," Lauren repeated.

"Well, how else do you want to ge—"

"Hey *wena*! What are you doing here?"

Heino and the girls stuttered over each other. The ominous, gargled voice caught them off guard, much like when a stranger raps on your door at midnight— it might be soft and gentle, but it still startles and unsettles.

The bright light flashed in Heino's eyes. "Relax *boet*. We were just looking around," he replied, shielding his eyes with his apelike hand. "Will you stop shining the light in my face?"

The light blitzed to the wall, fixing on the ventilation shaft, and moved quickly down to the floor. "And that?" the man asked, bouncing a beam of light up and down on the dubiously positioned grate. "You do realise this is not only trespassing, but damage to property as well."

Busted.

Heino had no answer, and neither did the girls who quickly shuffled behind him. However, not a single peep from Darren. Where the hell was he?

"Get out of here." The man switched off the flashlight and turned around. "Go home."

Heino scratched his chromed head. "How much?"

The man spun on his heels. "Excuse me?"

"How much for us to look around?"

"Sir, this is private property. I'm not accepting any money from you or your friends to look around." He waved them away. "Come back in 2017. The hospital should be reopened by then."

Heino didn't expect that, looking offended that his bribe wasn't accepted. "Oh, come on. Let us have a look around and you can make a couple of extra bucks for doing nothing."

A long, uneasy silence lingered. "Do you *know* the story of this place?"

"Of course I do," Heino scoffed. "It used to be a popular hospital in this area. Then, one day, poof! Everyone just dropped their shit and left and no one knows why. Been empty since 1995. Everyone says the place is haunted.”

“1996,” the man corrected him. “And your story is wrong.”

Heino smirked and flexed his muscles. His neck bopped like a peacock’s, ready to settle a farmyard score. This guy was obviously getting a little too clever for his liking and Heino didn’t like being shown up in front of *his* girls.

“Do you know what really happened?” Lauren asked, fiddling with her blonde locks and looking like a cow chewing on a piece of grass.

“*Ja*. Do you?” Justine added with a hint of excitement and anticipation in her voice.

“I do.”

“You know, we’ll just have a look around for ourselves instead of listening to some old wives’ tales, thank you very much,” Heino interjected. He wasn’t about to let some random guy interfere with his plans to get the girls alone, considering Darren had already tried his best. “We can negotiate. How about R100 for the three of us?”

“*Nee*, Heino,” Justine protested. “We want to listen to . . . sorry, what’s your name?”

“Thabiso,” he replied.

She nodded. “We want to listen to Thabiso’s story.”

“I agree,” Lauren said. “He must know a lot more about this place than anyone else. Will you tell us the real story of this hospital, Thabiso?”

Seeing how the night had already unfolded, Heino didn’t even need to guess the answer.

Thabiso replied, “Come with me. We can sit outside and talk.” He shot Heino a stern look. “And I won’t take a cent of your money.”

Lauren rubbed her hands and smiled. "Ooh. I'm excited."

"Me, too," Justine said. "We should probably tell Darren it's safe for him to come out now."

"Who is Darren?" Thabiso asked.

"A *poephol*," Heino rudely responded. He whipped out his flashlight and shone it toward the edge of the building where his friend had been keeping watch. "Darren, you can come out now, you *mampara*."

No reply, and no sight of Darren, either.

"The bloody wimp probably ran away when he heard you," Heino said to Thabiso. "Ag, whatever. His loss."

Thabiso said nothing, choosing to step into the arch of darkness that stood between his new acquaintances and the parking lot. Keeping a close eye on him, Heino instantly trailed into the shadows, his eyes narrowed as he tried to mirror Thabiso's footsteps. The girls played a game of follow the leader with Heino, latching onto his arm and letting him lead the way through the scented path of sweet jasmine. The hospital had been abandoned for years, but the garden was certainly kept in a good condition.

Thabiso turned the corner and staggered towards the stairs at the bottom of the entrance of the massive building. The dirty, face brick structure towered high above them. The lurching white courtyard roof caught Heino's eye in particular—mostly due to the missing lettering, which resulted in the building being named SITL.

The parking lot's lamp shone a warm, orange glow upon Thabiso, like an unwitting spotlight. Extremely tiny, almost childlike, he swam in an oversized brown jacket, yet his peppered hair and rough, scarred skin told another story of a lifetime's worth of pain. He laboured to the top step and sat down. The girls squeezed up next to each other on the second step. Heino, however, remained standing like the last toy soldier at Christmas. The breeze softened, replaced by crickets chirping away in the serenity of a December evening and the unmistakable smell of nightfall.

"Do you know the story of Jan van Riebeeck?" Thabiso asked his audience.

"Of course we do. He founded South Africa," Heino boasted like a child who believed he'd be smarter if he spoke up the quickest and loudest in class.

"No. South Africa had already been founded by numerous tribes and settlers," he corrected him, not for the first time.

"*Ja*, but they were still *kakking* in the bushes and lacking any real civilisation, until Oom Jan came along."

Others might've reacted in anger to the disparaging remark, but Thabiso didn't take the bait. Thabiso continued, "In 1652, van Riebeeck landed three ships in what would eventually become Cape Town. Aboard the one ship, the *Goede Hoop*, there were a handful of stowaways."

"What does this have to do with this hospital? I don't need a history lesson about South Africa," Heino protested. "Next thing, you'll start talking about the struggle and all that other nonsense."

The alpha male parade took its toll on Justine who let out an almighty sigh. "Just shut up, Heino. If you don't want to listen, go sit in the car and wait for us."

Thabiso rubbed his rough white stubble and

resumed his story. "When the *Goede Hoop* arrived in South Africa it didn't just bring van Riebeeck's crew; it also brought something far more sinister with it. It brought the *Goedereede* group."

"Sorry? The what?" Lauren asked.

"The *Goedereede* group. A group of witches from the Netherlands."

"*Voetsek*, baba," Heino rumbled. "Don't start with your sangoma stories here." He began to strut towards the parking lot, motioning for the girls to follow him. "This guy is taking the piss now. Let's go. We might still make happy hour at Masquerades if we leave."

Justine clicked her tongue. "Heino, enough. Either shut up or bugger off." She softened her demeanour as she spoke to Thabiso, "I'm sorry for our friend's behaviour. He's from Brakpan and doesn't have any manners."

"I'm from Dalpark, not Brakpan!"

Justine pursed her lips and looked him straight in the eye. "Are you going to stop your shit and sit down?"

"Stuff this," Heino said. "You two can find another way home. Ask your new *friend*, Thabiso, for a lift."

Lauren shook her head, while Justine sighed and rubbed her temples. "I'm sorry for his rudeness . . . Will you please go on with the story?"

Thabiso's eyes stayed glued to Heino as he stomped his way through the parking lot, out of the light's sight and into the night. He cleared his throat and continued, "There are things in this world that hold no real purpose but to cause immense suffering and misery to the rest of us. They're a type of anarchy that is simple and driven only by evil. The *Goedereede* witches embodied this unrepentant wickedness. They didn't wear pointy black hats, nor did they fly around on broomsticks and brew potions. No, they existed only to cause extreme pain to others. Their only satisfaction was feeding of their bloodlust. They fed off this destruction, grew through it, revelling in the death of civilisations.

"Unlike the rest of Europe, where witchcraft was a common occurrence, there wasn't a concern in the Netherlands until 1585. The three Dimmensdr sisters and their half-sister were tried for witchcraft in Schiedam and Goedereede. Of the four, the third sister, Eeuwout, and half-sister, Joosgen Costers, were found not guilty. Despite the verdict though, when the accusation of witchcraft hangs over you a court's judgement will not protect you from mob mentality. So Dimmensdr and Costers fled into Europe, leaving behind their families . . . and the real witches in their community. But lurking in Goedereede were the real perpetrators of the heinous crimes. While innocents stood trial, these witches prowled the villages for another pound of flesh. They were shape-shifters, tricksters, evil incarnate. No one was safe. They'd steal and then eat your heart."

Lauren and Justine hung onto every word as if their lives depended on it. They were shocked but oddly curious. Lauren, in particular, wanted to know more. "But why did they eat hearts?" she asked.

"The heart is the symbol of life, and witches seek immortality. They believe that by feeding off someone else's life, they gain more of it," he explained.

Lauren unleashed an almighty, ear-drum piercing scream that could've woken the dead. Justine wrenched her body around to see if her friend was okay. "Laurentjie, what's wrong?"

"T-t-that!" Lauren nervously pointed to the ground.

Justine's eyes grew wider after she saw what Lauren pointed out. Her lips twisted into a frown and her hands shook. Scampering into the parking lot were two mice—not rats.

But not a chuckle or grin from the storyteller. While others might've had a good laugh at the girl's expense, Thabiso remained stone cold and far away in his own world.

After regaining her composure, Lauren apologised. "I'm sorry about that . . . Please continue."

So he did. "Three members of the group—Carn, Gael and Angel—decided that the Netherlands had become too small for them. With the pack breeding at a rapid rate and spreading to the rest of Europe, they decided to expand their frontiers and find a new place for their clan. They snuck their way onto Van Riebeeck's ship and sailed to the southernmost point of Africa," he said.

"Did they also cause *kak* when they arrived here?" Justine asked.

"What do you think?" Thabiso asked.

Lauren scrunched her nose. "Okay. I don't mean to be rude, but what do the witches have to do with this hospital? I mean, they landed in Cape Town, but this hospital is in Johannesburg . . . "

"Africa is full of natural abundance and beauty. The *Goedereede* arrived in a paradise. A paradise to be corrupted," Thabiso said. "Due to the lack of an established government, they went wild—slaughtering and massacring to their hearts' content. They made no secret of their existence and freely killed and savaged in human and animal form. As time progressed and the first regime was established, the government realised it needed a solution to protect its 'primary' citizens. At first, the regime offered its slaves as sacrificial lambs. In the centre of the town the people would tie up their slaves and leave them there. The witches would come and take them away in the middle of the night. Sometimes, the slaves would be found . . . in pieces. For years it was a silent understanding between the regime and the *Goedereede*. It seemed to work out well . . . Well, until slavery was abolished in the 1800s."

A crackling sound in the bushes prickled Lauren's senses. "Can we perhaps sit inside the building?" she asked, her nerves getting the best of her. "These rats are creeping me out."

"I don't think that will be a good idea."

"Just in the reception area. We don't need to go any further." Lauren flashed a smile in hope that it would sway Thabiso. However, the sizeable gap between her front teeth ensured that any smile would look far goofier than charming.

It must've swayed Thabiso, who simply nodded his head in agreement and said, "Okay."

Lauren high-fived Justine. "You see? If Heino wasn't being such an idiot, he could've gone into the building, too."

Thabiso lifted himself up and limped to the glass doors. He dug around in his jacket pocket, shuffling around a rattle of keys. Once he'd settled on a key, he placed it into the keyhole and unlocked the door. With a heave-ho, he managed to slide the door to the right just enough to let out what was inside. A wisp of dirt shrouded the air and polluted Thabiso's lungs. Hastily, he buried his mouth and nose into his jacket sleeve, coughing and gagging, yet still managing to widen the doorway.

The girls ran up the stairs, coughing and waving away the dust storm. "This place needs a real spring clean," Justine said to Lauren. They cupped their hands over their face and stepped through the doorway into the abandoned hospital's reception area—and right into 1996.

The lights from the parking lot lit up patches of the reception, most noticeably the dusty *You Magazine*, which featured *Jerry Maguire* star Tom Cruise—with his eyes scratched out—on the front cover. It lay on the floor next to a brick-shaped Motorola Startac. In the corner of the room, dead orchids sprawled out of the pots, putrid and as inviting as a rancid meal. On the reception desk stood another forgotten relic: a white Packard Bell desktop computer.

"This looks like Uncle Koos' house." Lauren giggled.

Thabiso dusted off one of the green plastic benches and made himself comfortable. The girls followed his lead, but decided to cover the seats with their jerseys before sitting down.

He took in the moment, staring at the abandoned room and its untold stories.

"Once slavery was abolished, the tensions arose between the *Goedereede* and the people of the land. With no more sacrifices, the witches went back to their old ways. The governments didn't know what to do; their people were suffering from the torture and violence—particularly in the isolated farmlands of the country. Years went by, governments came and went, but the *Goedereede* stayed. South Africa was their home and hunting ground."

Justine's eyes began to wander around the room, scanning the dust-laden wheelchairs and peeled walls. A murky-looking jar, situated on a table across the room, really piqued her curiosity.

"It was the Apartheid government that finally took action, realising it was mostly the Boers who were suffering at the time. Taking a page out of their ancestors' book, they devised a diabolical scheme: a public hospital was to be opened near an infamous township area. A hospital in no man's land. The *Goedereede* were handed the keys to this hospital and told that it was their piece of hell to do with as they please."

"But how was this possible?" Lauren asked. "I mean, during Apartheid, other countries were aware of all the wrong going on here. I don't see a hospital being run by witches as something that can be overlooked."

Thabiso looked annoyed. "Real nurses and doctors were hired to appease any inquisition, and prevent international parties from asking too many questions."

With her eyes still firmly on the suspicious object, Justine quietly lifted herself up from her seat and gravitated towards the mysterious jar.

"As a result of this very hospital, the *Goedereede* always had more than enough meat walking in through those doors. Plus, the hospital seemed legitimate in everyone else's eyes. They tortured, abused, tested . . . and cannibalised their 'patients'. It wasn't too long when the news of what was going on spread. But when the questions were asked aloud, the inquisitors disappeared quickly. While the real doctors and nurses treated patients as they would any hospital, they were well aware of what was going on. However, they decided to remain quiet, fearing for themselves and their family's safety."

Lauren's blue eyes lit up as she realised she had something valuable to contribute. "My mother once told me that she had a friend who had her baby in this hospital. On the same day when she gave birth, she saw a doctor take away another lady's baby, which apparently didn't look human at all. It looked like a jackal," she whispered. "I always thought it was a ridiculous story, because why wouldn't a doctor report something like that?"

A hellacious scream erupted in the reception area.

Justine sprinted back to her seat and wrapped her arms around Lauren. She repeatedly uttered, "Oh my God."

"What's wrong, *maatjie*?" Lauren asked, while she stroked her friend's hair.

"T-t-that j-j-jar . . . "

"What about the jar?"

"It's a tiny b-b-baby. W-w-with h-h-hooves. It has hooves instead of hands!"

Lauren's tweezed eyebrows shot up. She measured Thabiso with a concerned look.

He shrugged. "I told you they experimented. For them, it became much more than just death or sex; it was about toying with people. You should see the first floor—that is far scarier than a mutant foetus in a jar." The white of his eyes gleamed as he described it.

"I want to see," Lauren said.

"Are you mad?" Justine barked and shook her friend. "Look, I know I'm the one who likes the gory stuff, but even I'm freaked out by that bloody jar."

Thabiso stood up and began to tread further into the darkness of the building. "Are you coming?"

Lauren looked at Justine, who furiously shook her head from side-to-side, then back at Thabiso. "Yes, we are." She stood up and extended her hand to her friend. Justine dropped her head into her sweaty hands and took a deep breath. She stood up, sighed and reluctantly followed.

A slight opening between the elevator's doors invited them, but the patchy yellow tape offered a word of caution. They choose to use the stairs instead. Thabiso held onto the grubby railings and gingerly lifted himself up the staircase.

Sticking close together, the girls blindly followed.

Concentration and caution remained at optimal levels, as each foot was carefully placed on the next step, in order to avoid a humiliating tumble in the dark.

Similar to the ground floor, the dust and night's darkness wrapped around them, but the passage and shut doors suffocated the space, making it feel more like a tunnel. Thabiso pushed open the second door on the right, which creaked with a sound synonymous to a cat's mating call. The girls nervously peeked over their shoulders, into the pitch black staircase, before they rushed after him. Once in the room, the cold reflection of the silver panels showed them exactly what the room had been.

"Is this what I think it is?" Justine asked.

"What do you think it is?" Thabiso responded. He

grabbed his flashlight and shone it around the room, revealing the splatters of crimson on the operating table and hand smears down the cabinets.

The sense of disbelief choked out the already tense atmosphere.

"What happened in here?" Lauren asked.

Thabiso flicked his flashlight over a soiled plate with a gnawed bone. "Dinner."

"I think we should go and find Heino and Darren," Lauren said, glancing at Justine who nodded in agreement. "Thank you for taking the time to tell us the story, but it's getting late and this is getting a bit too freaky for us."

"But don't you want to know why the hospital was abandoned in 1996?"

"No, it's okay," Lauren said. "I'm sure as a security guard you probably have to do your patrols soon."

"I never said I was a security guard . . . "

A harrowed shade of white coloured Lauren's face. "Excuse me? But don't you work here?"

"No."

"So why are you here then?" Lauren and Justine had slowly started to backtrack in the door's direction.

"To enjoy a little piece of paradise."

The time for politeness ended.

The girls rushed to the entrance, leaving the stranger behind.

"I wouldn't run if I were you. It'll be less painful if you stay," he said.

They didn't heed Thabiso's warning.

Instead, they ran straight to where I wanted them.

My sharp nails sunk deep into their throats and suffocated the hope out of them before they could set foot out of the door. I squeezed a little bit tighter just to see them squirm, to make me quiver with glee.

I whistled and my brother heeded. Gael scurried through the parking lot, dragging the remains of Heino and Darren's bloody carcasses with him, crunching and gnawing away on loose bones like the hungry dog he was. The bastard hadn't waited for me, again.

"Your performance tonight was incredible. I really like this Thabiso alias, Carn. It kind of suits you," I said, biting my bottom lip and gazing into my prey's petrified gaze. "I'll be sure to leave some for you, too."

"I'm displeased that Gael has practically finished the ugly, bald one. The big mouths are always juicier."

Lauren mouthed "Heino".

"But can I at least finish the story first, Angel?" Carn asked with a hint of disappointment in his voice. "They always come here to find out the truth, but ultimately die before I get to the good parts."

I tightened my grip even tighter on Lauren and smiled. "Does it really matter?"

BIOGRAPHY: *Self-described as a creativist, Sergio Pereira works as an editor and writer by day and writes fiction and other nonsense at night. He is the author of* Fixation, The Smile, Tom Wilson, Don't Steal from the Devil, Tidal Wave *and other stories that you (should) love. He also enjoys writing about himself in third-person narrative and reading it back to others in Christopher Lee's voice.*

The Reaper's Fire

KENNETH W. CAIN

As a child, Dana watched her father die. He'd saved her first. Then, after assuring her he'd be okay, he ran back into the blazing cornfield to try to extinguish the fire. She'd been alone when he started screaming and she realized he wouldn't be keeping his promise.

Five years later her friend Fran became the third to die in that same cornfield. Dana remembered every detail: the way the sparse clouds drifted across the night sky, the smell of burning stalks, how the charcoal black smoke slithered up into the sky like an ominous snake, and the crackle and pop of corn beneath fiery husks. Dana had barely made it out alive.

All three fires occurred on a night children shouldn't have to worry about such crimes. Their only concern should have been stuffing their bellies with sugary delights. But, living in Rustin came with a price, and that meant one could not just ignore what went on in the cornfield. It was part of them, every last one of them.

As a high school senior, candy didn't have the same

allure it had on children. By then Dana had enough money to buy whatever treats she desired. She got good grades, was the head of the cheerleading squad, and had been voted into the homecoming court in both her junior and senior years. Being both attractive and tough, she'd been popular and would attend a prominent university soon enough. As such, she deserved a break now and then, and what better night for mischief than Halloween?

She'd come to this field each year to honor the dead. It comforted her, thinking this hallowed ground was the lone place she could connect with her deceased father. Not some silly stone, but the precise place he'd died. Maybe, given the right circumstances, her dead father might be capable of conveying some message to her.

Noticing Jesse's smile, she suspected he came for other reasons. *It's all he thinks about.*

She twisted her father's wedding ring on her thumb. Mom would be upset if she found out, but the ring relaxed Dana, enough so that she could drink the peach schnapps Jesse brought along.

She took a long hard swig, the liquor sweet and sour all at once. Wincing, she handed the bottle back. Too bad the schnapps couldn't keep her warm. Not even Jesse's jacket offered much relief. But none of that mattered because her thoughts were a mile away, thinking of her dad and how he'd given her the ring to hold before running into that fire.

A noise alerted her, pulling her out of her thoughts. She stared off through the many rows of stalks surrounding this small clearing and saw nothing. But she heard the squelch of a radio and knew what it had been.

The police patrolled the perimeter of this cornfield throughout the night. Constant patrols on foot and by car were vigilant of anything unusual. But they rarely entered the field itself, and likely couldn't see her even if they did a fly over.

"You don't *really* think they'll come back, do you?" he said after a long while. "It's been a long time."

The blond hair hanging in his face made her grin. He could be so cute.

"Who, the police?"

"No," he said. "The killer. Or *killers* for all we know."

She shrugged. "I don't know." She picked up the wooden bat he'd brought along, feeling its weight. "I hope so."

"You've come out here every year since Fran died. And the times I came along I've never seen anything the least bit suspicious. Heck, the most action we saw was that year the cops chased us."

She remembered that time.

Frustration came out in her words. "That doesn't mean they won't come."

"Well, you know what they say." He smiled, leaned over and took the bottle. "Three strikes and you're out."

She loathed his persistent baseball references. It was a dreadful game with far too little strategy for her tastes. She preferred a good game of chess or Risk or maybe even Dungeons & Dragons. A game that forced you to think, strategize beyond the occasional bunt or shifting your infield.

She dabbed at her lips with his jacket sleeve. "I hardly think another baseball reference is apropos."

His Adam's apple bounced as he swallowed. When he finished, he handed the bottle back and she drank. Already she felt woozy. She would need to slow down if she meant to keep her wits about her.

"What the hell does apt pro po mean?"

She shook her head. "Never mind. Jeez, jocks. Do you ever listen to the things you say?"

"What I'm trying to say is why would they come back with all these cops around?" He paused, his expression somber. "Besides, aren't we kinda crazy just for being out here?"

Disappointment filled her. "Why do you think that?"

"Come on, if a fire starts, we're goners."

Her eyes went to the sky as her thoughts drifted back. "I made it out okay."

When she looked back, his expression had softened.

"I'm sorry. I know Fran was your friend and all, but sometimes I think we should avoid this place like the plague. Especially on Halloween."

She stared at him long and hard, her thoughts interrupted by a chainsaw buzzing followed by the piercing screams of children. This would be in response to the Tanner's, who always put on the best amateur haunted house for as far back as she could remember. Mr. Tanner would no doubt be wearing an old hockey mask and tattered clothes, running around chasing kids with an old chainsaw that no longer had a chain. Not that the kids ever picked up on this last detail.

Somewhere to her right, a larger group of kids sauntered along the outer perimeter. She reminisced how the older kids used to dare the younger ones to venture into the fields. Some of the kids she hung out with still succumbed to that sort of pressure. It had been the reason she'd been out here the night Fran died.

She recalled the way Fran stared back at her, the fear apparent. Fran cried, unable to reel in her emotions. Dana tried to calm her with a story, but as the details intensified, so did Fran's unease. Soon after, the fire had separated them. Both she and Fran ran, but only Dana's route led to safety.

A vivid image of Fran bursting out from the fire remained etched in Dana's memory. The flames consumed a staggering Fran. The girl fell dead on the ground a few yards from where Dana stood, the smell of death still fresh in her memories.

When the police arrived, Dana hadn't been able to stop crying long enough to explain. But the police were patient, much more so than Fran's parents. Thankfully, time healed most wounds. Although Fran's death left horrible scars on all involved, they all moved on in their own ways.

It hadn't been Dana's first dare, but it was the last time she surrendered to peer pressure. It had also been the day Dana started smoking. Thinking of it, she withdrew a cigarette and her lighter. She held her hair back with one hand and used the other to light the cigarette. She sucked in deep, watching the smoke spiral out of her mouth, forming mesmerizing shapes. All the while she twisted her father's ring on her thumb.

"Whatcha thinking about?" Jesse asked.

She narrowed her view on him and took another drag. "Nothing."

"Come on." Then, as if the thought had just popped into his head, "Were you thinking about that night?"

"Of course I was, stupid."

He sat quiet for a long moment. "Sorry."

"It's okay. Don't be."

She'd always been stronger than most girls. It hadn't been hard for her to accept death. She'd seen too much of it for a girl her age. Death was an imminent consequence of life.

"What did it—"

He sucked in a deep breath and appeared to regret his words.

"For Heaven's sake, Jesse, just ask already."

"What did it feel like being trapped in that fire?"

She thought hard. "Not as bad as you would think."

"No?"

"Well, for one thing, I don't remember being afraid. I felt the heat and all, smelled the smoke, but my thoughts were elsewhere. Danger, the fire, those things never crossed my mind until afterward. Next thing I know I'm staring down at my dead friend and I can't stop thinking about what happened. I still can't shake that feeling, the numbness."

"Numb?"

She nodded. "I suppose it still hasn't set in after all these years . . . that she's gone."

"I miss her," he said solemnly.

She caught herself glaring at him. Did he miss her? Or had he said this for her sake?

Of course he said it for your benefit. Not that it matters.

But in a way, it did.

"Seriously? Did you ever even talk to her?"

Doubt obvious in his frown, he nodded. "Yes, I did."

"No, I mean *talk* to her?"

His eyes veered away, perhaps trying to create some special moment. But he said nothing. How could he? His ignorance took root in her thoughts and she might have ridiculed him if it hadn't been for the sudden manifestation of blue and red lights on the horizon.

Both of them watched, hearing a squelch from the radio as an unseen officer spoke. Then she heard the squeal of brakes. Seconds later younger voices spoke. Soon enough the lights moved on and they watched until the glow could no longer be seen.

"Thought the jig was up," he said.

"Nah, they're just harassing the kids. Making sure they don't come out here in the corn. Remember? They did the same damn thing to us."

He nodded.

"Soon," she said, "they'll all go inside. It's almost curfew, and there won't be so many cops. Doubt they'll bother us anyway." She winked. "But you never know, one of those donut eaters might get nosey."

His eyes widened. "What if . . . "

"Stop doing that."

"What if a cop did it?"

She couldn't draw her gaze away. "Come on, do you think one of Rustin's finest could do such a thing?"

"Yep," he said, raising his eyebrows. "I mean, maybe. It could've been anyone, so why not one of them? Who says it's even someone from our town?"

She examined his face as she pondered his words. He was on to something.

"Thing is," she said, "it could be you for all I know."

Nervous laughter escaped him and for a long moment he said nothing. "It isn't, you know?"

She grinned. "Isn't what? One of the cops?"

"No, I mean it isn't me," he said. "I could never do . . . *that.*"

"I know, dumbass."

She smacked him hard on the shoulder and took another swig of the schnapps. Handed the bottle over to him and took a final drag off the cigarette. She stabbed the butt into one of the few stones on the ground, blew the smoke into his face, which made him cough. That also made her laugh.

He grinned, and shifted closer to her. For now, she let him. They lay there staring into each other's eyes, their lips close, until she was sure he could stand no more. She breathed in and let him kiss her.

His hand caressed her shoulders. Down the small of her back and to her ass, where he groped and pulled. His other hand snaked under her shirt, struggling to wriggle past the underwire of her bra. When he finally managed this task he squeezed and pinched.

They kissed deeper, their tongues dancing. He smelled like peaches, shaving cream and sweat. Then she heard someone approaching.

She pushed him away, rose to one knee and tugged her shirt down.

He came up behind her, his hands still searching, willing to ignore any and all intrusions.

She shook him off, but he kept at it. She couldn't blame him. To use one of his references, she'd let him steal second base and then called the game prematurely.

"Behave yourself," she said. "Someone's coming."

"It's okay," he said, reassuring her and pawing around to her belly. His fingers moved up her shirt again. "No one ever comes in this far."

We did. But only because she'd invited him.

"They might," she said.

Entranced by her body, his voice sounded miles away. "Nah."

His hand cupped her breast and she felt like smacking him. Her eyes remained on a short span of cornstalks, everything beyond them concealed in darkness. Her eyes pried deeper into the thicket, still seeing nothing. Then she did see something.

Feet scurried from one position to another. There, the whites of two eyes peered out from the dark.

Do they see me?

She pulled away from Jesse's groping hands and shrank in behind him. Redirected his eyes to those eyes.

"There," she said, whispering.

Now he saw what she'd seen. He grabbed the bat and rose fast, charging into the stalks.

The young girl burst out into the open, eyes fixed on Jesse. It was long enough for Dana to identify their intruder.

Linda Lenore had sold Girl Scout cookies to Dana's mom for the last three years. If the girl had been wearing much more face paint, Dana might not have recognized her.

Jesse chased the girl far into the darkness, returning seconds later alone.

"We should go," he said. "She might tell the cops."

"Okay, okay. Give me a minute will you."

Dana breathed deeply, still catching herself.

Jesse kneeled beside her and sat the bat aside. He acted as though he cared, although she suspected this was a ploy to continue his pursuit of home plate at some other location.

"Do you think she saw me?" Dana said.

"Not a chance." He grinned, dimples deep in his cheeks. "She couldn't take her eyes off me."

"Yeah, right."

"Why would she look at you with me chasing her?" He wore a devilish grin. "I think she peed herself."

She wasn't so sure. Still, she grabbed the bat and rose. With her appearing playful, he let her come closer. Then, she brought the bat around hard and fast against Jesse's temple.

Shocked, he stumbled to all fours.

Fast as ever, she stood over him and struck him over the head again. She stared down at him for a split second and although she regretted it, she brought the bat down on his head again.

Finally he collapsed.

Justifying her actions, she considered his motives. *All he wanted was to cop a feel. I'm so sick of people, always pretending to understand when they clearly don't. Liars, all of them. They're all so self-absorbed.*

She retrieved the lighter from her pocket and struck it. She held the flame to a bundle of dried husks, which ignited fast, and watched the flames grow, encouraging them and lighting several locations surrounding Jesse.

When she finished, she stood a good distance away and watched it burn. Felt hot and excited, so alive.

After a while Jesse stirred and they stared at each

other through the wall of flames. Together they broke for freedom.

Jesse burst through the wall of flames toward her, still ablaze. He lifted his hands, begging for help she would not provide.

"Help me," he said. "Please."

She ignored his pleas. She'd come here for other reasons. Besides, she didn't see Jesse. She twisted the ring on her thumb.

"Daddy?" Tears streamed down her face, hot as fire. "I'm sorry. I didn't mean to—" She started again. "You said you'd come back."

She wiped her tears away. Slowly, the flames diminished. She didn't notice Jesse until they were nearly out.

Having seen the smoke, red and blue lights brightened the horizon once more. They'd be here soon, but she waited, ever hopeful. But her daddy didn't come back.

That wouldn't keep her from trying.

Conceding her failure, she fled. Exited through the same drainage ditch her father had used to save her that first time. It dumped out into the woods, obscuring her in a canopy of leafless trees.

Far away now, she glanced up at the moon and lit a cigarette. She watched the sky fill with dusky smoke, and her thoughts turned to Linda.

Kenneth W. Cain

BIOGRAPHY: *Kenneth W. Cain is the author of The* Saga Of I trilogy (These Trespasses, Grave Revelations, and Reckoning), United States of the Dead, *and two acclaimed short story collections:* These Old Tales *and* Fresh Cut Tales. *His short stories have been published, and are forthcoming, in several anthologies and publications. He lives in Chester County, Pennsylvania with his wife and two children.*

Effigy

KATE JONEZ

Tiny white lights looped off the trellis surrounding the patio of Sampang Café and reflected off the tops of the glass tables. For just an instant Gwen felt off balance, as though she were supposed to remember how to pick out a meaningful constellation from the sea of artificial stars. Someone told her once or maybe she read it somewhere that the constellations helped ancient people remember their history. That seemed unlikely. There was no meaning in the stars, not even the real ones. Why should she even try to remember that stuff? It was hard enough to remember how to navigate the city.

"Gwen," a man called out.

Gwen hurried toward his table then remembered to slow down so she wouldn't draw attention to the fact she was fifteen minutes late. He wouldn't notice unless she made a big deal of it.

Probably.

It wasn't her fault. She'd left her phone on top of a stack of boxes in her apartment. Without it, it had been a nightmare finding the Culver City restaurant. Luckily, she'd written the address on a scrap of paper. Most people would have given up, but Gwen didn't have that option.

The air was heavy with the smells of curry and fish. Without being too obvious, Gwen peeked at what people were eating. She didn't recognize anything. She hoped Indonesians didn't eat fish bladders or chicken beaks. She should have researched that ahead of time, especially since she planned to land this job as a nanny. Living with the family, she'd surely have to partake of the cuisine.

Gwen smiled as the man stood up to shake her hand. Victor Sunjaya, *Soon-jai-ya*. He wasn't old or young; good-looking or ugly. He was exactly in between. He was the same height as she was, five foot seven. She thought he'd be taller.

For a man who ran an import/export company he didn't look especially distinguished.

She should keep an open mind. Judging people by their appearance was wrong. She was going to be his nanny not his wife, so his looks didn't matter.

It was a little odd to meet for a job interview in a restaurant at night. A little odd, but not all that much. Not every Craig's List ad was posted by murderers and rapists. He was probably busy in the day importing and exporting or maybe traveling to the company's main office in Jakarta. Once she was hired, she'd be travelling around the world in no time. Nannies got to do that.

"Did you find the place without trouble?" he asked as he sat down again, gesturing for her to do the same. He didn't have an accent exactly but there was something about the way he strung words together, *without trouble*, which seemed like it took effort. His teeth were remarkably white and straight.

Gwen smiled without showing hers. She couldn't remember if she'd brushed.

At the next table, a tall, dark-haired man with a fashionable haircut hissed at his wife. As if she were being purposefully defiant, she took her time letting her eyes wander back from Mr. Sunjaya and Gwen's table. The man said something in a language Gwen couldn't place. Indonesian obviously. The woman narrowed her eyes at him and tucked a lock of her long expertly coiffed hair behind her ear.

Gwen wished she'd gotten the nice haircut she wanted rather than the ten-dollar Supercut. She felt like a scarecrow compared to the woman at the next table. Saving the money didn't matter in the long run. She still came up short. First paycheck she pledged to get her hair done properly.

"No problem at all, Mr. Sunjaya. Your directions were good, thank you." Gwen hoped he would say she should call him Victor because his last name didn't exactly roll off her tongue. He didn't, but that would come later, once he got to know her better.

His eyes darted across the patio to the archway she'd just come through. They flitted back to her then again to the archway as if he were nervous or waiting for someone. That was probably where the waiters lingered, waiting for a sign from the guests. Maybe he was looking for a waiter, although the archway looked just like an exit to the parking lot.

"Would you like something, a coffee?" Mr. Sunjaya asked. "Waiter," he barked at a waiter who did not appear through the archway but looked up from a nearby table. Mr. Sunjaya's voice was surprisingly loud for such a small man. "Coffee."

The waiter nodded. He didn't seem at all annoyed that Mr. Sunjaya interrupted him. Victor must be an important person.

Gwen wasn't especially fond of coffee, but it was too late now. She'd drink it. It wasn't that big of a deal. When she was his nanny she'd make hot chocolate for the child and always make extra for herself.

She reached into her bag and pulled out her resume and slid it across the table. The thin white paper, not cream-colored and fabric-like made her cringe. She'd spared no expense to get the very best resumes, only she'd forgotten to pick them up from the printer. Maybe it wouldn't matter. The type of resume paper an applicant used wasn't that important.

Mr. Sunjaya took the paper from her. He seemed a bit distracted like there was somewhere else he'd rather be. He glanced at it and set it down. He looked into Gwen's eyes.

For just an instant she thought she saw a hint of something . . . sympathy maybe . . . but it quickly passed.

His eyebrows were bushy with a few long stray gray hairs. He'd look ten years younger if he took care of that. Someday, when she was considered a member of the family she'd mention it.

The waiter placed a miniature cup filled with ink-black liquid in front of her.

"Thank you," Gwen said.

Without asking, the waiter placed a delicate looking glass in front of her and filled it with water from a pitcher.

"How old is your child?" Gwen asked. "Your daughter, right?"

Confusion flashed in Mr. Sunjaya's eyes for a second, but he quickly recovered. "Right, yes, my daughter." He glanced at the archway again.

The tiny lights climbed up one side and down the other. They were so much brighter than the stars in the sky, but just as meaningless. How could stars ever help anyone remember their history? There were so many. They were so random.

Gwen sipped her coffee. It tasted like someone had soaked cigarette butts in hot water. She resisted the urge to spit. That's not the kind of thing a nanny would do.

"Would you like to meet her?" Mr. Sunjaya pushed Gwen's resume away without taking a second look at it.

"I have references if you'd like their numbers."

Mr. Sunjaya waved his had to dismiss the idea. All the while his eyes darted back and forth around the patio.

Gwen's stomach lurched. According to the notice the sheriff pinned to the door of her apartment, at midnight tonight, in just a few hours, she was going to be locked out. She envied those people she ran into from time to time who could move home to Iowa or wherever when things got bad. How lucky they were to have the family home to run to when they needed to rebound from failure and nurse their humiliation. Those people acted like it was the worst that could happen. They were wrong.

"I'll bring her here." He slid back his chair and stood. "And you can meet her. You wait. Wait here until I return with my daughter and you will be her . . . *pengasuh* . . . babysitter."

"But . . . ?" Gwen said. "Can I tell you about my experience with children?"

Gwen had none, but Mr. Sunjaya didn't need to know that. She had references that said she did. Gwen was going to love being a nanny. She never got to be a kid, not the way most kids did. With that thing that happened with her mother and her father nowhere to be found. When she was a nanny she was going to play all the kid games and read all the kid books and eat all the kid food and be happy and safe and secure.

"I am giving to you the job." Mr. Sunjaya said without looking at Gwen. His eyes seemed to be focused on the tips of her fingers. "You should not try so hard."

"You are?" It felt like the sun bloomed inside her. A hundred questions flooded her head. She glanced at her resume. What piece of information had secured the position for her? What did she say? What did she do? She couldn't even guess.

"I am going now." Mr. Sunjaya leaned toward her. Even though he was small for a man, he loomed over her. The mass of his body blocked the constellations of decorative light. Gwen tensed, and a flash of fear exploded in her chest as he reached down. This was an odd reaction to a man who had just given her a job. Mr. Sunjaya didn't put his hand on Gwen's shoulder as she thought he was going to do. He grabbed a box from the chair next to her and placed it on the table. "Please take care of my package while I am going to get my daughter."

"Okay." Gwen's voice rose at the end like she was

asking a question. This was a perfectly normal request. He would bring the child back and then Gwen would be her nanny. It was perfect. It was the best possible outcome.

The box didn't take up much more room than a dinner plate. It was cardboard and looked like a shoebox except the printing on the side wasn't English and a strip of silver duct tape sealed it. Someone had stabbed a few holes in the top with a sharp object as though a small animal needed air.

Gwen poked the box. Nothing moved.

"No." Mr. Sunjaya said. There was a brittle edge to his voice. "Just watch it. Don't touch it for now."

Gwen peered at the box. She opened her mouth to ask a question, but Mr. Sunjaya cut her off.

He stepped back from the table. "I will go now."

"Okay," Gwen said.

"You will stay here with the package?"

"Yes." Gwen was surprised by a spike of annoyance. She made sure it didn't show on her face. She was going to be the best nanny ever. She would never get angry or forget to read a bedtime story.

"Do not leave the package here," he said.

"Okay." This time, even though she tried to prevent it, a little irritation crept into her tone. Did he think she was stupid? She knew how to keep an eye on a package.

He turned to the archway and walked as though he were in a hurry.

"Mr. Sunjaya?" Gwen called after him.

The people at the next table looked up. The man looked away and made a warning noise into his dinner plate. He said something that sounded a lot like *stay out of it*, but maybe he said something else entirely. The woman's eyes lingered on her a moment before she too turned back to her meal. She wore a pink cashmere cardigan just like the one Gwen had admired at Nordstrom's but hadn't had the money to buy. Maybe she'd get that sweater with her first paycheck.

"Mr. Sunjaya," Gwen said again.

He turned.

"What is her name?"

Something terrifying happened behind Mr. Sunjaya's eyes. As though a shadow had fallen over him, his expression darkened. There was another emotion surging through him that Gwen couldn't quite identify, confusion maybe or dread.

"My daughter," he said. His words marched out of his mouth meticulously as though he had to search for each one.

"I know. What is her name?" Gwen's voice was too loud. She wasn't the kind of person who yelled across rooms let alone across restaurants. Most people learned that kind of thing from their mothers. Gwen had figured it out on her own.

The woman at the next table shifted her eyes to the side, gazing at her through a curtain of hair. The rope of pearls she wore nestled against the soft nap of her cardigan. She was casually elegant as if she didn't know the value of the things she wore. Gwen wished she was more like her. She would be before long. First she'd be a nanny, then a personal assistant, then who knew?

Mr. Sunjaya held Gwen's gaze for a moment, then a moment longer. He forced the corners of his mouth into a smile that no one could pretend was genuine.

He tilted his head at her as though he'd answered her question.

"I have given you the job."

Too quickly, at almost a run, he passed through the archway and disappeared from sight.

Gwen folded her hands in front of her at the table. The moments spooled out before her. She felt weird sitting alone in the restaurant. She felt as though her head had swollen to the size of a good carving pumpkin and was wobbling precariously on her shoulders. She couldn't catch anyone, but she could feel their eyes on her.

One after another, the diners finished their meals, pushed their plates away, paid their checks and drifted through the archway into the night. Gwen felt a little less uncomfortable as the people left.

Mr. Sunjaya's box sat on the table, taking up space like her dinner companion. Gwen entertained the idea of drawing a face on it with lipstick and engaging in conversation just to pass the time, but decided against acting so childish in public. A kid would appreciate something like that. She was going to be the best nanny ever.

The silver duct tape wasn't fully stuck down on one side. Gwen worried it with her fingernail. Someone before her had opened the box and resealed it. Mr. Sunjaya would never know if she looked inside. She hesitated. It would be just her luck Mr. Sunjaya would return the moment she opened the box.

The waiter stopped at the edge of her table. He refilled her water glass. "Are you ready to order?" His hands trembled slightly as he held a pencil to a pad. He wouldn't look directly at her. Maybe it was cultural taboo. Gwen resolved to learn all about Indonesia and Indonesian ways.

"I'm going to wait for . . . " What should she call him? Her dinner companion—creepy. Her boss—too much information. "I'm going to wait."

The waiter bobbed his head and hurried away from the table, never looking at Gwen once.

Gwen glanced at the glittering lights of the archway.

Where was he? Mr. Sunjaya should be back by now.

Minutes ticked by.

Gwen found the Big Dipper in the twinkling lights on the railings. She couldn't imagine what story this might trigger. The whole business of stars as tools to aid memory seemed preposterous. More minutes passed. Gwen stared into her cold coffee then traced drips of condensation on her water glass. After many more minutes ticked by, she returned her attention to the box.

She tried to read the label. Not one of the words meant anything to her. With false confidence she poked at it, tipping it up on its side and letting it fall.

The man at the next table, the only one still occupied, made the sound of the letter "S" clipped short. "Finish now," he said to his wife, "we're going to be late. Even *you* don't eat this slowly."

"Don't rush me," the woman said. She lowered her voice and in a whisper, "she's only a girl."

Something inside the box moved around. Whatever it was wasn't packed too well. There didn't seem to be any paper or air packs for shipping. It wasn't heavy though. It didn't seem to be a rabbit or a kitten or a frog. Whatever it was didn't scurry like it was alive. Gwen pondered the air holes. Maybe it was cheese or something that needed to breathe.

Where was Mr. Sunjaya? It felt like it had been an hour already. Gwen glanced at her phone. Only forty-five minutes. Still that was a long time.

The waiter cleared the plates from the couple next to her. It was the only table on the patio still occupied. The beautiful woman in the pink cashmere sweater murmured to her husband. Gwen couldn't understand, but when she was a nanny she would learn. Gwen listened, picking out a familiar sounding word from time to time but not enough to understand what they were talking about.

The couple rose and walked toward the archway as Mr. Sunjaya had done.

A shiver worked its way through Gwen. The evening was much colder all of a sudden. All the people were gone and the heaters had been turned off. What else could it be?

The woman hung back a little as if she didn't want to leave yet.

Gwen realized she'd been staring when the woman glanced over her shoulder. She held Gwen's gaze like she was trying to tell her something. It made Gwen so uncomfortable that she had to look away.

When she looked up again, the woman and her husband were passing through the archway. The crunch of their shoes on the gravel grew softer and softer.

Gwen counted the lights as first one then another of the constellations flickered out. Maybe their batteries were dying. She glanced up at the actual sky with the actual stars but could only see dim faraway flickers. Where was Mr. Sunjaya?

Even though her footsteps were far away, Gwen heard the woman exclaim. A moment later the soft pink of her cardigan and the sheen of her pearls appeared in the archway. The woman rushed across the patio back to her table and grabbed her Prada bag. There was no relief on her face. It was like she'd known exactly where it was all along. As if she'd left it there on purpose. Who would leave a bag like that unattended?

The woman dropped down beside the chair she'd vacated only moments ago and said in a hushed tone, "You must keep it safe and feed it."

Gwen jumped at the sound of her voice. The woman looked out of place squatting between the tables. Someone dressed in such lovely clothes wouldn't hunch down and whisper to a stranger. It made her words carry more weight.

Gwen studied the woman's intense brown eyes. "Me?"

"Yes, you must keep it safe and feed it." She jabbed at the box with a perfect almond shaped nail. "Or it will turn against you."

An angry crunch, crunch, crunch of leather shoes in the parking lot let Gwen know that the woman's husband wasn't far away.

Gwen reached out for the box and slid it closer to her.

"You feed it, okay." The woman placed her hand on Gwen's leg. "Keep it safe." Her pinky finger was gnarled and mottled and missing from the second joint. She rose slowly. The expression on her face was somewhere between pity and revulsion, an expression that seemed more appropriate from someone who had just seen a horrible accident.

"It belongs to Mr. Sunjaya. He'll be back in a minute."

The woman's eyes reflected the last of the stars still flickering out along the railing. Her eyes glittered as if she might cry.

"He is never returning."

Gwen knew this. She did. She knew it several times over, but she'd pushed the evidence out of her mind. Filled up her head with dreams of her wonderful new job instead.

"How am I supposed to . . . what is it?" Gwen grabbed the edge of the silver tape and yanked it off.

"No. Feed the jenglot before you look." The woman grabbed Gwen's hand. She held it in both of her own. A faint scent of perfume Gwen had only sampled at cosmetics counters wafted from the woman. She wrapped Gwen's fingers around her water glass and squeezed. The hideous decapitated finger pressed against her.

Gwen tried to pull away but the woman was stronger than her fuzzy pink sweater would indicate.

"You can be okay. You may survive if you do what I say."

"Wani, come away from her." The man materialized in the archway. "Stop."

The woman didn't flinch at the sound of his voice. She gripped Gwen's hand tighter, squeezed harder.

"Let go," Gwen cried as she scooted her chair back, swung her head around searching for the waiter. The windows were dark and the door closed. Everyone else was gone. "Let go of me."

The woman squeezed tighter.

The man reached out and grabbed her arm.

The glass snapped in Gwen's hand. Water splashed over her arm. Shards of glass tinkled as they hit the floor. A stream of red welled from the gash in her finger and blossomed over her skin.

The woman pulled Gwen until her hand was over the box. Blood dripped on to the cardboard. The woman jerked Gwen so the drips fell through an air hole. "Feed it every day, every day, every day. Never miss a day." She squeezed Gwen's finger tight. Blood drops fell faster and faster. The jenglot will help you get whatever you want, but you must never forget."

Tears streamed down Gwen's face. "That hurts."

Nothing moved in the box. Nothing scurried or scattered or erupted in a puff of smoke. Nothing happened at all.

"I know," the woman said. "It will always hurt."

"Let's go now, Wani. There's nothing more you can do." The man put his arm around the woman's shoulders and guided her away. He never once looked at Gwen.

"I could call the police, you know." Gwen applied pressure to her finger to stop the bleeding "You assaulted me," she called after the woman. She knew she would never do this. Even though the accident was not an accident, in her heart she knew the woman was trying to help her. How and why, Gwen couldn't be sure.

The woman glanced back. "Never forget to feed it."

As their feet crunched across the gravel, Gwen heard a sob and maybe she heard, *a careless girl like her is doomed.* Or maybe she didn't because how would she know.

All of the constellations twisted around the rail had gone out. A grim darkness that only dwelled in the unlit corners of cities flooded the patio and spilled out into the night.

Gwen checked her watch. The hour had passed when the sheriff had locked up her apartment. She lived in the darkness now. She gripped the tape and ripped it off the box.

Big glassy eyes, almost human, stared up at her from a face made from something like desiccated leather, or like a mummy Gwen had seen in a museum once, with ropey muscles and bone-thin arms and legs, as stringy as forgotten turkey wings from the back of the fridge a month past Thanksgiving. Its black hair, human hair, fell over its eyes in a tangled mop.

Gwen reached into the box and picked up the figurine. It was warm to the touch like a living thing.

"If you want to reach for the stars," the jenglot said in a dusty old voice, "I will help you reach them."

Gwen nearly dropped the doll. She hadn't seen its mouth move but maybe it had. Maybe it had moved just the tiniest bit. Nothing seemed impossible.

"What do you want from me?"

"To be safe and well-fed.

"Me too. That's exactly what I want." Gwen's heart fluttered in excitement. She'd found a kindred spirit. "We're going to be wonderful friends."

"You'll forget about me before long."

"I won't forget. Not ever," Gwen said.

"Oh yes you will." The jenglot cackled its dry, dusty old woman laugh. "Yes indeed you will."

Kate Jonez

BIOGRAPHY: *Kate Jonez is the author of the Shirley Jackson Award nominated novella* Ceremony of Flies *and the Stoker Award® nominated novel* Candy House. *Her stories can be found in many anthologies and magazines.*

She is also chief editor at Omnium Gatherum, a small press dedicated to publishing unique dark fantasy, weird fiction and horror. Several Omnium Gatherum titles have been nominated for awards.

Scents of Fear

STEVE JENNER

The first time I ever met Veronica Brooks she saved my life and I really kind of liked her for that.

At least that was what I thought at the time. No tender administering of the kiss of life to my cold blue lips or frantic pounding of my unmoving chest to galvanise a stuttering heart. No, nothing quite so ordinary.

It was simply a piece of immaculate timing that left her supine on the floor with a bullet hole in her temple and me crouching safely behind a marble statue with the woman's handbag in my lap.

Not theft, I hasten to add. Just a coincidence of chance trajectory.

I wondered, as I patiently sifted through her belongings, what quirk of fate had brought her so close to me when the shot was fired. Unfortunately, her possessions provided very few clues other than her name. Veronica Brooks.

I peered around the stone plinth but could find no danger to face. No foot soldiers rushed in to clean up the shooter's mess; no plan B, it would seem. This suited me. Arrogance and an edgy trigger finger would certainly get somebody killed but it wouldn't be me, not today anyway. Then I thought of the dead girl lying on the cold floor only a few feet away and realised that being right was not always a comfort. Alright. Enough of that. Time to leave.

Distant sirens convinced me the sniper would soon be in retreat and that the encroaching museum crowd, ashen-faced and wide-eyed at the tragedy, would provide me with adequate cover to make my escape too. As I edged towards the forming circle, shaking my head in false outrage as I went, I scoured the four corners of the exhibition hall for my doubtless frustrated assassin. Meanwhile, Veronica Brooks lay silent amongst the stone figures, her body heat ebbing to match their cool detachment. Anger began to pinch at me as I searched.

I spied no protruding rifle barrel through the balcony struts and no fleeing figure draped in weapon-concealing attire. What I did see was the pale face and green eyes of a young woman, motionless and serene, unconcerned about the hole in her head. Something about her lost expression reached me. Touched me even. I am no stranger to violent death. In fact we're old friends.

Time to get reacquainted, I thought, and headed out after her killer.

Men in uniform hurtled past as I walked away from the scene of the crime. Museum curators dived in every direction, desperately holding on to unsteady exhibits as armed police burst into their midst to point their weapons in accusatory thrusts.

Professionals were always in such a hurry.

I slipped through glass doors and out into the cool morning air. Was that what had happened, I wondered, with the one earlier? The one who had taken his shot too early and murdered Veronica Brooks? I would have to find him and ask, before I reached down his throat to tear out his heart.

Out on the street, the city odours were stale and noxious but not enough to hide his reek. I almost shouted when I filtered out the first trace of him, such was my eagerness. The ensuing laughter was silent. My attacker might be in the wind but that wasn't going to save him from me. I puffed out my cheeks and sighed.

So, not a peaceful day out to the museum then. Instead a manhunt.

I could live with that.

For more than a minute I stood by the busy road with my head back and my eyes to the sky. I watched the white jet trails cut across the pale blue as the urban roar swelled towards a mid-morning crescendo. The taste in my mouth was metallic and bitter. It was a sensory cyclone into which I was about to plunge.

Ah well, no peace for the wicked.

Inhaling in shallow sniffs, I fine tuned my olfactory compass and dived in.

Through the organic stink I searched until I located a singular human scent. The same one I had caught so briefly inside the museum before the thick stench of death had smothered it. I breathed in again. My sense of smell was so very acute I could easily detect one individual strain in a thousand. This one was so ripe it stood out like a freshly-buried corpse in a graveyard.

I stared into the distance.

Not so far behind after all, I realised.

Ignoring the rage that boiled within, I allowed a little calm to creep in, to soak through my muscles, enough to stop them thrusting me forward too recklessly.

Overeager, I knew, meant over too soon. Couldn't have that.

He was running scared now, that much was certain. But not fast enough. No, not nearly fast enough.

I bit my tongue and spat blood on to the ground. This was too easy. Too fleeting. Though I could not see him, his spore filled the air like the jet trails above. It carried the death scent of Veronica Brooks in its flow, yet was so tangible I felt I could simply grab it and haul him in. My jaw hardened. It was time to stop daydreaming and get serious. Time to get moving. Time to hunt.

Fury and elation competed for control of my nervous system. I had experienced the sensations before but this time the thrill coursed up and down me as if I were a storm-struck lightning rod. Hot breath hissed between my teeth as I grinned. Ah, it was good to be alive when the blood sang. My twitching fingers clenched tightly. I was ready. Ravenous. Damn, it's hard not to scream with anticipation at times like this.

In a dozen agile steps, I had zigzagged through the grinding traffic to reach the far side of the street where a set of wrought iron gates were open and inviting. Grassland lay beyond, exuding a hundred hazy perfumes of summer bloom. It was a great relief to leave behind the sour carbon of endless exhausts but if he thought this heady blend of aromatic flora would confuse me then he was gravely mistaken. I knew his signature now. I was closing in.

With my emotions just about in check, I looked around. A black path stretched away in a mild curve that reached a line of trees and then disappeared over a green crest. In between, groups of women lovingly tended to gurgling children on the grass while men in pin stripes sat on nearby benches enjoying a break from the office. All blissfully ignorant. All exuding the most innocuous aromas. People ambled past, unaware that the air around them had been tainted by the acrid scent of a fleeing killer. I envied them their ignorance, but only for a moment.

The smell of his fear hung like a beige miasmic trail through the musky garden ahead. It would grow more rank as he sensed my breath upon his shoulder. I flexed my limbs in preparation for the chase, and a jolt of exhilaration electrified me again.

Coming ready or not, I growled.

Veronica Brooks and her soft green eyes sprang into my head. She smiled wickedly, urging me on into merciless pursuit.

I kind of liked her for that too.

Along the tarmac path I moved with deceptive speed. Passers-by glimpsed me in motion only as blur at the edges of their perception and even then, just as an ordinary man in a hurry. Dogs barked occasionally at my heels but for the most part, the world let me pass without objection or opposition. I surged ahead. The distance between myself and my quarry eroded so rapidly that the rancid trace of his terror increased a hundred fold. He was venting fear and the emissions excited me. Blood pulsed through my veins like a sharp drug. I thundered on.

When I reached the end of the path, the park narrowed to a thin strip of trees then to a single track which was barred by another set of heavy gates. This time they were closed and locked. I wondered if my prey had accomplished this himself or enlisted help. If it were the latter then the hunt grew more intense. And, of course, more appealing. He may well have access to a vehicle now and perhaps more weapons trained on me as I deliberated. A potentially perilous predicament indeed. Stimulating, nevertheless.

I sniffed the air but sensed only a slight increase in tension. Just the tart smell of agitated bowels and maybe the salty tang of tears rippled through the breeze. As I tuned into his decay, I heard his heart begin to labour. I cackled with satisfaction at the distraught thump. It must have come as quite a shock to turn around and find me so close. Still, he better not have a heart attack yet. We still had unfinished business.

An image of Veronica Brooks nodding her approval cheered me so I scaled the metal barrier in careless leaps to continue the chase.

Only when I landed neatly on the other side of the gate did the real danger become apparent. I felt the bullet graze my sleeve a fraction of a second before throwing myself to the ground and rolling behind a tree. Another projectile gouged a strip of bark from the trunk inches from my head. A third ploughed up dirt just to my right. The smell of cordite choked me. I considered retreat, but only for a second.

Veronica Brooks would not hear of it and I agreed.

Beyond the roar of gunfire, I heard the sniper's pulse throbbing again. This time it was loud and fast.

For a few seconds, the odour from up ahead changed to a sweet flowing stream of jubilation that gradually waned as he realised his failure. I wanted to call out to him that not only had he missed his target again, but had now ensured a lingering death. He had fired at me four times and I would take a finger for each shot.

If he fired a dozen or more times, I sniggered, then I would just have to use my imagination.

The sound of a vehicle engine coughing into life made my heart sink. He would be difficult though not impossible to catch if he put too much ground between us. I could not risk the possibility that the growling motor was no more than a ruse to lure me out so I shuffled cautiously forward into the deep shadow of a tree to await an opportunity. A grumble of frustration built inside me. I wanted to feel his flesh rip in my hands so badly.

The engine revved angrily a few times as if in challenge and then finally, I heard the gears engage. The crackle of tyres skidding on gravel indicated the car's hasty departure. I leaped to my feet and skulked silently forward, but only the unmistakable hint of mocking triumph still hung in the air.

Veronica Brooks tutted her disapproval and I didn't like her for that much.

I watched the clouds of dust rise in the vehicle's wake as it sped away and considered my best course of action. To pursue on foot would be wearisome and tedious. Not to mention infuriating. Nevertheless, as no other form of transport immediately presented itself, it would be necessary to give chase at running pace. I mentally chalked up another entry in my assailant's growing list of crimes and wondered which body part I would claim for this inconvenience.

I started out at a loping sort of jog, which ate up the ground but was no match for my quarry's tireless combustion. Dust clogged my pores as the scorching sun raked me but it was internal heat that finally made me sweat. The desire to reap havoc was an inferno inside me. I felt empty but for the bile that rose and fell, searing my chest like a burning stake. My stomach rumbled mournfully.

They say that people thirst for revenge but it always made me hungry.

I inhaled deeply of the air as I ran. It was bitter and tasted of corruption but always, in amongst the vapours, was that tell-tale strand of a man's growing dread. It pulled me along; almost like the reeling-in of a tiring fish that thrashed wildly, uselessly, in its diminishing and futile attempts to flee. For all of his bullets and bravado, this killer's nightmare was well upon him. I stifled my bloodlust and conserved my breath for the hunt.

Finding the car abandoned after only five miles was an agreeable surprise. A quick look inside told me two things. My assassin may be adequately skilled with a firearm but was certainly no mechanic. Some part of the vehicle's innards had expired from excessive use, causing it to overheat and stop; a problem to which he could apparently find no solution other than flight.

You'd better run, I thought grimly. Run until your lungs burst because you will have no use for them later.

I also detected a second scent now; one which coiled with that of the creature I trailed, like intertwining serpents. It almost beckoned as it twisted on the breeze, slowly but surely leading me back into the city.

So, there were two of them now, I thought and salivated.

Two hearts erratically beating the drums of retreat. I got the message.

Sorry boys, but surrender was no longer an option. There wasn't a white flag big enough to clean up the mess I was going to make.

The air thickened around me again and this time I heard their misery. Two spineless laments, discordant and so full of whining remorse it sickened me to listen. Their combined scent, however, was quite familiar. Not because I knew them but because twin terror is a pungent cocktail that emits a powerful appeal. The drifting vapours nourished me. They helped satisfy my appetites. I licked my lips. Ground my teeth. Then smiled and moved in.

There was no longer any need for haste. I tempered my murderous instincts with caution as I had no wish to fall victim to yet another ambush. The blood still pounded in my veins and my tongue grew dry but I steadied myself with the thought that somewhere up ahead, two men were sick with mounting fear. The concentration of their odours told me so.

If Veronica Brooks were here to experience such spirited anticipation, would she thrill to it as eagerly as I?

A not-so-mild flash of green eyes just behind my own left me in no doubt.

Steve Jenner

Through a maze of side streets, I kept up the relentless chase. The miles I had lost pursuing the car were no longer of consequence as my stealthy yet swift advance had cut down the deficit in minutes. At the corner of the next narrow junction, I sank into a crouch before whipping my head around the brickwork for a careful reconnoitre, then quickly pulled back again to avoid any gunfire.

No lethal projectiles came my way but the exciting sight of two men running together, only a hundred or so yards ahead down the road, almost overbalanced me. It is easy to become rash on such occasions so I regulated my breathing to just vigorous. Cars flashed past in the afternoon sunshine but I hardly saw them. I hardly saw anything bar the two of them, panting with fatigue but too afraid to stop.

I gave them my silent promise.

You will rest soon.

As I gathered my energies for the final push, a thought occurred to me. Certainly, this man had lay in wait for me at the museum, presumably expecting a simple kill, but if he was so confident, so cool, why were he and his accomplice so petrified now? Did my reputation really precede me so savagely? If so, how could they have been so sure before and so pitiful now?

Veronica Brooks, whose voice I had never heard in my life, mocked my uncertainty with graceless derision.

Then a notion struck me. Perhaps a man who lived by the gun, who killed so impassively from a distance, secure with his faithful weapon, suffered much more when that trusted tool was rendered obsolete. I wondered idly what use a man with no fingers might find for a rifle anyway. But then, of course, the time he would have to ponder such concepts would be so short that the question became moot.

A peal of laughter in my head told me that Veronica Brooks was back on side and the time for speculation was now over.

From my vantage point I watched them cross the street and enter a building I didn't recognise. Still, my knowledge of the city was hardly comprehensive and this part of town had held little attraction for me in the past. I waited until there was a lull in the traffic then sprinted forward to halt a few doors down from where I had last seen them. Flat to the wall I edged along until I was at the imposing wooden portal through which they had disappeared. A glance at the brass lettering on the wall outside did not fill me with confidence either.

I was also irritated to discover that the intensity of the men's scent had diluted to a less profound horror. As if the edifice in which they were hiding was somehow a filter for their fear or even a refuge for killers of innocent women. I read the sign again. It was an urban church of secular design and home to no denomination of which I had ever heard. The notion revolted me. If they planned to claim sanctuary here they would find that no pagan litany would prove a deterrent to my brand of inquisition.

It took only a few seconds to find the rear entrance and just a few more to deem it impenetrable. A church with bars on the windows and a deadbolt on the door surely had something to hide. I intended to find out what it was. My focus had not changed. Blood would still be spilt in generous crimson splashes, but my senses were now alert to new possibilities. Perhaps someone here could explain the attempt on my life and the subsequent destruction of Veronica Brooks. It was unlikely that the perpetrator would have the time or a tongue to do it.

My curiosity was piqued, as was my anger. The murderer and his accomplice taunted me with their smug conviction that one such as me might recognise their asylum.

My laughter rumbled like the growl of a hungry tiger.

It was a simple matter to scale the side of the building using the single drainpipe which ran from top to bottom.

I peered in through two more windows on the way up but heavy drapes prevented me from seeing anything other than more iron bars.

When I reached the flat rooftop, I was surprised to discover that the fortifications did not extend to the skylight. I peered down into semi-darkness.

Could it be a trap? Let's hope so. My limbs were tight from running and could do with a stretch.

I paused for a moment to sniff the air but sensed only confusion without intent. No signs of life were apparent in the room below so I effortlessly detached the glass from its frame and let myself drop noiselessly inside.

The column of pale sunlight from above failed to penetrate the furthest corners. It took less than a moment for me to adapt. My night vision, though not the equal of my spectacular sense of smell, coped easily enough with the musty gloom. The several rolls and shimmies I had performed upon landing proved unnecessary as all was still and quiet. All that was new here was my probing shadow.

Breathless and tingling, I straightened up in anticipation of a challenge but nothing presented itself. Disappointing, but I could wait.

Amongst the dusty aromas of antiquated furniture and fusty carpets, I detected an unpleasant undercurrent seeping up from below. As sinister as it was familiar. People had died in this building. Lots of them. A disturbing thought perhaps, yet encouraging nonetheless. If this was some sort of private abattoir then surely a few more cadavers wouldn't hurt. Still, the cloud of death particles here was vile and ultimately I would be glad to conclude my investigations and leave.

The door clicked open to my touch but there was no one in the passage beyond to witness the trespass. There was however, adequate lighting thoughtfully provided for the next stage of my hunt.

Despite the convenience of my unobserved access, impatience was gnawing at me. There was a dryness in my throat which I attributed to the foul atmosphere and suppressed impetuosity.

Keep steady, I told myself.

It had been a long journey from the museum and it would be madness to allow my passion for dismemberment to betray me now.

I refined my olfactory keenness to pierce the dense presence of ruinous death everywhere, in order to locate my own pair of killers who were taking shelter somewhere below. They would not be difficult to find despite the killing echoes that still bounced around the building. Their scents in this charnel house were like a sour breath on a wind of decay.

Steve Jenner

Veronica Brooks wrinkled her nose and I knew just how she felt.

A movement down the hall caught my eye. The ugly snub nose of a revolver poked around the corner but I did not wait to identify its owner. In three strides I was upon him, tearing the weapon from his fist along with three fingers. He opened his mouth to cry out but the sound never arrived, issuing instead from the foaming gap in his throat which I had provided for him. I let the twitching body slump to the floor. He was not the one I sought.

More men were coming.

As I slunk away to choose my ground, the rush coursed through me in a cascade of adrenaline.

I sniggered. The first kill of the day always juiced me.

Two men in dark suits ran up the stairs to block my passage. They stopped. Took aim. Weapons were discharged. They missed. I didn't. Scarlet ribbons draped the walls. Onwards. The metallic smell of blood was making my head spin. I charged on regardless. Down the stairs, two at a time. More men. More blood. No time even to take a breath. I burst through a set of double doors where I knew the killers waited. My bloodstream was a raging torrent of red aggression.

The assassin cried out in alarm as I swept messily through the line of men assigned to protect him. The red spray did not hide him. No projectile viscera delayed me. Nothing could keep me from his throat. In behind, the accomplice had sunk to his knees in supplication, mumbling appeals to an indifferent god whose name was unfamiliar to me. I did not need keen senses to know he had soiled himself.

After all that chasing and climbing, I should have just laid waste to the place and everyone in it. Instead I took the assassin's rifle and used it to bar the doors, frustrating the deadly attempts of further intruders. Then I delivered a ferocious blow to the grovelling assistant to quieten his snivelling. In the end, as it was always going to be, the murderer of Veronica Brooks and I stood a few feet apart; he with his deadly weapon out of reach, me with mine at my fingertips. I recalled my earlier desire to remove some of his integral parts and, unusually for me, curbed my enthusiasm. It would not last long.

"Why did you take a shot at me?" I asked, not unreasonably.

"You really don't know, do you? What actually happened here. Perhaps it's true then. You are overrated," was his rather rude reply.

"You killed an innocent woman. Why?" I continued calmly.

"Innocent? You wish," drawled the assassin, who had recovered some of his poise even though his odour was still steeped in vinegar.

I considered this remark for a moment but quickly decided that analysis would take far too long and so crushed four of his fingers instead. I enjoyed his shocked expression as he held up his ruined hand in front of him and screamed. I waved my own index finger from side to side. Stop whining, it said. They were mine to take. I had promised myself his tongue too but that would seem counterproductive under the circumstances.

When he had stopped shrieking, I asked the question again. It was not the first time that someone had indicated their aversion to me by hiring a killer to do their dirty work but it was the only time that an innocent had died in my place. The concept of others dying instead of me was not so very terrible, of course, but the sight of that sad, green-eyed girl with the hole in her head lying twisted on the marble floor had moved me in unexpected ways.

From a place deep in my mind, Veronica Brooks agreed with my methods, I was sure.

"You have six fingers left. Tell me!"

"Screw you!"

Crack!

"Five! Now tell me!"

I had thought that I was the fastest guy in town, certainly in the room, but a man with only five working digits, dripping and seeping as they were, can still be pretty quick on his feet apparently. Even with me all over him. When my unsuccessful assassin suddenly burst into life and ran towards me with his bleeding hands flapping in my face, I admit that it took me by surprise. I even staggered backwards over a chair as a result. It only thwarted me for a few seconds but it was enough.

An unsuspected doorway in the wall was hanging open when I finally turned around and the fragrance of pure panic permeated from the corridor beyond.

A secret passage! Ha! My day was complete.

Into the darkness I drove.

My eyes acclimatised instantly but I didn't need to see where I was going to follow this man. The ripe aroma, or should I say bouquet, of sour perspiration and secreted urine was a pure trail for a connoisseur like me.

Twenty steps ahead. Full speed. Then a sharp skidding left. Five more strides. Slowing down, but not much. Down some stairs in a single leap. Thinner air brushed me here, still riddled with its acidic stain, but cool now, as if from somewhere dark. I inhaled and followed the draught. Through another door. How did he open it with boneless fingers? Straight on again. Fast. Only my footsteps rattled the woodwork. A pungent shadow, just up ahead. I pounced.

It really was a day full of surprises. The room into which I had crashed was empty and cold. Well, not quite empty. The assassin I had been pursing all day long lay stretched out on the floor with a golden dagger protruding from his chest. Life vacated his body as I watched, his scent curdling in wretched clouds above him. They dissipated as he breathed his last. Only the red stain around the blade moved as it spread.

The sight was unexpected but I had no time to enjoy it. Spinning around, I scanned every surface for another false panel but no exit was immediately evident. When the door slammed shut behind me and an electronic lock engaged, I silently lamented my impatience.

Always rushing in where angels fear to tread.

Shaking my head in increasing frustration, I cursed my misfortune. Mostly at missing out on the kill.

Alright. Time to go to work. The killer's body provided no clues except one. I was sure he could not have stabbed himself considering his ebbing strength and mangled hands. Certainly no one had passed me in the passage. So, somewhere in this apparently featureless room was another sneaky portal which had only recently been used. I took a deep breath but no singular aroma reached me other than that of recent death which was now coating the chamber with its cloying film of misery. Growling my dislike of confinement, I struck the door viciously a few times and immediately felt better.

It took a few minutes to test the stones for anomalous echoes. I started off with a series of innocuous taps, hoping to locate the escape route quickly, but soon I was thumping the walls soundly with my fists as my anxiety increased. Despite my earlier eagerness to catch up with my prey, enforced incarceration with his draining corpse had not been part of the plan. Eventually, more by luck than judgement, a cunningly concealed crevice revealed itself to my unsubtle probing and I was away once again.

Away indeed, but to where?

Veronica Brooks had been avenged albeit not by me. The scents ahead of me were not overtly threatening and after witnessing the abject surrender of the accomplice, his fate could be left up to others too. Only one question remained: Who was behind the attack? Why send an assassin to do the job? What was going on in this church? Three questions then. And I didn't have an answer to any of them. I pressed on resolutely until I reached daylight.

It was a relief and a frustration to be outside again. True, I was away from the oppressive constriction of decay and free also from the prison that had held me for several unendurable minutes. But the whole affair had largely taken place around me with my own involvement being less than impressive. That was quite clearly unacceptable so there was only one thing for it. I was going back in and to Hell with the tradesman's entrance.

In the end, no wood required splintering, no locks needed to be sprung. A disappointment in many ways. I pushed at the front door and it swung inwards, silently inviting. Should have thought of this before. Lights flickered on as I moved along a narrow passage. Unsuspected technology at work behind ancient walls. Not a good sign. When the floor creaked with encouraging age, I recovered my composure and slid secretly on. Considering the day I was having, I shouldn't have been shocked by what was waiting in the next room.

The first thing that caught my eye was me. Lots of me, actually. Portraits, numerous statues, likenesses in gold and bronze on elaborate plinths. All unquestionably important pieces. Each one a stylised representation of me from my valiant youth right up to the mature version. I stood still and allowed my ego to be massaged while the rest of me searched for evidence of purpose.

The ancient and bloodstained altar in the middle of the room held all manner of troubling possibilities. It squatted toad-like, emitting an aura of bleak desperation that throbbed around it like a macabre magnetic field. I looked away and frowned at a particularly unflattering portrait of myself scowling like a trapped wolf and thought that it could quite easily have been rendered in the last few minutes.

"You are displeased with something?" a voice enquired from behind me.

I spun around to see that a man and a woman had entered the chamber. I was less than impressed to find the whimpering accomplice had recovered his backbone but startled at the scent of his ravishing new companion.

Flaming red hair. Wild emerald eyes. Scant room for a score of curves in a figure-hugging dress.

She had my undisputed attention already and had only spoken five words. Now what was it she had said? Displeased? Well, yes, you could say that. Still, first things first.

"The assassin is dead!" I snarled at the cringing man who was edging slowly in behind his more palatable ally.

"As he should be," the woman replied calmly.

I stopped still. Now I know that I hadn't really been on top of things all day and perhaps the fragrance of this exotic creature had soaked too deeply into my skin but I thought all along that I was the victim here.

Veronica Brooks sniffed her disdain but I didn't care.

This dazzling female was belittling my efforts. Standing in a room full of images with my face may do wonders for the self-esteem but my mind was spinning as questions outnumbered answers. Time to stand my ground.

"What is this place?" I asked, sweeping my hand around the room full of tributes.

Her eyes sparkled mischievously. "I'm surprised at you. Surely you recognise a shrine when you see one. You have a very loyal following, you know."

No, I did not know. This was certainly news to me as everyone I had encountered so far had either tried to shoot me, lay their hands upon me or lock me up. In my confusion, I resorted to levity.

"You mean I have a fan club?"

"A bit more than that. These people worship you. To them, you are a vengeful god."

Them, not us? Interesting.

The sallow accomplice was nodding and bowing in such an irritatingly obsequious manner that I considered buffeting him again to relieve my tension. In contrast, the woman seemed to have set herself apart from the fawning creature and was watching me intently. Not in reverent adoration, it had to be said, but more like a predator. I was acquainted with the expression. It was my own. Could it be that in this house of death and devotion, a serpent lurked? Let's hope so. Things had gotten dull in the last few minutes.

"Why did you kill the assassin?" I asked her.

"Revenge." Her tone was corrosive.

"Not for me." I knew this instinctively.

"No. Not this one either."

She could shift like greased lightning, I'll give her that. In a blinding series of moves, she cut to the side, took up the accomplice from his knees to his tiptoes and shook him viciously like a lioness with her kill. I listened to his neck break first. Then she flung him aside so violently that I heard the rest of his bones splinter. It occurred to me somewhat belatedly that I could no longer distinguish her scent from the rising stench of death in the room.

"You seem to be disposing of all if my tormentors," I said.

"Actually, not all," she replied, and then began to pace.

I followed her with my eyes as she paraded in lithe steps before me. I could usually learn all I needed to know from pheromones, but this one was a mystery. Any personal aroma that she might have exuded was now distorted within the cloud of hostility that flowed about her. I wondered if she could detect the doubt washing over me right now. She began speaking again which gave me hope. The talkers always got distracted.

"These people idolise you but you terrify them too. The assassin shot at you because you pursued him. He panicked. His fear overwhelmed him. The others here also reacted to your intrusion with violence. It is their way. But the assassin was not after you in the museum, though he did kill my sister who was. You did not sense her threat because the fool pointing the gun caught your attention. Three more steps and she would have torn out your throat."

So, I groaned inwardly, Veronica Brooks was a would-be killer. My would-be killer. I knew there was something about her I didn't like. I suppose the knife that I had found in her handbag should have been a bit of a clue but what with the sniper's scent and all, I really hadn't been thinking straight. Anyway, I like to think that I see the best in people. Veronica Brooks' sister was clearly a capable sort and apparently had not yet completed her explanation.

"This is a vile place," she spat. "Many of our kind have died here to satisfy the crude desires of these pathetic creatures and their evil reverence. This cannot go on. It is time that their object of adulation was finally expunged from this world."

Expunged? That didn't sound good. And what did she mean "our kind"? Was she including me in that? Surely she didn't think that we were related. Several courses of action sprang to mind but I decided on the path of least resistance. Ask her. I stood up straight, put on my most misunderstood expression and attempted to appeal to her better nature. I was sure she had one somewhere. Her basilisk smile was not encouraging.

"Help me out here," I pleaded. "Who are you?"

"You don't know us but we know you," she snarled. "Your great pride has made you oblivious to all but yourself. The barbarians who infest this building venerate you, however, and slaughter innocents in your name. They are merciless and they are many. They murder your brethren in the mistaken belief that we are a threat to you. No appeals for clemency penetrate their fanaticism. Sadly there aren't very many of us left now. In fact, now that my sister has departed, only you and I are left in this city."

Strange words indeed, I thought. My brethren? I knew no equal. Shared no blood. The world I inhabited was filled with hatred and fear, it was true, but I was too quick for any of it to stick to me.

Quicksilver retained its sheen regardless of collisions. This bewildering woman sought to tarnish me; hold me somehow responsible for the actions of zealots. I couldn't bring myself to call them maniacs considering the object of their devotion. I returned her cool gaze. It betrayed no sympathy for my confusion.

In an effort to absolve myself, I was about to describe my admittedly unusual lineage and being, up until now, its solitary surviving member when it occurred to me that she either already knew or didn't really care. My sad story of neglect and abandonment would not move her. The tale of my years of struggle with my unnatural self could not scratch her surface.

When she finally shrugged off her cloak of civility and threw herself at me with teeth and nails bared, it became clear that my sensitive nature had failed to stir her and the time for chitchat was over.

I would like to say that her feverish attack was gracefully repelled and decorum was restored quickly and quietly. I would like to report that the blood she drew, my blood, yes, my blood, was a lucky shot and that my response was measured and restrained. In fact, the first dozen or so slicing arcs from a whirlwind of limbs were so fierce that I was obliged to take several steps backwards to parry the onslaught. A shock, since retreat was almost unknown to me.

Murderous blows rained in thick and fast from all directions. It was all I could do to preserve my dignity as this flurry of feminine ferocity clearly considered no anatomical target off limits. So quick. So ruthless. I could not help but be impressed. Some of her moves were so reminiscent of my own that it seemed almost churlish to strike back. It was ironic, I supposed, that in this temple devoted to me, something she so evidently despised, nothing was a greater compliment than her imitation. Of course, my ego did not allow for any other explanations. Including sibling parallels.

For an hour I was a blur of defensive co-ordination as she darted around the room, a tempest of slashing violence, until fatigue finally gripped her and I made my move. In between ducking two brutal swipes towards head and heart, I slipped inside her guard to take a lethal hold upon her throat. Before she could lash out in response, I drove forward at breakneck speed to collide with the stone wall, a move that resulted in a sickening crunch. Not too sickening, naturally, as it wasn't me making first contact. Her eyes glazed. The tension in her muscles drained away as she slumped semi-conscious into my arms. I was alert for deception but no inside jabs sneaked through.

Regardless of the abrasions that criss-crossed my face and arms, my composure remained intact which certainly saved my beautiful assailant's life as self control was not usually high on my list of attributes. But I was intrigued. Could this fiery and fascinating woman really be "my kind"? I glanced up at a portrait on the wall and then into her cold green eyes. My eyes. And the cool olivine stare of Veronica Brooks also flickered in my memory. A relation? A sister? Did I mention that I always kind of liked her?

I relaxed my grip. She gulped in air. Slowly, new energy restored her and I felt her body tense once more for action. My hand stroked her forehead. She rose in agitation then fell back. Significant pressure at her throat stilled her violence. Her consciousness departed in a hiss of despair. I noticed from the corner of my eye that our altercation had overturned a number of candles and a considerable conflagration was now in progress.

Time to leave. But what to do with this exquisite creature who may or may not be my only living relative?

If I took her with me, I would be responsible for her. Possibly, she might eventually restrain herself and tell me of our history. Of our kind. Or, she may blame me for everything and renew her frenzied attempts upon my life at the first available opportunity. Of course, if I left her behind she would most certainly burn in the now seething inferno. My new family all gone. A difficult decision which would require all of my renowned compassion and empathy. With flames at my heels, I acted for the best.

I ripped my way through the door she had locked and raced out in the smoke-dense passageway. No brawny dark-suited gunmen awaited me there.

Dead or fled, I assumed.

In seconds, I had reached the front entrance and stepped casually out on to the street where the first plumes of smoke were already mixing with the city exhausts. On the heated breeze, I caught just a hint of burning flesh and recognised its taint as similar to my own. As I walked away from the crumbling building, I considered how close I had come to no longer being alone in the world.

Ah well, easy come, easy go.

Veronica Brooks cursed my name as I strode away, but I still kind of liked her for all that.

BIOGRAPHY: *Steve Jenner lives in a village on the edge of Greater London where he composes his dark, quirky tales, quite often in broad daylight. He has been writing for about twenty years mainly for his own entertainment, but having been an avid reader all his life, hopes to one day place one of his own modest efforts in amongst those authors to whom he owes so much.*

A Hand from the Depths

DAVE DE BURGH

The air vibrated with ululations when they came for Manolo. He was small, not yet ten summers, and his parents had lost themselves in the Day of the Dead celebrations. He clutched the conch shell his father had given him, as if holding onto it would somehow keep him from being swallowed by the swirling crowd.

Hands slipped in under his arms and lifted him. He was still smiling, laughing, in wide-eyed wonder at the sublime chaos around him. It was only as the person who had picked him up began moving away from his parents that he began to realize he was being taken *away*.

When he began wailing to be let down, no-one heard him. When his legs began kicking, no-one saw.

***

Manolo was in a small room, smaller than his room at home. There was a narrow slot in the wall, not even wide enough for his fingers. When he pressed his head to the slot he could just make out the opposite wall, and sometimes a suggestion of light during daytime.

Dave De Burgh

The room was seven paces in length, two in width, and he sometimes walked the space trying to find some kind of escape in the rhythm of his steps. No lights, nor switches against the wall. Other times Manolo sat down, bare back to the cold, grimy wall, and just held himself. He tried not to think too much, but his thoughts always turned to the life he had been taken from. Memories flitted through his mind, familiar and heart breaking, but he tried to hold onto them when the darkness became too much. He remembered living outside—remembered the sun, and the touch of the wind. His parents. His father's strong arms. His mother's soft hair.

He picked up the conch shell and blew into it, but the mournful sound reminded him of all he had lost, and that he would probably never see the ocean again. He remembered the grown-ups whispering that his father had fought some kind of sea man-monster for the shell. Monsters could be men, too, like the people who had taken him and brought him here.

He had thought his mother was making up stories to get him into bed, every time she told him about how this child or that child had gone missing. His world had been one of cartoons on weekends, his crate of toys every afternoon; the stories of the kidnapped children were just stories, after all. Nothing to be afraid of.

Daytime was a blur of sickly brightness against a dimly seen wall. Nights seemed everlasting and were terrifyingly devoid of every other sound, except those he made. Rough-hewn bowls contained bits of meat, fat and shreds of vegetables, which he found upon waking, never seeing who brought the food. And the innumerable times he'd pounded against the cell door, against the walls, hours spent screaming with his face pressed to the narrow slot.

Once the cell door rattled when someone outside unlocked the door. His eyes had opened in time to see the shape entering—robed, a cowl framing a shadowed face, tall and swift. He could only manage a squeak of fear before a cold, long-fingered hand clamped over his mouth.

"You are Chosen," the robed man whispered, his Spanish laced with a strange accent Manolo hadn't heard before. "You and the others. The Ones Below are stirring, and they cannot be allowed to wake. We must offer blood. Such is the cycle, such is the way." The hand clamped even harder and he whispered, seemingly to the air, "This we offer, so that You may ever sleep."

Manolo understood the words, but not what was being said, and it terrified him. The hand lifted away. The man retreated.

The door closed and was locked again.

***

There was nothing in the room with which to occupy Manolo's mind. Even the conch sat forgotten in a corner. Manolo stopped remembering the cycles of day and night. At times he screamed his throat raw—other times he mumbled nonsense words, trying to voice the thoughts in his mind with words he had never been taught. Time passed, broken sporadically by visits from the strange, robed man. Manolo grew taller.

Puberty was terrifying and painful, a process which he hadn't been prepared for. For a while he thought he was becoming some kind of monster. When his voice broke he sat in a corner of the room, crying, wondering if his body could change enough so that his mother and father wouldn't recognize him if they ever saw each other again.

Did they miss him, too? Did they remember him?

Eventually he stopped calling out to them, too.

***

After a long while Manolo stopped talking to himself. He had come to hate the sound of his voice.

He took to sleeping most of the day, and he ate less. Not out of any need to rebel, but because the lack of movement simply made him less hungry.

It may have gone on too long, this not eating, because Manolo eventually received another visit. Not from the robed man, but from a broad-shouldered, hard-faced, silent man and his smaller companion. They wore denims and black shirts with sturdy boots. The big man held Manolo still, while the smaller man forced food down his throat.

He tried to explain to them that he would eat but he had forgotten some of the words he had known. They forced him to chew and swallow and ignored his tears. Afterward, remembering the sounds he made when being force fed, he thought he was becoming an animal of some kind.

Maybe that was what they wanted—to see if re-making a person into an animal was possible.

Manolo was woken that following day by the lash of a whip across his bare back. The big man continued until it seemed that the world was pain, pain, pain.

He was whipped every day after that.

***

Manolo eventually learned to wake before they came.

He stood against the wall, face pressed to the narrow slot, focusing on the only hint of freedom he knew as the whip began to lash his back. Eventually the pain changed into something else—a way for him to travel inward, deep into himself where his remaining memories hid and the pain lessened.

The pain became his ally.

When he no longer cried out as the whip struck him, the blows stopped falling. Later that night he was visited again by the robed man. The guard with him held a small video camera. He was surprised that he remembered what it was.

The robed man's voice issued from the shadowed cowl. "You have learned your first lesson as Chosen. Your remaining existence will be divided between the glory of pain and the craving of it. You are a simple animal now, but you have an important part to play."

Once again the words had meaning which he understood, even though he had forgotten how to shape most of the sounds with his lips.

The robed man paused, as if waiting for an answer.

After a spell of intense silence, he nodded, turned and left the room. The big man set the camera down, drew the whip off the ring on his belt and stepped forward.

****

On the day that everything changed, two men entered his cell. One carried the video camera and whip, the other carried a bag.

Manolo's eyes lingered on the bag for a long moment, curious.

One of them zipped open the bag and upended it—old, dirty clothing fell onto the cell's grimy floor.

Dave De Burgh

The guard tossed the empty bag aside and gestured for Manolo to approach. He did, and kept as still as possible as the guards proceeded to dress him.

His skin wasn't used to the feel of clothing against it. Though he itched terribly he didn't dare move. When the guards were done he stood in the center of the cell, unsure of what to do.

They each seized an arm and pulled him along with them, out of the cell. Panic seized Manolo—he snarled and tried to pull himself free but they were stronger.

Manolo never saw that cell again.

***

Manolo had forgotten that the robed man had mentioned other Chosen—others like him. When the guards dragged him to the chamber and tossed him to the ground, the first sound that came to him was the soft murmur of movement.

Manolo looked up, reeling as too-bright light speared into his head, and he couldn't help moaning through clenched, aching teeth.

It took a while for the vague blobs before him to resolve into knowable detail, and when he understood what he understood the sight of it, a surge of fear thrilled through him.

This new room was large, and the ceiling high. Four cameras jutted from the four corners of the room, moving left to right and back again. Four long, thin lights blazed white from the center of the ceiling.

The room was filled with people.

Other Chosen.

They were dressed as he was, their skins pale amid patches of dirt and grime, their eyes wide, while some gibbered fearfully. They all had snarled hair, long or curled, and they stood apart from each other. Scared of each other.

After a moment Manolo scrabbled back onto his haunches, every muscle tensed, fighting the urge to run because a part of him knew there was nowhere to run to. When he turned he saw that the door was closed. He was trapped in here with them.

He scuttled into the closest corner, panting his fear and bewilderment. His entire world had changed.

Sudden movement caught his attention—a thin, wiry man with protruding teeth accidently touched the elbow of the person closest to him. That person flinched away with a cry, knocking someone else off their feet.

More screams. More lurching movement, which quickly became shoving as those who were closest allowed their fear to take over. And then everyone erupted into violence; screams became snarls, fists fell and swung with brutal intention, knees rose and feet stomped.

Some flinched away from the fight, shoving away anyone close enough. While Manolo felt an urge to join in the violence he realised he wouldn't last long against them all. Some of the fallen stopped moving, tears in their clothing revealing ragged gashes in their flesh. Red water flowed from the injuries and the smell of it caught at the back of his throat. It didn't smell like the water he had been brought day after day.

Others lay twitching; their heads stomped into a messy pulp. He glimpsed a lone eye, separated from a head. Those who stumbled and slid in the red water left footprints as they limped away.

The red water flowed towards a small hole in the center of the floor.

Manolo focused on one of the fallen during a moment of silence, watched with fascination as the eyes blinked rapidly and then abruptly stilled. The chest deflated and a last exhalation sounded.

His eyes moved to the others and he noticed that some were still moving—weakly, haltingly. But still moving.

A word blossomed in his mind, strange and alien, a remnant of a life he hardly remembered anymore.

Alive.

Manolo uncurled from the corner, rose slowly and then moved forward. As he approached the dying and the injured he noticed how the torch-light made sharp dazzles in the thick red water.

Not water. *Blood.*

The word sounded right. He remembered that the robed man had used the word.

Manolo stopped beside one of the injured and looked down. Red bubbles inflated and popped between his blood-smeared lips. A bite-wound in the man's throat was leaking blood in steady spurts and he made gurgling, choking sounds as he trembled. His hand rose, wavered, the fingers curling and uncurling with a need he couldn't put words to.

Alive. Blood.

No, there was something else, a different sound with a different meaning, connected to the *blood-*sound.

That was what he had to do, what they all had to do. What had already begun.

Manolo went down on his knees and trapped the

dying man's head between his hands. He gripped the snarled, dirty hair, lifted, and then slammed the head down. And again. Again. A hand clutched at him, scrabbling, nails scoring trails through the dirt on his skin.

Drops of blood sprayed and spattered with each impact until the back of the man's head broke open. The man stopped moving. One eye sank slightly into his head.

Dead. Yes, that was the word. That was what they had to do here. The injured had to be made dead because they were weak. They couldn't be allowed to get up.

If they were, *he* might be the next to fall. He didn't want to be made dead.

Releasing the corpse's head, he turned, looking for the next person, and then moved over, ignoring the wordless plea that struck his ears.

***

The dead were dragged out by two guards.

He could feel eyes on him and there was a sense that something important had changed. He couldn't put words to it.

He had changed.

The door opened again and the robed man stepped into the room, followed by three guards. The man had pushed his hood back and Manolo saw that his face was thin, his eyes protruding, his lips pressed together in a pale line. He had no eyebrows, no facial hair. His tongue darted out periodically to lick his lips.

"Those of you who remain, you Chosen, will now leave this place." He turned to survey them, slowly, as if looking for something in their eyes and faces. "Not all of you will survive the journey, but those who do will be offered. Such is the cycle, such is the way."

He turned on his heel and left the room as the guards began to herd them out.

He was the first to be taken up a nearby flight of steps, down a long stretch of corridor, and out of the building that had been his cage for most of his life.

***

Manolo was at the head of the group of Chosen as they were hurried down the streets and boulevards of the village, a truck filled with guards following them. He wept when he saw the great blue bowl of sky overhead. He smelled the scents of food he had forgotten existed and his stomach rumbled and cramped. This place was different to the one who had lived in with his parents. Nothing looked familiar.

Many people had gathered to watch the sacrificial procession.

They were silent at first, but gradually a strange sound rose from them. He saw that their lips were moving and that their eyes were closed. The guards kept urging them on, ignoring what was happening, intent, focused.

The meaning of the words became clear, the phrase he had heard so many times in the language he remembered so little of: *"Such is the cycle, such is the way."*

Buildings of different sizes and heights surrounded them; this place was larger than he had ever imagined. Knowing that it had existed beyond the slot in his cell wall and seeing it now stole his breath.

Eventually the group came to a tall, wide door set into a wall that reached toward the sky.

The wall stretched away to the left and right, surrounding the village.

The sudden creak of the large door splitting down the middle and then opening slowly made the Chosen flinch. The open door revealed a dusty path stretching away and off into the distance; more sky, arching overhead, seemingly without end.

The guards marched them through and the group continued forward. The ground was uneven underfoot and when Manolo swung his head back he saw some of the Chosen stumble, but not fall.

To fall, Manolo knew, was to die.

***

They walked until the sky became darker and the air around them colder. Manolo shivered, huddling with the others for warmth, ignoring the chattering of teeth and soft whimpers around him. When he looked up he saw that the darkness had been pierced all over by countless, distant, flickering points of white light. His mouth opened in stunned amazement.

When Manolo finally came back to himself he saw that the rest of the Chosen were similarly captivated. This was the *world*.

That was the word. *World*.

It had been hidden from them, denied them, and now they were in it, walking across it, huddling beneath it.

***

Manolo looked around, not recognizing anything. He realized there was only one direction they could be moving in

They were moving toward *The Ones Below*.

Sometime later they were allowed to rest and the

guards stood watch all around them. They wore thick jackets.

When the brightness of the sun began to spread across the sky, sending the darkness flooding away as if fearful, the guards roused the group of Chosen and prodded them into marching.

Manolo had never learned numbers and so didn't know how much time passed. During one of the cycles of day and night one of the Chosen dropped to the ground, too exhausted or weak to move.

Manolo watched as the guards prodded the dust-stained bundle of rags and stick-like limbs, heard the pleading and naked need in the moans drifting toward him. The guard took out something black and pointed down at the Chosen, and Manolo flinched in shock as a loud bang reverberated through the air. A section of the man's head exploded, spattering over the dirt. He was dead. Manolo wasn't surprised.

The weak were being removed.

One of the other guards approached the body, carrying a jug. He caught the flowing blood in the cup, being careful and taking his time.

The guard then poured the blood into a large container which the guards transported on their truck.

And then the group continued on, leaving the dead man behind.

***

The guards brought out their whips again when the group slowed.

Most of the Chosen were staggering, mouths agape, lips cracked, wheezing. They continued to stagger even as the blows began to fall.

Manolo felt the whip's kiss but only as distant

vibrations that ebbed through his body. He was focused on his breathing, and on walking. Nothing else mattered.

Not even his thirst could pull him out of the daze he was in. His eyes remained locked on the horizon, locked on that place not yet visible.

The place where it would all end.

When they stopped in the evenings it was to collapse into exhaustion. The guards came round with jugs of water and measured out five sips to each of them. Most of the guards slept in the back of their truck and the Chosen slept on the naked ground. The next morning three more were dead.

The ritual from before was repeated, their blood collected and poured into the container.

When they resumed marching, the bodies were left behind.

***

Eventually they came to an area where the ground alternately rose and dipped—steeply in some places, gradually in others. He began to notice colors other than the drab browns and reds, colors that reminded him of what he had seen on all the chanting people outside the cells. Greens and blues dotted the surface, and a multitude of different scents began to pervade the air.

When they were eventually ordered to halt, the remaining Chosen swayed on their feet, eyes staring blankly. Manolo became aware that he had stopped walking. He took a reflexive step forward, then another. Wheezing air into his lungs to fuel his aching body, three words escaped his lips like a sigh:

"The Ones Below."

Dave De Burgh

He took another step and felt an increasing pressure around his elbow. It seemed to take an eternity to turn his head and look down, and he eventually understood that he was looking at a hand. Looking up he saw a man's sweat-slicked, bearded face. Another eternity passed before he realised he was looking at one of the guards.

The man pulled him back, gently so that he didn't stumble, and led him into the group of dazed Chosen. Manolo was close to collapse. Only force of will kept him upright.

The guard gestured and Manolo watched as a different guard poured the water from the jar out onto the ground. The Chosen stuttered forward, scrambling on hands and knees, clustering around the muddy patch in the ground. An ache trembled through him before he realised that his body was reacting; his first step forward became a lurch of desperate movement.

Water.

He reached the nearest of the Chosen, clamped his fingers around the back of the man's neck and lifted him away, already focusing on the next Chosen. He grabbed an ankle and pulled, yanking the woman toward him. She twisted and grabbed his leg; he snarled and lifted it, pulling her arm along until she let go, and then stamped on her hand. The crackle of her fingers breaking was lost in the slurping and gurgling coming from the middle of the huddle. So was her scream of pain.

He tangled his fingers in the next Chosen's filthy thatch of hair, pulled his head up, then gritted his teeth and twisted the head sharply to the left, cutting off the beginnings of a hoarse scream.

The woman's hand clawed at his ankle. Manolo turned, stamped on the back of her head until she stopped moving, and searched for the next water-thief.

The attacker hit him from behind, smashing him off his feet. They struck the group of Chosen, flattening one into the dirt, someone else crying out in surprise and dismay. Manolo struggled against his attacker, pushing and shoving until he was on his back, and saw a circle of muddied, enraged faces staring down at him.

The blows began to fall, fists smashing against his forehead, nose, lips, chin; glancing blows to his ears, a punch to the throat. Fists struck his chest and abdomen, exploding the breath from his lungs. His body rocked, pain blossoming and expanding.

His back was wet. He had reached the water they had been drinking. And with every blow his world became darker, the tunnel of his vision retreating.

The last thing he saw was a guard shoving between the attacking Chosen, raising his gloved fist. It flashed down and darkness fell.

***

Manolo woke as cold wetness enfolded him, the shock of it pushing a scream from his lungs. The sound of it was strange, muted, and an explosion of bubbles roared from his mouth. He thrashed around but hands gripped him tightly and he couldn't free himself. He gulped water and began choking. Fear lashed him.

And then he was being lifted out of the water, gasping, coughing, spluttering, life-giving air filling his lungs. He glimpsed a large span of ripple-covered water, a shore that stretched out to his left and right, and far ahead, on the opposite side of the lake, a dark, looming forest.

A guard spoke in Spanish: "You have been blessed in the tears of The Ones Below. Such is the cycle, such is the way."

Something hard hit the back of his head and he fell into darkness again.

*****

Manolo woke in fits and starts. The world swayed around him, topsy-turvy. He felt pressure around his forearms and ankles. His body sang and pulsed with pain. He moaned, blinked, and caught a glimpse of bars. Something moved beyond the steel, a massive thing with a long, circular body and a wide head. It watched him pass, weaving slowly from side to side. Hissing.

More cells passed on either side and some of the things he saw hurt his mind and made him feel an incomprehensible fear.

He closed his eyes, accepting the pain. It scoured away the images of the terrible things he had seen in the cells and eventually he managed to wonder about his fate. Lifting his head took a lot of effort and when he opened his eyes again Manolo saw guards; four of them, carrying him by his legs and arms.

The ceiling above them was rough-hewn rock and stained with jumping, flickering shadows. The air smelled of dust and blood.

Manolo moaned again and one of the guards spared him a quick glance. He was surprised to see sadness in the man's lined face.

Eventually the ceiling changed, sloping higher, and he saw smooth walls, a smooth floor, and flat slabs set into the walls.

Jagged figures had been carved into the slabs.

Two guards stood at a section of the chamber

where the floor met the ceiling. They struggled with a familiar container. When they tipped it blood slopped and flowed out, falling into an open gap between the floor and wall.

The guards released him without warning and he struck the floor. The back of his head struck the stone and his vision flashed white. When he could see again, one of the guards was reaching for him.

Manolo tried to bat the hand away but he was so weak that his hand only twitched.

The guard looked into his eyes and said, "Such is the cycle, such is the way."

Manolo's eyes widened a moment before he felt the blade kiss his skin and then slice into his throat.

Pain lanced through him, blinding him, stunning him with its ferocity. Warm wetness. Blood, his blood, spilled across his chest and spurted against the guard's grimacing face. The guards pulled him upright and set him against one of the slabs, holding him so that his blood painted the slab and the stone floor red.

The scene darkened around him and he heard the wet, desperate gurgle of his own breathing. He glimpsed another, larger open space where the floor ended and the wall began. He looked into the space, saw the great chasm with its rough walls, lit by distant, immense flames.

Something . . . something massive was at the very bottom.

Something that moved. Turned.

A hand.

He looked at an unimaginably massive hand.

The guards tipped his body into the space and as he began falling, his last thought was: *The Ones Below*.

Dave De Burgh

BIOGRAPHY: *Dave de Burgh is a bookseller and writer living in Pretoria, South Africa. His work has been published in AfroSF, eFantasy, eSciFi and the forthcoming African Monsters. His novel,* Betrayal's Shadow *was re-published by Ticketyboo Press on the 1st of December 2015, to be followed by the sequels in 2016 and 2017. Dave is an avid reader, writer, Pekingese-dad and* Star Wars *fan.*

The Bet

AMY GRECH

David Sheffield, a lanky sophomore, clutched a knapsack full of knowledge as he took long strides through the crowded hallways of Albany High. His small, brown eyes darted from side to side, searching for a clear path as he hurried to his next class.

Jim Hanson, a short, stocky senior, leader of the pack known as The Black Death, watched him like a hawk circling his prey. He yearned for the taste of sweet victory his encounter with David would surely bring. Jim tapped John Roth, a burly gang member, on the shoulder and whispered in his ear.

John grinned and rushed over to David, who stopped walking and stood his ground when he saw him approach.

"What's up, John?" David shoved his hands into his jeans' pockets, trying to look casual.

"Meet Jim behind the tennis courts at three. He's got an offer you can't refuse." John slapped him on the back.

David cringed, dreading the worst. "Count me in."

"Be on time—Jim hates to wait."

He nodded. "Don't worry, I'm *always* early."

John rolled his eyes. "Later, Sheffield. I'll let him know you'll be waiting."

David walked to his English Literature class quickly; puzzled—he had no idea why Jim picked him—he didn't consider himself Black Death material. He wondered if he was the victim of a cruel joke. Curiosity got the better of him. David dismissed his skepticism as nervous excitement.

John headed over to the lockers where Jim and the other members of The Black Death stood to deliver David's reply. "He's thrilled you picked him. He wants to meet up after school."

"He's probably scared shitless right now," Jim said, grinning. "Let's go have a smoke."

Jim led his gang out to the deserted football field. The Black Death sat in the center of the grassy area near the train tracks that ran alongside the school. Each of the six members removed a Marlboro and a red Bic Lighter from their sleeveless denim jackets. They lit their cigarettes, took a drag, and pocketed their lighters.

"Have you boys thought about how we should break in our last recruit, David Sheffield? We need another member." Jim studied his disciples. "That way we'll have seven, one member for every day of the week."

Everyone exchanged glances and nodded.

Keith Travis spoke first: "We should tell him to ask Sara Parker for a date. She's the prettiest girl in school. He won't stand a chance." He ran bony fingers through his spiked, brown hair.

Jim shook his head. A shiny switchblade sprung from the pocket of his jeans. He admired his reflection in the flawless metal, where dark blue eyes shimmered on the smooth, sharp blade.

"That's cruel. We all know Sara gave you the cold shoulder, Keith. Remember, David is *really* smart. He'd never fall for that."

John punched Keith. "There's one important rule: The dare *must* be fair!"

Keith rubbed his sore arm. "Okay, okay, you made your point."

Brian Nicholas tossed his smoldering butt into the tall grass behind the football field. "Make him tread water for thirty minutes."

"You've got to be kidding!" John chuckled.

Dan Troteli chimed in, "Yeah, David's a weakling. He'd drown in no time."

Brian winked. "That's the idea, numb-nuts!"

Peter Baker scratched his head. "Let's make good use of his genius instead."

"What do you have in mind?" Keith gave Peter a dirty look. "David's a geek! He's only good with books¾he hasn't got life skills."

"That's not true, Keith." Jim cleared his throat. "I've seen him outrun you dozens of times when you tried to chase him. Hey, that gives me an idea. I've got a dare for David that's both challenging and fair." He lit another cigarette and blew a stack of wobbly smoke rings skyward. "Let's make him stand in the middle of the tracks that run alongside the school without moving until the nine-forty-five is about to hit him."

No one had any say once Jim made up his mind. Now David's fate was sealed.

***

At two-fifty-eight, David wandered over to the green fence that surrounded the tennis courts and waited for Jim to show. He knew fists would fly. Not his, he didn't believe in violence. Besides, his scrawny arms were no match for his idol's massive biceps.

Jim showed up at three o'clock. He spotted David¾an easy target¾leaning against the fence, looking anxious.

David watched him approach and took a deep breath. "What's up, Jim? John told me you wanted to meet up."

"Yeah, that's right. I'm here to offer you a chance to join The Black Death." Jim grinned. "If you're up to it."

"What do I have to do to become a member?" His Adam's apple bobbed like a frog trapped in his throat.

"Prove yourself." His dark blue eyes burned with fierce intensity.

"How am I supposed to do that?" David asked, puzzled. He focused on Jim for a second then directed his gaze downward to his feet, afraid that if he stared at Jim he would seem too bold.

"Take a chance and win. If you lose, you won't live long enough to live it down. Meet me in the parking lot at nine o'clock tonight, if you're up to it." Jim's long red hair flickered like fire in the wind.

"I'll be there¾I love a challenge." David nodded and turned to go. He knew Jim wanted to see him make a fool of himself, but David didn't mind, because if he pulled the stunt off he would finally earn some respect.

Jim sped off in a black Thunderbird with a bumper

sticker that read: **IF YOU DON'T LIKE MY DRIVING, DIAL 1-800-EAT-SHIT.**

David started his navy blue Mazda 626, checking cautiously for traffic before heading home. Along the way, he wondered what Jim had planned: Does *he want to drag race, or will he make me stand in front of his car while he speeds around the lot and tries to stop before my face collides with his windshield? Does he expect me to beat the odds, or does he want the odds to beat me?*

When he stepped inside the house, David walked into the kitchen to answer the phone. His mother called to see how his day was. He wanted to tell her the leader of The Black Death told him to meet him in the parking lot at nine o'clock, but David decided not to mention it. He knew she wouldn't let him go if he did. The gang had a bad reputation; the police were after at least three members for armed robbery and the mutilation of several defenseless animals. He told her he got an 'A' on his English Literature exam instead.

Then David went up to his room and took a nap.

David stood in the middle of the train tracks by Albany High School, while Jim stood off to the side, grinning.

David saw the train's headlight in the distance. A bolt of lightning flashed in the sky; followed by the roar of distant thunder. A deluge of rain began to fall, drowning his fear.

As the train sped down the tracks, the thunderclaps grew louder and louder, until they were deafening. David clasped his hands over his ringing ears, trying desperately, to muffle the maddening sound. When the nine-forty-five overtook him, the sound of screeching metal brought him to his knees . . .

The front door slammed, waking him from a sound sleep. His parents had returned from work. He heard his mother whine because he forgot to lock the door again. His father told her to quit complaining. David rolled over to glance at the clock next to his bed, seven o'clock.

He went downstairs for dinner. His parents had Chinese food waiting in the dining room. His favorite.

He took his usual seat at the table and polished off his Wanton Soup in record time. "Hi, Dad."

His father smiled in between sips of soup. "You mother tells me you got an 'A' on your English Literature exam. Congratulations. You're a regular Hemingway."

David nodded. "Thanks, Dad. I try my best." He shifted in his seat, trying to get comfortable. "Mom, can I go over to Peter's house after dinner?"

"What for?" Mrs. Sheffield sipped her Martini.

"We have a math test tomorrow. He asked me to help him study."

"All right, but don't stay out too late. It's a school night." His mother smiled and set a full plate down in front of him.

David nodded. "You won't even know I'm gone."

After dinner, he went back up to his room and sat on the bed to think. He looked at the clock, eight-twenty-five. David looked out his window while he convinced himself that a chance to join The Black Death by Jim was worth it. He didn't think the train in his dream would outrun him, if Jim *really* did want him to play chicken. At least he hoped not . . .

***

At eight-fifty-seven with minutes to spare, David pulled into the empty lot. He wiped his sweaty palms on his jeans, got out and sat on the hood of his car; he found its warmth oddly comforting. Seconds later, a black Thunderbird came to a screeching halt inches from his legs.

Jim cut the engine and hopped out.

"Did I scare you, Sheffield?"

"Yeah, you caught me by surprise." David couldn't stop shaking. He looked down and noticed that one of Jim's sneakers was untied. David decided not to tell him—it might be fun to watch Jim trip over his own two feet.

"You've got to calm down, David. You're wound too tight." Jim shook his head. "Let's take a walk. It will help you relax." He led the way, his loose shoelace flapping rhythmically on the ground, marking time.

He shoved his hands into his pockets. "Okay, sounds good to me."

They made their way across the deserted football field to the train tracks adjacent to the school, and started walking down the center. David stared at the starry sky while Jim reached into the pocket of his denim jacket for a Marlboro and his Bic Lighter. Caught off guard, David flinched when he heard a series of faint clicks—whispers in the dark—that created sparks and eventually a flickering flame.

The tip of Jim's cigarette glowed like a miniature sun in the darkness. "Want a smoke?" He pressed it to his thin lips and inhaled.

"No, way. Those things will kill you," David

shouted, still watching the sky. Now, dark, menacing clouds obscured the stars.

"Hey, it's your loss." Jim shrugged. "You don't know what you're missing." He blew a stack of smoke rings at his latest recruit, who was too nervous to notice. He tossed the smoking butt onto the tracks, took the lighter out again and pressed the button, causing its flame to waver. Jim held it up to his watch, which read nine-thirty-four before pocketing his lighter one last time.

"Hey, Sheffield." Jim tapped him on the shoulder.

David stopped looking at the sky and stared at him. "Huh?"

"It's show time." He stopped walking. "Are you ready to rock?"

"I dunno . . . What if something goes wrong and I get hurt? I don't think this is a good idea." David stopped dead in his tracks.

"Come on. Don't be a pussy. You'll never live this down if you back out now. Besides, if you get hurt bad enough, you'll wind up with a wicked scar and bragging rights. What more could you want!" Jim punched David's bony arm so hard he bruised his hand. "Son of a bitch. See what you made me do."

"Ow! That really hurt. Why did you punch me?" He rubbed his arm and frowned.

"I wanted to knock some sense into you¾I think it worked." Jim rubbed his aching hand. He felt it swell up.

"Sorry, Jim. I tried to get out of the way, but you're too quick for me." David kicked some gravel scattered across the tracks.

"Stand here when the nine-forty-five comes. You

can't move until the train passes the line I draw. Understand?" Jim pulled a piece of chalk, stolen, no doubt, out of his jacket and made a mark on the left side of the tracks. "Remember, don't move until you see the train. If you do, the deal's off and I'll tell everyone you're a coward." He stood next to David and rested his foot on one of the rails, accidentally tangling his loose shoelace in the metal.

David froze and looked around. He saw overgrown bushes and brown grass on either side of him. When the tracks began to vibrate, he stared at the white line inches from his feet and crossed it, bolting from the tracks. He stood a comfortable distance away¾off to the side in the overgrown grass—close enough to see the action, but far enough to watch the train pass unharmed.

"What the fuck. You got it all wrong. Didn't you hear what I said? " Jim slammed his foot down on the tracks "Get back here, coward. You're *never* going to live this down. I'll make sure of that."

David raised his right hand slowly and gave Jim the finger—it glowed in the eerie white light cast by the rapidly approaching train, like a beacon. "It looks like you're fucked, Jim. Are you just going to stand there like an ass? Why don't you come over here and beat the crap out of me?" He leaned over for a closer look. "Looks like you're tied up."

Jim stared at his loose shoelace in disbelief when he realized it had fused with the smooth shiny rail of the tracks and shrieked. "David you've got to help me. I'll do anything you want if you get me out of this mess!" With a trembling hand, Jim fumbled for the switchblade in his pocket. It slipped from his grasp and clattered to the tracks just beyond his reach.

Jim saw a bolt of lightning, followed by the sound of thunder rumbling in the distance as a torrential rain began to fall . . . His dark blue eyes were awash in fear, reflected in the tarnished, discarded blade at his feet. When Jim tried to drag it closer with his free foot, he slipped in the muddy gravel and landed smack on his ass.

The train's whistle shrieked as it barreled down the tracks.

Fascinated, David watched the spectacle unfold, unsure how it would end.

The train was almost on top of Jim while he strained to yank his foot out. He tugged at his leg, feeling as though everything was moving in slow motion—except for the train—still speeding towards him like a bullet.

As Jim felt the white-hot pain shoot up what was left of his leg, he knew he was trapped. Fascinated, he shrieked and watched as the high arc of blood shot from the artery in his severed leg.

David watched him struggle to get free, like an animal caught in a snare.

"I thought you were smarter than that, Jim! Did you really think I wanted to join The Black Death? I know you invited me because you wanted to see me make a fool of myself. It looks like you're the fool." He laughed and walked away, leaving Jim to die.

Every night at precisely nine-forty-five there have been numerous sightings of Jim Hanson, ghostly pale, wearing a sleeveless denim jacket, with a missing leg hobbling around the train tracks next to Albany High, where he met his gruesome demise.

Without fail, he vanishes when the train speeds by in one big silver blur.

BIOGRAPHY: *Amy Grech has sold over 100 stories to various anthologies and magazines including:* Apex Magazine, Beat to a Pulp: Hardboiled, Dead Harvest, Detectives of the Fantastic, Volume II, Expiration Date, Fear on Demand, Fright Mare, Funeral Party 2, Inhuman Magazine, Needle Magazine, Reel Dark, Shrieks and Shivers *from the* Horror Zine, Space & Time, The Horror Within, Under the Bed, *and many others. New Pulp Press recently published her book of noir stories,* Rage and Redemption in Alphabet City.

She has stories forthcoming in Creepy Campfire Quarterly *and* Tales from The Lake Vol. 3. *Amy is an Active Member of the Horror Writers Association who lives in Brooklyn. Visit her website: http://www.crimsonscreams.com. Follow Amy on Twitter: http://twitter.com/amy_grech.*

The Monster of Biscayne Bay

ROXANNE DENT

New Year's Day
1975

Last night I dreamt of Biscayne Bay and the monster that ate the hearts of all my friends.

It was the summer of 1955. School was out. I was ten and on a plane to Florida with my seriously ill mother. My father was an out of work actor and had a new family. It was decided we should take my aunt up on her offer to live with her and Uncle Reg until my mother got back on her feet.

My aunt promised to hire a live-in nurse to care for my mother, a bicycle for me and a community swimming pool I could walk to.

The instant I stepped off the plane at the Miami Airport, the hot, moist air hit me. The long drive to my aunt's house seemed to stretch on endlessly as my aunt drove past vast tracts of flat land. This land was home to hundreds of car dealerships, one-level homes with terra cotta tile roofs, giant, red poinsettia bushes and diners that sold fried chicken and grits.

My aunt's home was a bungalow with four bedrooms and a garden in the back with banana and coconut trees. A bright, plastic, pink flamingo decorated the front lawn. I thought it looked scared but then I never lacked imagination.

True to her word, Aunt Wilda hired a doctor who visited twice a week and a live-in bossy nurse named Mrs. Babbitt.

Once we were settled, Wilda informed us she and Reg were leaving on a European tour that would take up most of the summer. We would be alone except for the nurse and the dailies. So long as I didn't make a mess, Shirley the cook and Edna, the housekeeper left me alone.

A few days before they left for Europe, my aunt took us to visit a Seminole Indian village . . .

We got a late start and it took longer than expected. We didn't arrive until late afternoon I didn't expect to see the village enclosed by a fence, or houses with three sided, open air, thatched roofs.

I learned the Seminole people had their roots in the Creek culture but also mixed with runaway slaves and free Negroes. The men wore jeans and colorful shirts and the women wore long multi-colored skirts and peasant blouses.

My mother and aunt returned to the car to rest. Curious, I wandered off. The Indians ignored me as they built fires outside and began cooking the evening meal.

I noticed several children sitting around an old man. It looked like he was telling a story and I went over.

"It's true. When I was a boy, I was hunting with my father and uncles and saw an Ishtikini."

"What did it look like?" a boy of about seven whispered.

"Exactly like a man. An Ishtikini can change into anything, man, woman, a wolf, anything."

"How did you know what it was if it looked like a man?" a little girl asked.

"His eyes were dead and, even from far away, he stank of blood."

I knew the creature was after my heart. An Ishtikini will go after a man or woman, but children's hearts are tender and the blood sweet so they hunt them first."

An older boy spoke up. "Tell us how they kill."

"They like to wait until its dark. Then they crawl or fly into an open window, dig deep into the child's mouth or chest with their razor beaks, and rip out the heart, like this." He demonstrated with his hands and the children gasped and shrieked. "By eating the heart, the Ishtikini become human again."

"What happened when you saw the Ishtikini?" one little boy asked.

"My father shot at it, but the creature took the shape of the Horned Owl, and flew away. We built a fire and stayed up all night keeping the fire going. They fear fire. We never saw it again."

The shadows became darker and it began to rain. Thunder rumbled in the distance and everyone scattered, heading for home. The old man stood up. We were alone. He didn't look my way but when he spoke, I felt he was talking directly to me.

"The Ishtikini are clever, and . . . move like the

wind. Some people have the gift to recognize them in their human form."

Shivering, I watched him walk away in the rain. One minute he was there, the next he was gone. The fires were out and the village was empty as the people went indoors. I heard an owl screech and my imagination made me hear the flapping of wings. I felt sure it was the Horned Owl and ran for the exit.

That night I dreamed the Ishtikini was after me. I could smell his foul breath on the back of my neck as I ran, one step ahead of him. Once the sun came up, I felt a little silly. Monsters weren't real and yet the nightmare lingered just beyond consciousness, ready to pull me in the moment I let my guard down.

The next day, I went out exploring on my new, red bike. All the houses in the area looked exactly like my aunt's bungalow except for one. The peeling, yellow, two-story, wooden house down by the bay must have been built before the bungalows came. There was an air of neglect and sadness about it. It looked haunted.

I was standing with my bike out front, sure I'd seen movement on the second floor, when a girl rode up on her bike and stopped. She looked about my age with long, tanned legs, and short, dark brown hair. She wore a pair of pink polka dot shorts, a sleeveless, white shirt and scuffed, white sneakers. Next to her, I looked like a ghost with my pale skin, wrinkled white shirt and shoulder length, dirty blonde hair.

"Creepy isn't it?" she whispered.

"Whose house is it?"

"Some old lady who used to be in movies. No one famous. She comes here in the winter for a few weeks and throws cocktail parties but the house is empty now."

"I thought I saw someone upstairs."

"Not unless it's a squatter and squatters don't come around here on account of the patrols. My name's Dixie."

"Lilly."

"How long will you be staying, Lilly?"

"Don't know."

Dixie mounted her bike. "I like riding down by the beach. Wanna come?"

As we rode away, I glanced back. I saw the shape of a man at the window and peddled faster.

***

Curtis and Billie Jo were the only other permanent residents. Billie Jo was two years older than me. She wore dresses and her mother's red lipstick. She also smoked. Under her left eye was a yellowing bruise she tried to cover up with makeup. The rest of the kids in the area were visiting relatives and would be gone in a couple of weeks, so the four of us hung out together.

Curtis was the oldest at thirteen. He disliked me as soon as he heard me speak. "Ya'll must be a Yankee," he snarled.

"So," I snapped.

"You lay off, Curtis Marshall," Dixie ordered, stepping in front of me.

"Northerners make trouble," Curtis muttered.

"Lilly's okay."

"Suit yourself."

Curtis could have knocked Dixie out with one punch but Dixie was one of those people who could stare you down.

Dixie and I often took Rosie, Mrs. Archer's black Chihuahua, on long walks. Rosie flat out refused to go anywhere near the yellow house. She'd dig her little feet into the sand and whined.

"Why do you think she does that?" I asked Dixie one day.

She shrugged. "I had an Irish Setter once who wouldn't go down a street. We never found out why." Her blue eyes lit with ghoulish delight. "Maybe there's a dead body buried in the back yard."

I laughed but sympathized with Rosie. The house gave me the shivers. It was Curtis who first challenged us to enter the moldering, yellow house.

We were walking on the beach and he stopped abruptly. We were only twenty feet from the house. I bumped into him and he whirled on me. "I bet you're too scared to go in and look around."

"That's breaking and entering," I said.

"I declare, Curtis Raymond, one day ya'll gonna be on a chain gang," Billie Jo drawled as she puffed on an Old Gold filtered cigarette.

"It's not breaking and entering if you got a key." Curtis opened his palm. On it was an old brass key.

"How did you get that?" Dixie asked impressed.

"I saw where the old bat keeps the spare. She hid it under the cactus on the porch." He laughed. "Talk about dumb."

"It's not right," I protested.

"We won't take nothing. That would be a crime," Curtis agreed. "We'll just look around. It's owned by some old actress. There must be tons of interesting stuff in there."

Billie Jo dropped her cigarette and stepped on it. "I heard the place was haunted."

"If you're scared, then don't come."

"Let's do it." Curtis said heading toward the house. Nobody spoke up.

"Hold on," Dixie said, grabbing Curtis's arm. "It's daylight. Suppose someone sees us? Let's wait till everyone's at supper."

My mother won't let me out at night," Billie Jo muttered.

"Your mother will be dead to the world by six," Curtis said nastily.

Dixie punched his arm and Billie Jo flushed.

"Mrs. Hamel's six year old granddaughter Patty went missing," Billie Jo said shivering. "Folks are saying she was kidnapped from her own bed. What if there's a kidnapper roaming around looking to take kids?"

"Who would want to grab you? We'll all be together. I'll even walk ya home," Curtis promised.

I turned to Dixie. "Do your parents let you out after supper?"

She shrugged. "They don't care what I do so long as I don't interrupt their programs."

Curtis nodded. "Okay. Let's make it late. Everyone swear to be here by eight sharp. It'll still be light out."

We each swore an oath and went home.

It was five o'clock. We had three hours before we met. I felt sick and barely touched the fried chicken, instant mashed potatoes and collard greens or the peach pie and whipped cream.

I didn't want to go.

I couldn't shake the image of a monster lurking in the shadows upstairs waiting to rip out our hearts.

***

At seven twenty-five, I yawned and stretched. Nurse

Babbitt was watching *Captain Blood*, an old Errol Flynn movie. My mother was asleep in her room.

"I'm going to bed," I announced.

"So early?" Nurse Babbitt asked without looking up.

"I'm tired."

When she didn't turn around, I snuck into the kitchen.

My aunt and uncle were somewhere in Europe. it was only Mrs. Babbitt, my mother and me.

I grabbed a filleting knife Shirley used for skinning fish, and slipped the knife into the beaded, suede, fringed sheath I purchased at the Seminole village. I attached it to my waistband. In my aunt's bedroom, I picked up the silver, monogrammed, cigarette lighter she forgot to take, and dropped it into my pocket before sneaking out my bedroom window onto the soft grass.

The humid, perfumed air hit me like a wet blanket Jasmine from Mrs. Archer's yard drifted on the faint, evening breeze. Smoky, grey clouds floated across the moon. I shivered as I made my way to the house by the bay, swatting at the swarm of mosquitoes determined to suck out every drop of my blood.

As I neared the house, a putrid smell made me gag. It was worse than a pile of rotting fish. I almost ran away.

The others stepped out of the shadows like ghosts.

"What is that nasty smell?" Billie Jo whispered.

"Who cares? Let's go in,' Curtis muttered impatiently. He walked up to the house, inserted the key and opened the door. The rest of us followed. Inside, mildew and mold hit me right away.

Underneath was that awful stink. The air was stiflingly hot and still.

"Smells like a pack of rats died in the walls," Dixie said holding her nose.

By eight thirty, it would be pitch black.

I stumbled into Billie Jo who let out a tiny scream.

"It's a good thing I thought to bring a flashlight," Curtis said shining the light around the hall.

"What if the patrols see the light," I whispered nervously, releasing the catch on my sheath.

"They won't, stupid. I timed them," Curtis crowed. "They only go by every two hours and they just passed."

He headed into what looked like the living room.

Framed movie posters of long dead, silent stars hung on the walls. Over the white fireplace was a portrait of a young blonde. She wore a blue satin dress. I thought it might be the owner when she still dreamed she'd be a big star one day.

"Wow, look at that," Curtis exclaimed.

Along with the posters hung an African mask and the head of a snarling, stuffed tiger who looked like he was about to leap off the wall and tear us to shreds.

On the mantle were all sorts of knickknacks of carved wooden figures with big eyes and bellies. There was a layer of dust over everything. A large spider crawled along the ceiling.

Billie Jo grabbed my hand and I squeezed it.

"She must have gone on safari," Dixie said enviously. "I'd like to do that someday."

Upstairs, the house creaked. We all stood still holding our breath.

"It's an old house," Curtis said scornfully. "They

always make sounds. Nothing to worry about." He led us into the kitchen where a flock of palmetto bugs flew at us.

"Ew, get them off me," Billie Jo screamed.

"Come on, let's go upstairs," Curtis said excitedly. "Maybe there's a safe with jewels in it."

We followed him to the second floor. There were four closed doors. I opened the one nearest me and looked in. It was a bedroom. The bed had been stripped and it was stifling hot. Flies buzzed around a dark stain.

"What's that?" I whispered hoarsely.

Curtis went over and shined the light on the spot. It was almost black but there was a reddish sheen.

Dixie asked what I was thinking. "Is it blood?"

"Course not silly," Curtis said. "Probably wine."

I felt the sweat pouring off me and itched to flee.

"I want to go home," Billie Jo whimpered.

"Nobody leaves until we find something really interesting," Curtis growled.

Storming into the hall he yanked open another door and stopped dead.

I was right behind him, looking over his shoulder, and saw the body of a six year old girl in green and yellow Tinkerbelle pajamas sprawled on the floor. Her long, blonde hair fanned out behind her. Her mouth was sliced wide apart, her tongue was missing and her face and upper body was covered in dried blood.

Billie Jo let out a high pitched shriek and ran for the stairs.

The Ishtikini grabbed her. He was over six feet and had bulging, yellow eyes, a deformed beak, black talons and razor teeth. With one sweep of his claws, he split open her chest and plucked out her still beating heart with his beak. He swallowed it whole, his gullet swelling and tossed her body over the balcony. She landed with a thud.

Dixie tried to run past him. He caught her by the leg. While she screamed and punched, he grabbed her hair. Yanking her head back, he was about to slit her chest open. I grabbed my filleting knife and stabbed him in the back. He screeched and threw Dixie against the wall. I heard a crack and she was still.

The creature turned to me, a wild look in its eyes. I would have been next if Curtis, in a blind panic hadn't started yelling like a banshee and ran past, knocking me out of the way and smashing the Ishtikini in the face with his flashlight, taking the stairs two at a time.

Furious, the Ishtikini leaped over the banister and landed in front of him with the easy grace of a dancer. When Curtis tried to run past him, the monster reached out and jerked Curtis up, dangling his body off the ground. Curtis' feet helplessly kicked the air. He sobbed and screamed for help. The Ishtikini's head cocked to one side. His golden, owl eyes gleamed. He never spoke. Curtis swung at him, twisted and kicked, but nothing he did had any effect.

The giant opened his mouth wide. His double tongue flicked before he drove his beak smack into Curtis' chest. Grunting, the beast tore out his heart, greedily gobbling it down. Curtis stopped struggling.

It all happened in seconds.

The spell of horror broken, I ran into the first bedroom, locked the door and tried to open the window, but after years of dampness the wood around it had swollen. I grabbed a vase and smashed the glass, crawling out onto the rotting balcony.

The peeling wood was bowed in the middle and looked unsafe. I didn't care. It was my only way out. I cut my arms and legs climbing through the jagged glass but didn't feel a thing until much later.

I dropped to the ground, spraining my ankle and scrambled to stand.

When I looked up I saw the monster at the window.

For a second, blind panic made me want to run, but I knew I couldn't outrun the Ishtikini. I thought of my mother who slept with an open window and the dead, little girl in the bedroom upstairs. When I jumped, the knife fell out of my sheath. The blade lay on the ground a few inches in front of me. I felt my pocket. The cigarette lighter was there. My heart was pounding so loud, it sounded like thunder in my ears. I picked up the knife, headed back inside. Tearing off a curtain, I lit it and set fire to the other curtains and the rickety, wooden stairs. They went up as if they were soaked with gasoline. The Ishtikini appeared on the landing.

Changing into the Horned Owl, he flew right at me.

I threw the knife with all my strength. It hit him in the chest. He let out a piercing, ear-splitting screech and fell halfway down the stairs changing back into a man with black hair and a beard. The flames rushed up the stairs crackling and spitting, engulfing his body. He tried to stand but his charred flesh fell off him in chunks until only his skeleton was visible for a second before he collapsed in the flames. I fled the house as the flames licked my feet.

Outside, I took a back way home, limping as fast as I could.

Out of breath, I climbed in my bedroom window, shut and locked it. Sneaking into my mother's bedroom, I closed her windows and locked them too. I stripped off ripped clothes that stank of fire, and took a quick shower before crawling into bed. I heard the fire engines roar past.

The next morning, I had dark circles under my eyes and hurt all over from the cuts I received climbing through the broken window and spraining my ankle but did my best to hide it. Shirley asked me where the filleting knife was.

I told her "No."

When the police determined along with the bodies of four children, a man in the inferno had a knife buried in his ribs, she stopped complaining and bought another. It would do no good to have a Negro admit a knife used to kill a white man, was missing from her kitchen.

That's when the nightmares and sleep walking began.

***

All that happened twenty years ago. My mother died shortly after and I returned to New York to live with my father and his new family. I told no one about the Ishtikini or my part in the fire. The nightmares and sleepwalking gradually receded. I almost came to believe it never happened.

Last night I partied with friends dancing to some of my favorite songs, ushering in not only the New Year, but my thirtieth birthday. I drank too much of the spiked punch and spent a couple of hours in the bathroom wishing I was dead. All that liquor must have released the nightmares.

Roxanne Dent

I took a hot shower to relax, and played the boom box as I dressed.

The song *Cats in the Cradle* blared out. I'd heard it last night and the music triggered a memory I froze. I was drunk and weaving to the music. Everyone was happy. Musky incense mingled with the pot smoke.

A girl was standing in a corner all by herself, watching everyone. She had the face of an angel and wore faded hip huggers, a peasant blouse, and large silver hoops. Her long, straight blonde hair fell to her waist. I didn't recognize her. She looked about fourteen, too young to be at an adult party and I wondered who she was. More people joined in the dancing and the crowd surged. I ended up close to the girl.

At that moment she looked up. Her black eyes were dead and underneath the sweet perfume was a faint, putrid odor that reminded me of the monster I killed in 1955.

She smiled.

I knew she knew I knew.

BIOGRAPHY: The Janus Demon, *Roxanne Dent's ninth novel is a paranormal fantasy, Great Old Ones Publishing. "Heart of Stone," a short horror appeared in* Enter at Your Own Risk: Dreamscapes Into Darkness, *Firblog Publishing. "The Haunting of Jemima Nash," a ghost story is included in the anthology,* Zombies, Tales of the Supernatural, *an anthology created for the Whittier Museum based on a Whittier poem. Roxanne and her sister Karen collaborated on "The Death of Honeysuckle Rose," a mystery written for the anthology,* Murder Ink, Thirteen Tales of New England Newsroom Crime, *Plaidswede Publishing.*

The Song at the Edge of the Unfinished Road

JACK BATES

Richard Forsythe couldn't remember if he was the first resident or the last resident of the Sprawling Oaks development. He did know that the oaks were few and far between inside the gated entrance of the eight house community. Four houses lined each side of Thornhill Lane. At the east end waited a roundabout with a little extension of pavement that at one time suggested a future expansion. Now that unfinished road reminded the residents of an untimely end to any further developments.

Before Phase One of Sprawling Oaks could be completed, the builder seemingly had a nervous breakdown. They found him in a nearby creek. Face down. Floating under a fallen tree limb. Fish had eaten his face. Speculation was he had gone to hang himself, but the limb broke under his weight, trapping him beneath the surface. Problem with that theory was no one ever found any rope.

How many years had Forsythe stared beyond the end of the forgotten road?

Jack Bates

Once he even walked over to it, actually walked out onto it and put a foot to the gravel. He didn't step completely off the unfinished road. Something warned him not to go any farther. He simply stood there, both feet firmly on the pavement, and watched the moon rise in a pale indigo sky. Since then he only went halfway down—or was it up—of the segment.

Paul Benton, a neighbor, walked up behind Richard. "Hey. What's out there?"

Forsythe shrugged. "A field, I guess."

Benton shook his head. "Nah. Gotta be more. We should get flashlights and go take a look."

"I don't think so." Forsythe couldn't explain why. He'd feel foolish saying that the one time he did step off the end of the pavement he felt the ground shifting, as if a giant beetle was rolling around beneath the stone and dirt.

"Come on. It'll be fun. We'll go to the top of the next hill and we'll explore. When we were kids we would've run there and back by now. Maybe twice."

"When we were kids we stayed out till the first streetlight came on and then it was home before the boogey man scratched you."

"See? Life was exciting back then. Mysterious. Full of wonder. Now we read things on portable screens that scare us into staying inside."

"We're not inside."

"No. I saw you out here staring off at the darkening horizon. Thought maybe I'd get you to go for a walk to that next hill."

"What's so fascinating about that next hill?"

Benton shrugged. "It's there."

"That's it?" Forsythe had hoped for more. A

collaborator. Someone else who felt rolling beetles beneath their feet.

Benton stared off into the distance. "No. There's something more."

Forsythe watched his neighbor. He waited. He thought he knew what Benton was going to say. When the man didn't speak, Forsythe prodded him. "What is it, Benton?"

Benton's mouth moved. Nothing came out. He walked back along the roundabout to his house. Forsythe watched his neighbor stagger, turnabout with uncertainty.

"Benton? What's the matter?"

"Nothing. I just got a bit dizzy. I wasn't certain I knew where I live."

"Where you live? You're right there. Next to that couple with the child."

"Couple with a child?"

"Don't they have a child?"

"I thought the other houses were empty." Benton stumbled up to the third house from the gate on the south side of Thornhill Lane.

Forsythe watched Benton go inside. He looked at the other homes. Were the other homes all empty? Was it just Forsythe and Benton in the whole community? He swore he saw other neighbors. Wasn't one of them a child? Oddly, they did all look similar. Minor differences. The addresses, for example. Forsythe lived in number sixty-seven. Benton lived in number seventy-six. The couple with the child owned number fifty-eight. The house immediately west of Forsythe's was number eighty-five.

He wasn't a numerologist, but the combinations,

when added together, all equaled thirteen. He also wasn't superstitious but when thirteen was added together the sum was four. He knew some cultures viewed the number of four as a symbol of death.

Nonsense.

The quarter moon stretched higher. Just like its pull on tides, it pulled at Forsythe. It begged him to come to it, to come out into the field, to walk to that next hill.

His toe touched the gravel.

The ground shifted. He felt uncontrollably nervous. Richard Forsythe pulled his foot back. The anxiety still burned within.

"Maybe I'll feel better in the morning."

Behind him, porchlights automatically snapped on.

***

Forsythe woke the next morning—he assumed it was the next morning.

Sometimes when he woke he wondered how long he had been asleep. Not by hours but by years. Sometimes at night he felt like he could slip into another time, another reality. Sometimes he opened his eyes expecting to see his wife.

Ridiculous, of course. Forsythe had never been married.

Had he?

His head throbbed like he'd had one too many nightcaps. A loud, engine-like hum filled not only his head but his house as well. He pulled on a robe and looked out his upstairs window.

Below, Benton faced the rising sun, his arms raised high and hands reaching.

And he was as naked as the day he was born.

The Song at the Edge of the Unfinished Road

Forsythe quickly put on his own clothes. He hurried down the carpeted stairs stopping long enough to slip his bare feet into a pair of loafers. Forsythe ran from the house to the roundabout where he draped the robe around Benton.

"No. No, no, no . . . " Benton sobbed. "No. Don't go."

It was hard to hear over the hum. Just beneath the whirr of a power engine there was a ribbon of something else. Forsythe thought of an underground river, water rushing over rocks. Faint to the untrained ears.

Benton bowed his head. He kept his arms raised. Tears fell to the white concrete beneath his bare feet.

"Don't go. Come back." His voice was much softer.

"Are you talking to the sun?"

"The sun?"

Nothing but bewilderment on Benton's face then. He looked down at the robe. "Forsythe? Why am I wearing this robe?"

Forsythe laughed. "I put it on you this morning."

"This morning? Why?"

"You were standing here naked, talking to the sun."

Benton put a hand on Forsythe's arm. "Oh dear God, Forsythe. I just haven't been myself lately. I woke up to the most beautiful singing. Chant actually. A single sound running through a variety of octaves." He closed his eyes. Hummed. Pointed with a long, narrow finger at the faraway hill. "It came from over the hill. And then I saw them."

"Saw who, Benton?"

"Our neighbors. The people who used to live in these houses."

"What are you talking about? People still live there."

"Do they? Who else have you seen here? I swear it's just you and me. Forsythe, may I ask you a personal question?"

"You're standing naked in the street. Anything you say seems personal." The jest fell flat.

"Forsythe, where's your wife?"

"My wife? You're mistaken, Benton. I'm not married. I've never been married."

"But you were, Forsythe. When you first moved here to Sprawling Oaks you were married. I want to say her name was Mandy."

"You're mistaken, Benton."

Benton half laughed, half cried. He shook his head. "No. I remember her. Very pretty. She loved you."

Forsythe could feel the anger rising inside him. "Stop it, Benton. I've never been married."

"Yes, you were. And she was friends with Kirstin and Andy who lived in number forty-nine."

The house number triggered something in Forsythe's head. "Pete. I have to ask you something now. Have you noticed all of our house numbers individually add up to thirteen?"

"And next to me lived Catherine and Jason and their daughter Allison, and on the other side of them were John and Ethel, and over there were—"

Forsythe shook his neighbor's arm. "Over there were who?"

Bewilderment returned to Benton's face. "Forsythe. Could you help me into my house? I'm suddenly very light headed."

"Of course."

"It's been a long day. Maybe I just need some sleep."

Forsythe looked at the sun going down behind the gate. Had a whole day just passed?

"Look at that, Forsythe. It's made another pass."

"What has?"

Benton laughed. "The sun of course. But don't worry. It'll return. It always returns."

They reached Benton's door. His neighbor looked up at the two numbers nailed above the door. "You're right, Forsythe. It does add to thirteen. Why do you suppose the developer numbered them this way?"

"Guess we'll never know."

"It's like he was trying to send us a message."

"About what?"

Benton patted Forsythe's hand. "Let not your mind be troubled over trivial matters. I think Shakespeare said that."

"You going to be okay?"

"Are you?" Benton smiled. "I'll return your robe in the morning."

Benton went inside. Forsythe stared at his neighbor's door before he turned and walked across Thornhill Lane. He stopped midway.

There were thirteen letters in the name of the street.

There were thirteen letters in Sprawling Oaks.

He turned back to Benton's house. The lights inside went off. Forsythe didn't know why but he no longer wanted to be out in the street.

An hour later he sat in his den, computer on. He searched the internet for meanings behind the number thirteen. There were the usual theories; thirteen attended the Last Supper, on the thirteenth of October King Philip the IV of France ordered the arrests of the Knights Templar. No restaurant would take a reservation for thirteen after the deadly fire at a popular night club. He got nowhere. Whatever the developer's message behind the use of the number thirteen was he couldn't decipher. Maybe if he knew more about the developer, he'd know. Forsythe couldn't remember the builder's name. He typed in the name of the gated community.

Nothing came up.

He typed it in again and got the same result. Just to be certain he hadn't broken the internet, he typed in 'gregarious cheese dust' and got over five and a half million hits. Forsythe found this amusing and troubling. He closed his laptop. It was late. He had to go into work in the morning, didn't he?

Didn't he?

He stood up to leave. Outside his window it sounded like heavy rain fell. He moved over to it in the dark and looked outside.

It wasn't raining.

Hundreds of giant, eight legged beetles clicked their mandibles and fluttered wings from beneath open shells on their backs. They marched or hovered or scurried from the unfinished road to all the empty houses. They pounced on the homes, and crushed them into dust. Behind them came tall, humanlike figures with four, long spindly arms. They wore Fedoras down on their brows to cover their egg shaped eyes, scarves to block their missing noses and sideways, figure-eight shaped mouths in case they were spotted. Black cloaks covered humps on their backs. Each arm held a long, tube-like worm. The worms' mouths opened and closed until the figures squeezed the worms behind the mouths. They held the worms over the powdered debris and sucked it up like a multi-hosed vacuum cleaner.

Above it all was that roar of a phantom engine, and beneath that the singing of a single note by a multitude of the damned. A doomed choir praying to its dynamo.

Forsythe couldn't believe what he was seeing.

He scrambled upstairs for his phone. He'd have to get pictures of this. Benton would never believe him without proof.

He was halfway up the staircase when a chill washed over him. No, more than a chill. Dread. It filled his thoughts and seeped into his bones. He sat down on the carpeted steps and leaned his face against the bannister railings. He looked down.

Mandy looked up at him. Once upon a time she had the prettiest green eyes. Now they were the color of ashes inside cracked eggshells. The luster of her smile had tarnished, her mouth twisted, her teeth gnarled.

"You came home," he said.

"I can't stay."

"No. Of course you can't."

"But you can come with me."

"I can't do that."

"I can't stay long. They let me out long enough to see if you'd come back with me."

"I'm not ready to go yet."

"You're not going to have much say in the matter. They want you to return with the rest of us. The thirteen passings are coming to a close."

"But I'm not ready."

"They've sent the grudes and the four-armed guards to eradicate the settlement."

"I know. I saw them. I was going to take pictures with my phone to show Benton. Then I remembered . . . I remembered . . . and here you are."

Outside some great beast bellowed.

Mandy looked up at Richard. She was less like him and more like who they were when they arrived.

"I have to go."

Richard nodded. "I know."

"You won't survive. You won't be able to hold their look or shape. They'll see who you really are and they'll hunt you down."

The beast outside roared again.

Richard looked away from her. "You'd better go, Mandy."

But she was already gone.

Forsythe no longer wished to photograph the grudes eating the empty houses, or the four-armed guards vacuuming the dust. He didn't even feel like going the rest of the way up the stairs to bed or down the stairs to close the front door. He leaned his head against the rails.

***

Morning sunlight lit the windows. Fresh coffee brewed. Forsythe whistled a single note in different octaves as he poured a cup. His doorbell rang. It occurred to him that the tone of the bell harmonized with his whistling.

"Good morning, Forsythe." Benton held out the robe.

Forsythe tossed it onto the back of a high-back chair in the living room. "Coffee, Benton?"

The Song at the Edge of the Unfinished Road

"Oh, one last cup for the morning won't kill me."

Forsythe took a cup from the cupboard. He poured coffee into it. Benton sipped.

"They took down the empty houses last night."

Benton nodded. "I almost called you."

"I was going to take pictures for you."

The neighbors shared an awkward laugh. Neither spoke for a moment.

"I remembered things last night, Forsythe."

"So did I." Forsythe looked at the stairs. The memory of seeing his wife was a fading shadow. Forsythe knew that soon the two would forget things again.

"So, are you ready to go back?"

Forsythe shook his head. "No. You?"

"No. I thought today I'd walk over to the hill."

"They won't let you come back."

"I know. Join me?"

Forsythe looked around the kitchen. He emptied the remainder of his coffee into the sink then ran a little tap water over the lingering puddles.

"What the hell."

The morning was warm. They walked in silence to the roundabout. The roar of the engine greeted them as they stepped to the end of the unfinished road. Forsythe realized he sang the single note of praise.

Benton put a hand on Forsythe's shoulder, and he looked at his friend. Benton was telling him something that appeared to be important. Forsythe had no idea what it could be, though. Benton's eyes filled with tears. He gestured to the distant hill. His hand trembled. Forsythe realized his neighbor was afraid, so he took hold of Benton's arm.

"It's okay."

Benton stopped talking. He looked bewildered, shook his head, pointed at his ears, and asked, "What?"

Forsythe laughed. "It's okay."

Benton still didn't register.

Forsythe stepped off the end of the unfinished road. He walked on the backs of sleeping beetles. Plumes of sand, stone, and dirt erupted around each of his steps. Benton fell behind.

Forsythe moved on.

A grude beetle jumped up from below the surface, and took Benton in its mandibles, snapping him in half.

Forsythe moved on.

He marched over the bones of the forgotten, over the carcasses of old generation grudes, over the end of the field, until he reached the base of the hill. He shielded his eyes and looked up at the sun.

Forsythe turned around.

He saw nothing behind him, although he thought there was someone else. He must have been wrong about that. His house was the only one on the lonely dirt road. He could still see the closed gate, the large 'No Trespassing' sign outside it. Below that warning, another in smaller letters proclaimed, 'Restricted Area Per Federal Regulation Thirteen'.

The roar of the engine was gone. All that remained was the incessant song of a single note. Forsythe turned his attention to the top of the hill. He made his way up the grassy slope. Each step appeared to increase the height of the hill. The music drove him to press on. He needed to see where the music came from. He needed to see who sang it.

The Song at the Edge of the Unfinished Road

After what seemed like a day of infinite hours, Forsythe reached the top of the hill. The loneliness of the song weighed heavily on his heart.

When he got to the top he collapsed onto his hands and knees. His head dropped.

The song came from a large hole in the ground, a hole wide enough to swallow all of reality.

The ground shook beneath his tired, used body. Herds of grude beetles charged past. They came up over the crest of the hill and headed down to the hole, toppling into the mouth in droves. Watching the beetles die made the melancholy from the song heavier.

Forsythe knew it was time.

The plan had been a failure. They had arrived thirteen years ago from their own dying world. The indigenous species was just primitive enough to make them think they could assimilate, but they couldn't. The four-armed guards had followed protocol and released the grudes to forever eradicate their colony. Forsythe was the last of the race.

The guards hovered over the rim of the hole. All four arms were raised to the alien sky. Their dual mouths formed perfect circles. They harmonized with themselves and beckoned for Forsythe to go down into the hole.

He could stay, he realized. He could turn and run back to his house and stay. He would open the gate to the inhabitants of the adopted planet and he would tell them who he was and why they came and—

The four-armed guards circled him. They each shoved a vacuum hose onto his head, carried Forsythe to the mouth. A giant tongue lapped at his feet. When the four-armed guards released him, Forsythe fell and the mouth swallowed him.

***

The one he had known as Benton stood over his bed. The body he'd had in the colony was replaced with his true form—an elongated face, the sideways figure-eight mouth, the egg shaped eyes.

"Good morning, Forsythe."

He rose up on the quad elbows of his four arms. "How did it go?"

"Same results. Every simulation ends with the same results. Our people just aren't suited for colonization. This is our home. We were condemned to be born here and then die here."

Forsythe sat up. Outside his window orange streaks swirled inside the indigo star that once gave life to their dying planet. The streaks swam over a dimming light. Before long the gas would ignite and the sun would explode and their planet would be swallowed in the explosion.

"It worked for a time, Benton."

"I'm sorry, Forsythe. It's not to be."

"Do you hear the music, Benton? It's the song from the unfinished road."

"It was always our people calling us home. Telling us they wanted us to stay."

"It's a sad song."

"It's a song only we will ever hear."

"Perhaps. Perhaps we should join the others and sing with them."

"I have no song to sing, old friend."

And Forsythe, who longed to return to his home on the other world, sang for him.

The Song at the Edge of the Unfinished Road

BIOGRAPHY: *Jack Bates is an award winning writer of short stories, screenplays, and children's books. He is a two time nominee for a Derringer Award from the Short Mystery Fiction Society.*

And now, an excerpt from
324 Abercorn
by Mark Allan Gunnells

PROLOGUE:
DREAM HOUSE

JUNE 2006

THE **HOUSE CROUCHED** *there on the corner of Abercorn and Wayne like something alive but dormant, a hibernating beast, which may soon awaken and swallow the world whole.*

Standing across the street in Crenshaw Square, Brad Storm thought he would describe the house in those terms in one of the horror stories he liked writing. Despite the tour guide's eerie tales about the place's rather macabre history, Brad only saw a gorgeous Greek Revival mansion. Sure, the house was neglected and in serious need of repairs, but the bones were sturdy. Brad could use his hyperactive imagination to see beyond the busted windows and missing shutters, the moldering brick and general air of abandonment, and envision the house as it must have been in its glory.

The building stood three stories tall, with slightly curving side-steps leading up to the main entrance on the second floor. The details were somewhat obscured in the dark, but on the right side there seemed to be a veranda running the entire length of the house on the ground floor, with equally long balconies stretching along the top two levels. Brad couldn't see it from here, but he knew there was a two-story carriage house around back.

"The house was built in 1868?" the guide said in a chirpy voice, which made every statement sound like a question. "General Benjamin Wilson lived here with his wife and daughter, at least until his wife died from yellow fever, leaving Wilson and his daughter alone in the house? The General had fought for the Confederacy in the Civil War, and was not too pleased when the Maverick School opened across the street; it was Savannah's first fully integrated school? He was even more displeased when he learned his young daughter was playing with some of the black children while they were on their recess break? To punish her, he tied her to a chair and sat her by the living room window, so she would be forced to watch the children from the Maverick School having fun at recess but not be able to join them? Back then, before air conditioning, these houses could get quite hot, and I'm sure you can imagine how miserable it must have been sitting right at the window? After a few days of this, the girl died from heatstroke and dehydration? Some believe she never left the house, that to this day her spirit still roams the halls, staring out the windows, still wanting to play with someone? In fact, a gentleman who went on my tour last year sent me a photo he took that night, and you can see the girl's pale face staring out from the bay window, above the front door?"

In true Pavlovian nature, everyone in the group, including Brad, looked up at the window on the third story.

The window jutted out like a cancerous growth, malignant and pulsing with evil.

Brad chuckled softly to himself. With the right words, one could make something as innocuous as a window sound malevolent. The guide passed around a grainy photo for the group to see. When an overweight woman in a "Crab Shack" T-shirt handed it to Brad, he glanced down at the image and shook his head. An indistinct white blur was visible in the bay window, more than likely a reflection of light on the glass. He supposed it might resemble a crude face, but only tangentially. Then again, he thought he remembered reading something in a Psych class once of how the human brain would often take senseless shapes and rearrange them into something the mind could comprehend, something familiar. The theory explained why people often saw images of Jesus or the Virgin Mary in their pancakes and oatmeal.

Once everyone had an opportunity to scrutinize the photo—eliciting gasps from a few of the more gullible members of the crowd—the guide continued with her spiel: "Some theorize the paranormal activity surrounding 324 Abercorn is strong because of its location? You see, the square we are presently standing in was once a slave cemetery? If you look around, you'll notice the lack of grave markers, so you may assume that means they moved the cemetery? But you would be wrong? They simply built right on top of the graves? The cemetery also was not confined merely to the perimeter of Crenshaw Square, but actually stretched out for several blocks, including right underneath 324?"

The ground beneath the crowd's feet seemed to tremble, not with an earthquake, but as if hundreds of bodies were clawing their way back up through dirt and rock, an undead horde hell-bent on retribution for the wrongs done to them in the past.

"What are you smiling about?" asked Crab Shack. "We're standing on top of poor dead slaves."

Brad shrugged. "I guess it's possible. They say Savannah is a city that walks over its dead."

"Then you should show a little more respect."

What do you want me to do, go hang from a tree limb? Brad thought, but he merely nodded and arranged his face into a solemn expression.

A young couple near the front of the group, whom Brad assumed were newlyweds based on their inability to keep their hands off each other, took two simultaneous steps toward the street. They paused, as if not daring to go further.

"How long has the house been empty?" the young man asked.

"Since 1973? The family who'd bought it lived here only a month or two, complaining of phantom forces choking and pushing them? They moved out of state, up north, I believe, and have not been back since? However, they refuse to sell the property because they say they don't want to inflict the horror on anyone else? So the house just sits here, radiating malice?"

Crab Shack raised her hand. When the guide nodded in her direction, she said, "I heard a group of teenage girls were killed in the house back in the 50s or 60s, and the crime was never solved. Is that true?"

"Yes, that is a rather grisly story? We're running a bit behind schedule, so I'll tell you the tale as we head down toward Mercer House?"

The guide led the group out of Crenshaw Square and down Abercorn, in the direction of Forsyth Park at the far end of the Historic District. Most of the crowd cast furtive glances back toward the house before moving on, but Brad lingered. He stepped into the street, raising his camera and taking a few shots, thinking he might like to come back in the morning if he had time and get some pictures in the daylight.

The house watched him as he watched it, as if it recognized him, as if their destinies were intertwined.

Laughing at his own foolishness, Brad hurried to catch up with the group. He cast his own glances back toward the house, but his were full of longing.

324 Abercorn was one of the grandest and most beautiful houses he'd ever seen, and he thought it a shame that it was deteriorating this way. He would love to be able to buy it, restore it, and make it his home.

But it would never happen. He'd barely been able to scrape up enough money to take this vacation to Savannah, Georgia. No, tomorrow he'd head home to his cramped studio apartment in Spartanburg, South Carolina, and pack the fantasy away with the one of him becoming a bestselling author. He could dream about living in such an extravagant house, but that was all it ever was . . .

A dream.

PART ONE:
NEW BOY IN TOWN

MARCH 2016

CHAPTER ONE
THE BOY IN THE BOOK LADY

BRAD WAS BROWSING the Mystery section in Book Lady on Liberty Street when he noticed the boy staring at him. Well, not a boy exactly. He was probably in his early twenties, more of a young man. The older Brad got, though, the younger everyone else looked to him.

Jesus, you're only thirty-six, stop casting yourself in the role of a geriatric. Although you are closer to forty than twenty. Hell, you're closer to forty than thirty . . .

Blocking out his own inner voice, Brad glanced back toward the staircase lined with stacks of books. The young man still stood there, practically in the children's section, still staring at him. He wore a pair of capri pants and a gray hooded sweatshirt, his black hair done up in meticulous bed-head, ample time spent to make it appear he spent no time on his appearance. Mild amusement marked his face. Instinctively, Brad reached up and brushed at his chin, wondering if a bit of his lunch had gotten stuck in his goatee.

The young man finally walked over to the Mysteries and said, rather abruptly, "I know you."

"Um, I don't think we've ever met."

"No, we haven't . . . but I know you. You're Bradley Storm."

"Oh, yes, I am," Brad said in a tone of voice suggesting he was admitting to something shameful like bedwetting or playing the ukulele. Even though he was a successful author with five bestselling horror novels and one short story collection to his credit, he still hadn't grown accustomed to being recognized. Truth be told, it made him uncomfortable. He much preferred the anonymity and solitude of sitting at his desk, plugging away on the laptop, to the public display of interviews and book tours. Then again, writers weren't exactly movie idols or rock stars; the instances of him getting recognized in public were rare. Being in a bookstore increased those chances a bit.

"You know," the young man said, "I read your first book, *Out of the Shadows, Into the Dark*."

"Well, thank you."

"Don't thank me yet. I didn't say whether I liked it or not."

This surprised a laugh out of Brad. "Touché."

"I'm just messing with you," the man said, wearing an infectious grin. "I thought it was a great book, creepy and atmospheric. The movie adaptation, on the other hand . . . that was a real stinker."

"I thought it turned out okay, all things considered."

The young man tilted his head and gave Brad a skeptical look. "You're just trying to be all diplomatic, but you have to admit they really dumbed down your story. Even the title change to *Shadow Monsters* was dreadful; sounds like something they'd air on SyFy after the latest *Sharknado*."

Brad tried to hold a neutral expression, but he couldn't keep the corners of his lips from curling. "Well, the check cleared, I'll say that much."

"I hear you. Didn't Stephen King say something once about how a bad movie version of one of his books can't actually tarnish the book; that it's still fine up on the shelf, something along those lines?"

"Actually, I think he was quoting James M. Cain."

"I'll take your word for it. You're the writer, after all." The young man held out his hand. "By the way, I'm Tobias Silver, but my friends call me—"

"Let me guess, Toby?"

"Bias, actually. I tend not to do anything traditionally."

Brad laughed and shook the man's hand. "Nice to meet you, Bias. You can call me Brad."

"Wow, you're the first real live breathing author I've ever met. What brings you to Savannah? Book signing?"

"No, actually I just moved here."

"Shut up! Really?"

"Yeah, I bought a house right here in the Historic District."

Bias grimaced and said, "Downtown."

"What?"

"If you're going to live here, you should know only tourists call this 'the Historic District.' Locals just say 'downtown.'"

"Ah, thanks for the tip. It's good to have insider information."

"I'm not a native myself, but I have lived her for three and a half years. I'm a student at S.C.A.D. That's the Savannah College—"

"—of Art and Design," Brad finished. "I do know a thing or two about the city."

"Cool. I have a little studio apartment on the corner of Jones and Bull. Where are you living?"

"I bought a house just off Crenshaw Square."

Bias instantly went rigid and his mouth fell open like that of a broken Nutcracker. At first he didn't speak, didn't even seem to breathe, and Brad wondered if he was going to be sick. Finally Bias said, "Are you shitting me? Are you the person who bought 324 Abercorn?"

"Guilty."

"Oh man, when I saw they were fixing up the place last year, I thought someone might have decided to turn it into a museum like the Juliette Gordon Low House, but you're actually going to *live there*?"

Brad laughed. "That's the plan. Why?"

"You know about the house's reputation, right?"

"You mean stories of spooks and ghoulies?"

"Yeah, it's one of the most haunted sites in all of Savannah and that's a verified fact."

Brad's tilted his head and looked skeptically at Bias. "You don't really believe in that stuff, do you?"

"Absolutely. Ghosts are my bread and butter."

"How so?"

"It's my job. I host a walking ghost tour around the downtown area. That house—*your* house—is one of my major stops."

"Thanks for the warning. I'll try to remember to close all the blinds before walking naked around the house."

"Have you spent the night yet?"

"Actually no, tonight will be my first full night in the house."

"And you're not even the slightest bit nervous?"

"Of course not. It's just a house . . . *my* house, as you said."

"I can't believe it. You're Mr. Horror, and you don't believe in ghosts? How is that even possible?"

"Okay, Bias, I'm going to blow your mind with one hell of a revelation about writers and their stories. I'm pretty sure Lewis Carroll never fell down a rabbit hole into a magical Wonderland; it doesn't seem likely that Anne Rice believes in vampires; and I highly doubt J.K. Rowling has met any real wizards. That's what makes it fiction and not *non*fiction."

"You're breaking my heart. Next you're going to tell me that Matthew, Mark, Luke, and John didn't even know Jesus personally."

The two men stared at one another for a moment before breaking into giggles. "Sorry," Brad said. "Didn't mean to sound like I was lecturing you."

"It's okay. I tend to get too passionate about the supernatural. It's one of a myriad of quirks and eccentricities I suffer from."

A silence settled between them and Brad's usual self-consciousness when interacting with people he didn't know well reasserted itself. He pulled out his cell and checked the time. "Well, Bias, it was great to meet you, but I really do have to run. The cupboards are bare, and I need to do some shopping before I head back home."

"Hold on just a sec." Bias took his wallet from his back pocket and dug through it until he came up with a slightly bent business card, which he held out to Brad. "My number and my email address are on there. Keep in touch. I'd love to come by the house sometime."

Brad took the card without really looking at it. "You would?"

"Definitely. I've been talking about 324 Abercorn on my tours for years. I'd kill to get a peek inside."

"Oh, of course. Maybe once I'm all settled in, I'll have you over and give the tour guide a tour."

"I'm going to hold you to that. Maybe you'll even sign my book for me."

"Sure thing."

Another awkward pause and then Brad shook Bias' hand and wandered off toward the exit. For just a moment, he'd thought Bias might've been flirting with him, but he should have known better. While thirty-six didn't exactly make him an old man, to a twenty-year-old he must seem ancient. Not that Brad was interested. After a rather disastrous six month relationship with a twenty-four-year-old back in South Carolina, he'd sworn off younger guys. Besides, though his gaydar had dinged a few times during the encounter, Brad didn't know for sure whether the young man was even gay. He was probably just imagining—

"Hey Brad."

Brad turned and looked back toward Bias, who still stood among the Mysteries. "Now that I know you sometimes walk around your house naked," the young man said with a crooked grin and a wink, "I'll be sure to snap a lot of pictures at the windows during my next tour."

Heat suffused Brad's face and he thought he could actually be blushing. After nodding at Bias rather dumbly, he hurried from the store. Once outside, he finally glanced down at the business card in his hand. On one side was a crude but strangely accurate caricature of Bias himself with a phone number and email address underneath it, while on the other side, in calligraphy script, were three lines of text:

Tobias Eugene Silver
Student, Artist, Paranormal Investigator,
And All-Around Awesome Dude!

With a smile, Brad slipped the card into his own wallet, and then headed off toward the City Market.

Finish reading the rest of this great novel by purchasing it wherever fine books are sold.

The End?

Not quite . . .

Have you read volumes one and two yet?

Tales from The Lake Vol.1—Remember those dark and scary nights spent telling ghost stories and other campfire stories? With the *Tales from The Lake* horror anthologies, you can relive some of those memories by reading the best Dark Fiction stories around. Includes Dark Fiction stories and poems by horror greats such as Graham Masterton, Bev Vincent, Tim Curran, Tim Waggoner, Elizabeth Massie, and many more. Be sure to check out our website for future *Tales from The Lake* volumes.

Tales from The Lake Vol.2—Beneath this lake you'll find nothing but mystery and suspense, horror and dread. Not to mention death and misery—tales to share around the campfire or living room floor from the likes of Ramsey Campbell, Jack Ketchum, and Edward Lee.

If you enjoyed this book, I'm sure you'll also like the following Crystal Lake titles:

Gutted: Beautiful Horror Stories—an anthology of dark fiction that explores the beauty at the very heart of darkness. Featuring horror's most celebrated voices: Clive Barker, Neil Gaiman, Ramsey Campbell, Paul Tremblay, John F.D. Taff, Lisa Mannetti,

Damien Angelica Walters, Josh Malerman, Christopher Coake, Mercedes M. Yardley, Brian Kirk, Stephanie M. Wytovich, Amanda Gowin, Richard Thomas, Maria Alexander, and Kevin Lucia.

Sarah Killian: Serial Killer (For Hire!) by Mark Sheldon. Follow foul-mouthed and mean-spirited Sarah Killian on an assignment from T.H.E.M. (Trusted Hierarchy of Everyday Murderers), a secret organization using serial killers to do the dirty work for their clients. Sarah's twisted sense of humor alone makes this Crime Fiction / Horror / Thriller a worthy read.

Blackwater Val by William Gorman—a Supernatural Suspense Thriller/Horror/Coming of age novel: A widower, traveling with his dead wife's ashes and his six-year-old psychic daughter Katie in tow, returns to his haunted birthplace to execute his dead wife's final wish. But something isn't quite right in the Val.

Run to Ground by Jasper Bark—Jim Mcleod is running from his responsibilities as a father, hiding out from his pregnant girlfriend and working as a groundskeeper in a rural graveyard. Throw in some ancient monsters and folklore, and you'll have Jim running for live through this folk horror graveyard.

The Final Cut by Jasper Bark—Follow the misfortunes of two indie filmmakers in their quest to fund their breakthrough movie by borrowing money from one dangerous underground figure in order to buy a large quantity of cocaine from a different but equally dangerous underground figure. They will learn that while some stories capture the imagination, others will be the death of you.

Tribulations by Richard Thomas—In the third short story collection by Richard Thomas, *Tribulations*, these stories cover a wide range of dark fiction—from fantasy, science fiction and horror, to magical realism, neo-noir, and transgressive fiction. The common thread that weaves these tragic tales together is suffering and sorrow, and the ways we emerge from such heartbreak stronger, more appreciative of what we have left—a spark of hope enough to guide us though the valley of death.

Devourer of Souls by Kevin Lucia—In Kevin Lucia's latest installment of his growing Clifton Heights mythos, Sheriff Chris Baker and Father Ward meet for a Saturday morning breakfast at The Skylark Dinner to once again commiserate over the weird and terrifying secrets surrounding their town.

Pretty Little Dead Girls: A Novel of Murder and Whimsy by Mercedes M. Yardley—Bryony Adams is destined to be murdered, but fortunately Fate has terrible marksmanship. In order to survive, she must run as far and as fast as she can. After arriving in Seattle, Bryony befriends a tortured musician, a market fish-thrower, and a starry-eyed hero who is secretly a serial killer bent on fulfilling Bryony's dark destiny.

Wind Chill by Patrick Rutigliano—What if you were held captive by your own family? Emma Rawlins has spent the last year a prisoner. The months following her mother's death dragged her father into a paranoid spiral of conspiracy theories and doomsday premonitions. But there is a force far colder than the freezing drifts. Ancient, ravenous, it knows no mercy. And it's already had a taste . . .

Eidolon Avenue: The First Feast by Jonathan Winn—where the secretly guilty go to die. All thrown into their own private hell as every cruel choice, every deadly mistake, every drop of spilled blood is remembered, resurrected and relived to feed the ancient evil that lives on Eidolon Avenue.

Flowers in a Dumpster by Mark Allan Gunnells—The world is full of beauty and mystery. In these 17 tales, Gunnells will take you on a journey through landscapes of light and darkness, rapture and agony, hope and fear. Let Gunnells guide you through these landscapes where magnificence and decay co-exist side by side. Come pick a bouquet from these Flowers in a Dumpster.

The Dark at the End of the Tunnel by Taylor Grant— Offered for the first time in a collected format, this selection features ten gripping and darkly imaginative stories by Taylor Grant, a Bram Stoker Award® nominated author and rising star in the suspense and horror genres. Grant exposes the terrors that hide beneath the surface of our ordinary world, behind people's masks of normalcy, and lurking in the shadows at the farthest reaches of the universe.

Little Dead Red by Mercedes M. Yardley—The Wolf is roaming the city, and he must be stopped. In this modern day retelling of Little Red Riding Hood, the wolf takes to the city streets to capture his prey, but the hunter is close behind him. With Grim Marie on the prowl, the hunter becomes the hunted.

Children of the Grave—Choose your own demise in this interactive shared-world zombie anthology. Welcome to Purgatory, an arid plain of existence where zombies are the least of your problems. It's a post-mortem Hunger Games, and Blaze, a newcomer to Purgatory, needs your help to learn the rules of this world and choose the best course of action.

The Outsiders Lovecraftian shared-world anthology—They'll do anything to protect their way of life. Anything. Welcome to Priory, a small gated community in the UK, where the only thing worse than an ancient monster is the group worshipping it. Is that which slithers below true evil, or does evil reside in the people of Priory? Includes stories by Stephen Bacon, James Everington, Rosanne Rabinowitz, V.H. Leslie, and Gary Fry.

Fear the Reaper anthology—Did you know Death was a girl? Ever wondered if it was possible to cheat death? To kill Death? Or that it's possible to escape and even become death? Includes Grim Reapers stories by legends like Rick Hautala, Gary A. Braunbeck, Joe McKinney, Richard Thomas, Jeremy C Shipp, Jeff Strand, and many more.

For the Night is Dark anthology—Darkness, our most primitive fear since shadows first moved.

Includes stories by Crystal Lake Publishing alumni like Gary McMahon, William Meikle, Jasper Bark, Tonia Brown, Blaze McRob, Daniel I Russell, Kevin Lucia, Armand Rosamilia, Ray Cluley, and many more.

Through a Mirror, Darkly by Kevin Lucia—Are there truths within the books we read? What if the book delves into the lives of the very town you live in? People you know? Or thought you knew. These are the questions a bookstore owner face when a mysterious book shows up.

Where You Live by Gary McMahon—Horror is everywhere, in the shadows and in the light. It takes on every shape, comes in every conceivable size. But most of all it's right where you live. With the WHERE YOU LIVE short story collection, Gary McMahon delves into the depths of dark and brooding horror in every day events, objects, and the ghost of human nature.

Tricks, Mischief and Mayhem by Daniel I. Russell—Tricks, Mischief and Mayhem. These are not just some of the themes lurking in this tome of horror, but the names of three mischievous carnival clowns. Along with them you'll meet some of Australia's most popular monsters and legends, along with a popular cast of ghosts, demons, and zombies. Hell, there are more than a few stories portraying nature fighting back.

Samurai and Other Stories by William Meikle—No one can handle Scottish folklore with elements of the darkest horror, science fiction and fantasy, suspense and adventure like William Meikle.

Stuck On You and Other Prime Cuts by Jasper Bark—A word of caution gentle reader, these tales will take you places you've never been before and may never dare revisit. They'll whisper truths so twisted you can only face them in the darkest hours of the night. They'll unlock desires so decadent you'll never wash their taint from your flesh.

Eden Underground horror poetry by Alessandro Manzetti—Another snake, another tree, another Eve. A surreal journey into obsessions and aberrations of the modern world and the darker side, which often takes control of the situation.

If you ever thought of becoming an author, I'd also like to recommend these non-fiction titles:

Horror 101: The Way Forward—a comprehensive overview of the Horror fiction genre and career opportunities available to established and aspiring authors, including Jack Ketchum, Graham Masterton, Edward Lee, Lisa Morton, Ellen Datlow, Ramsey Campbell, and many more.

Horror 201: The Silver Scream Vol.1 and *Vol.2*—A must read for anyone interested in the horror film industry. Includes interviews and essays by Wes Craven, John Carpenter, George A. Romero, Mick Garris, and dozens more. Now available in paperback, as well.

Modern Mythmakers: 35 interviews with Horror and Science Fiction Writers and Filmmakers by Michael McCarty—Ever wanted to hang out with legends like Ray Bradbury, Richard Matheson, and Dean Koontz? *Modern Mythmakers* is your chance to hear fun anecdotes and career advice from authors and filmmakers like Forrest J. Ackerman, Ray Bradbury, Ramsey Campbell, John Carpenter, Dan Curtis, Elvira, Neil Gaiman, Mick Garris, Laurell K. Hamilton, Jack Ketchum, Dean Koontz, Graham Masterton, Richard Matheson, John Russo, William F. Nolan, John Saul, Peter Straub, and many more.

Writers On Writing: An Author's Guide—Your favorite authors share their secrets in the ultimate guide to becoming and being and author. *Writers On Writing* is an ongoing eBook series with original 'On Writing' essays by writing professionals. A new edition will be launched every few months, featuring four or five essays per edition, so be sure to check out the webpage regularly for updates.

Or check out other Crystal Lake Publishing books for your Dark Fiction, Horror, Suspense, and Thriller needs.

Connect with Crystal Lake Publishing:

Website:
www.crystallakepub.com

Be sure to sign up for our newsletter and receive
a free eBook: http://eepurl.com/xfuKP

Books:
http://www.crystallakepub.com/books.php

Twitter:
https://twitter.com/crystallakepub

Facebook:
https://www.facebook.com/Crystallakepublishing/
https://www.facebook.com/Talesfromthelake/
https://www.facebook.com/WritersOnWritingSeries/

Google+:
https://plus.google.com/u/1/107478350897139952572

Pinterest:
https://za.pinterest.com/crystallakepub/

Instagram:
https://www.instagram.com/crystal_lake_publishing/

Tumblr:
https://www.tumblr.com/blog/crystal-lake-publishing

Patreon:
https://www.patreon.com/CLP

With unmatched success since 2012, Crystal Lake Publishing has quickly become one of the world's leading indie publishers of Mystery, Thriller, and Suspense books with a Dark Fiction edge.

Crystal Lake Publishing puts integrity, honor and respect at the forefront of our operations.

We strive for each book and outreach program that's launched to not only entertain and touch or comment on issues that affect our readers, but also to strengthen and support the Dark Fiction field and its authors.

Not only do we publish authors who are legends in the field and as hardworking as us, but we look for men and women who care about their readers and fellow human beings. We only publish the very best Dark Fiction, and look forward to launching many new careers.

We strive to know each and every one of our readers, while building personal relationships with our authors, reviewers, bloggers, pod-casters, bookstores and libraries.

Crystal Lake Publishing is and will always be a beacon of what passion and dedication, combined with overwhelming teamwork and respect, can accomplish: Unique fiction you can't find anywhere else.

We do not just publish books, we present you worlds within your world, doors within your mind, from talented authors who sacrifice so much for a moment of your time.

This is what we believe in. What we stand for. This will be our legacy.

Welcome to Crystal Lake Publishing.

We hope you enjoyed this title. If so, we'd be grateful if you could leave a review on your blog or any of the other websites and outlets open to book reviews. Reviews are like gold to writers and publishers, since word-of-mouth is and will always be the best way to market a great book. And remember to keep an eye out for more of our books.

THANK YOU FOR PURCHASING THIS BOOK